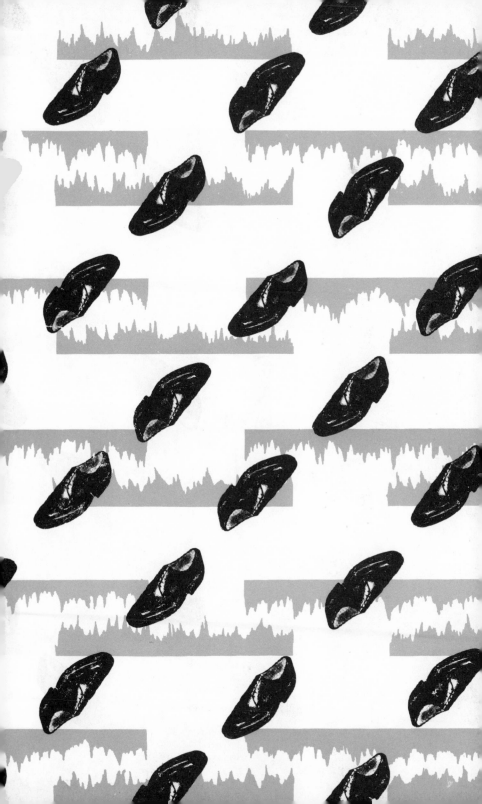

WATCHING THE BODY BURN

WATCHING THE BODY

Burn

THOMAS GLYNN

ALFRED A. KNOPF

NEW YORK

1989

THIS IS A BORZOI BOOK
PUBLISHED BY ALFRED A. KNOPF, INC.

A portion of this work was originally published in *The Quarterly, 7.*

Library of Congress Cataloging-in-Publication Data
Glynn, Thomas, [*date*]
  Watching the body burn.
  I. Title.
PS3557.L93W38 1988   813'.54   88-80772
ISBN 0-394-57176-2

Manufactured in the United States of America

First Edition

for John and Emmett

A I R

I S

T H E

H O M E

O F

T H E

S O U L

WATCHING THE BODY BURN

FIRST FIRE

MY FATHER IS ON FIRE. HIS HEAD IS BURNING. I DO NOT SEE the flames, but my aunt phones me to tell me about them. He fell asleep, a cigarette in his fingers. Perhaps his sheets would have burned first, but they were plastic because of his incontinence, which meant he shit and pissed in bed and may or may not have known it and may or may not have cared about it if he knew it. His pajamas burned, and then the flame leaped up to his hair, which was thick, white, and flat. My father had extremely flat hair, which he parted down the middle, and the flame touched both sides. The last thing my father said, according to my aunt, was, "Sis, look at this! Come look at this!" She said he sounded enthusiastic, the way my father sounded about everything.

But when I saw him in the hospital,

his face was puffed up like one of those creatures you pull from the bottom of the sea, creatures which, when suddenly released from tons of pressure, swell up and hide their features. His eyes were barely visible. The top of his nose had disappeared, and his mouth was swollen and distended. He couldn't talk. He was in a coma. His doctor told me his body was working furiously to replace the liquids that had been pulled out by the flames. He was full of tubes and doped up with painkiller, so I didn't know if he heard what I had to say. I screamed at him for an hour. For some reason, no one stopped me.

They put him in the burn ward and connected him to an electrocardiograph machine. An oscilloscope bared the secrets of his heart, and I could hear the beat chimed out over a small loudspeaker, a kind of medical Muzak. There was a bottle where liquids went in and another where they came out. His face, bloated like a pumpkin, had no eyebrows, and his hair was a ring of stubble around the back of his head. There was a salve on his face and his eyelids were crusted over. His doctor explained all this to me, and I took comfort in the description.

His doctor was a woman. My father had been cared for by women all his life. Women listened to him, believed in him. Women understood his arcane enthusiasms, were able to follow his logic. I could have spent hours listening to his doctor talk about his case, as if she were a biologist attempting to save some soon-to-be-extirpated species.

I liked renting a car for the drive to the hospital, and eating fried chicken on my aunt's Formica-and-chrome table in her ancient kitchen, listening to the sounds of the kids on the block. I liked the way she made coffee in an electric percolator, liked the smell better than the coffee, and was immensely comforted by the sound of the Chicago *Daily News* when it landed on her wooden porch, held in tight by a rubber band. She slept at night with the radio on to keep awake, because she never knew what my father was going to do.

My aunt was the whitest woman I have ever known. Her eyes

popped out. I don't know if she could shut her eyelids. My father had a name for her condition, as he had a name for everything. "Things don't exist," my father told me, "until they have a name." My father had four uncles who swore off women and lived together in a house they built on the South Side of Chicago near Sixty-ninth and Oglesby. They're gone, but the house is still there. The house my aunt and my father lived in was the house my grandparents lived in and also the house my uncle who really wasn't my uncle burned to death in. My aunt couldn't understand that. Two burnings in the same house were too much for her. Maybe it was the house's way of getting back at us.

When I saw my father in the hospital, I got the feeling there was something revolving inside him. I talked to the nurses about it, but they didn't want to know what I was talking about. The doctor smiled and blew cigarette smoke in my face. I didn't know what it was, but I kept hearing something, like a flywheel or a tiny engine.

I wanted to ask my father about it, but never did. He would have liked it. He always wanted to be a machine.

Waiting, I read the Chicago papers and watched television and walked over to the lake and felt the city pressing on my heart. I couldn't see the color of the air, but I could feel it, had the sense that it was being pushed down. Dry, quiet Chicago, a tortilla of the soul. The inside of my aunt's house was like a gray woolen muffler. She had small brass-framed pictures from happier times on lace tablecloths, and what struck me about the pictures is that when they were taken, there must have been times that were even happier before that, and so on, the whole thing receding back into some infinite ecstasy. At one time my father thought that the center of things was in trees. He brought logs home, dumped them in tanks in the backyard. He tested them, carved them up. I thought he wanted to make statues, but it was something else. "At the core of things is a river," my father said.

My father treated everyone with contempt. He waded through life nurturing this contempt, and I could always feel this in him, even when he was in a drunken stupor, having been brought home by a cabbie who had discovered him with his pockets picked clean, sitting in his own vomit in a men's room at a Clark Street bar. My father was contemptuous of the cabbie for having found him like this, for having to take care of him, bring him home, in this condition. His contempt spread, like kelp, threatening to cover even himself. He conducted many wars. He fought my mother, his friends, and anyone who employed him. He dared them to fire him, pressed forward to promote unpopular, wildly bizarre theories in the pharmaceutical companies that he worked for, to see how far they would trust him. When he got drunk, he advanced closer and closer to objects. Conversations were nose to nose, his eyes widened. He looked for something he had missed before: a line, a gesture, a small tic that betrayed a truth. He read when he was drunk, getting closer and closer to the page, believing that some overlooked data would jump out or that his mind would overpower the figures, pounce on the unsuspecting numbers, and extract the theory that lay hidden. At one and the same time he believed that things existed on the surface and that each thing possessed its own theory, or truth, the essence of which was overlooked by most people. This lay hidden, and yet was on the surface.

"The center is on the surface," my father would say.

My father would cut pieces of himself and look at them under the microscope.

"We are air," he told me. "We will evaporate." The second sentence he uttered at a board meeting to justify a theory of his, shortly before he was fired.

My father was a man of great enthusiasms. Almost embarrassing enthusiasms. I don't think I was up to them. I may have contributed to their downfall. His theories were both simple and arcane, anomalies, things that despite their strangeness, and newness, one couldn't help feeling were wrong. What he needed was someone to sort and edit his theories, to show him where he went off the track, to gently, with kindly corrections, rerail him. And yet he delighted in his perversity, the "wrongness" of his theories. Sometimes, when he started to explain one, and then went into the ramifications, it must have been obvious, even to him, to his scientific mind, that he was wrong. But his enthusiasms carried him beyond "wrongness." He glided over them. This was a mere impediment to a grander course he was charting.

He had his white shirts starched so stiffly the creases cut, and when he wore them they tended to break his body into sections. He loved compartments and gadgets of all kinds. He liked boxes, and putting things into boxes, and tools that performed obscure functions, one of which he used to try and kill my mother.

I think he felt that parts of him were defective.

Perhaps that's why he had tried to burn himself.

My father shared a ward in the burn unit with six other patients. I don't know if they were on their way toward life or death. There was a ring over his bed and a curtain that could be pulled around on it to hide his body, and when I saw my father there, revolving to his own peculiar drumbeat, I thought how huge and hairless his chest was. It reminded me of something pumped up and meant to float in water.

He was a tremendous swimmer. Or had been. He once swam ten miles toward the middle of Lake Michigan, stopping only to rest at a pumping station miles offshore. It was an obscure talent. He gave it up. There was no way to capitalize on it.

My father was a Catholic with a strong aversion to Catholicism that bordered on the maniacal. He was allergic to priests. In their presence he would erupt in hysterical gaiety, or quickly become morose and take off his shoes and socks and put them in his pockets. He preferred a turn on the rack to meeting a nun.

It is easy this way. I can say things at him. He is living in some tiny region of his mind, surfacing now and then with a flicker of his puffed eyes, and I wonder if he resents me seeing him like this and wishes I would get the hell away.

I am scared that he is going to die in front of me. I won't know what to do.

8

When I was sixteen, I discovered that I was stronger than he was. I felt ashamed. We were having chicken fights in the backyard, and I pulled him off his feet. He fell with a heavy thump, looking surprised, then amazed. He tried to push me over again and again, and I should have let him, but I could not. Something seemed to hold on to my legs, seemed to root them in the earth. Each shove met with the same result. He looked hopeless, angry, bitter. He wanted to spit at me. Finally he ended the game, storming into the house. I heard him breaking glass, kicking chairs and tables.

Then he began telling me things.

"Never marry a woman whose face is bigger than yours," he said.

I hadn't thought about marrying.

"I eat words," he told me, "I gorge on them, vomit them up."

He wrote letters to friends explaining his actions:

"Why do I do these strange things I do?"

Answering himself: "You must understand, nothing is strange."

He writes those who are after him:

"Don't try to follow me. You'll only get in trouble."

One day he turned to me suddenly, as if out of breath, and said, "Your penis will never stop growing."

On the subject of women:

"If you want to know what a woman's cunt looks like, look at her mouth."

He was mad about everything, and showed it. His quarrel was with existence. He was furious with the power it had over us, the way it bound us to this earth.

"What can we do about this life?" he once asked me.

And then he said, "Don't follow where I'm going. You won't be welcome."

Anger liberated him, stilled his mind, and also concentrated it. The triteness of "being oneself," of "finding oneself," he abhorred precisely because it was crucial.

Before he went to bed at night my father vacuumed his typewriter. He was waiting for words. He wanted to be ready when words came. He was very punctual about this vacuuming, and though there were many nights when I did not hear him typing, there were very few nights when I did not hear him vacuuming his machine. He was unhappy about dust.

The jobs, and the states, came and went. Illinois, Michigan, Texas, West Virginia. My father invented things. A typewriter that vacuumed itself. For some reason he put it on wheels. He had a paper published on soybean absorption. It was in a small journal, and it was printed on yellow paper. He invented a new system of calculus, which was more cumbersome than Newton's. He wrote embarrassing letters to his ex-secretary, who showed them to her boyfriend, who called up my mother.

And then several months later something happened. He got too close to himself, and recoiled in horror. "What is this?" he asks himself. "Have I been like this all along?" He pretends to come upon this for the first time, but in truth he has known it all along. He was afraid to tell himself that he knew. The stink of himself, the sweat of his own being, shamed him, repelled him. He must be this disgusting thing. He has been it all along.

He went mad. I romanticized this, but am cured of my romanticism when I see him in the institution. There I am confronted by a horrible sight. The inmates have normalized their insanity. Their bizarreness, perhaps the only valuable thing about them, has been worn down, made regular and repeatable. The doctors have managed to turn their madness into a sort of laxative that drained them. I think that is why my father was at his most ingenious, certainly his most inventive, in getting out of these institutions. He was willing to sacrifice just about anything in his search for the center, but not the joy of his aberrations.

He always got out.

We were sitting, talking. He looked too normal. I was worried that something bizarre was happening, that he would jump up and start shooting off his mouth or a pistol, or confess that he had an uncontrollable urge to explain things.

Between cigarettes, he did confess something.

"I have the feeling that people will call me up and apologize for wrongs they have done me years before. They will ask a favor of me, defer to me because of my position of power and authority, a position I have risen to since the time they have wronged me. They will ask my blessing, beg that I give a speech or write an article for them. I will, of course, do this. It is only in the granting of favors that one exerts one's authority."

He paused, to light another cigarette. He seemed incapable of talking without a cigarette.

"Good fortune comes about by phone. People I do not know will call up and offer public praise and private money for works I have accomplished in the past. Or for something I am about to do. An unreasonable amount of good fortune will also come to me through the mail."

While he waited for these honors, and fortune, he drifted toward senility. His face collapsed and gave way to a sort of sagging truth. He delighted in his senility. He giggled frequently, which upset me and in turn pleased him. Senility conferred on him a wisdom he had always lacked, though the price it asked of him was his brilliance. It was as though he had discovered a new toy, and wished to play with it day after day. I was haranguing him at some length about economics, explaining some obtuse point in childish terms, when he looked at me and said, "They say *that*, do they?" Then he giggled.

I watched him light a cigarette, his cataract-clouded eyes only vaguely aware of the match, his hand slowly guiding the flame to the vicinity of the tobacco. Once lit, the cigarette came out of his mouth and rested between his fingers, the ash growing until it became another finger, a clean gray extension of his hand. I wondered if he ever burned his fingers, if they were fireproof. His ashtrays were populated with barrel-like timbers of ash fallen haphazardly over one another in a mayhem of smoking.

It is February. Snow is falling in soft layers. His bed is next to a window. It has the plastic curtain around it and there is a steaming radiator that snaps and pops. I am afraid to touch him. His hand lies over the sheet like a slim fish. He has long, slender fingers with huge fingernails that cover the tips of his fingers. I am afraid to feel how cold his hand might be. Or how warm it might be. I am afraid to feel the skin: rubbery, smooth, too slippery, and yet crinkly, in folds, like creased wax paper. Several years before, when he came to visit, I hugged him, holding him tight, afraid he would slip out of my hands. We were both close to tears. It was the last time I held him.

My aunt and I visit him in the mornings and afternoons, and sometimes in the evenings. I am enamored with the routine, and grow to love everything about it except seeing him. I enjoy unlocking the door of the car I rent, seeing that my aunt is comfortably seated in the front, going around to the driver's side and slipping behind the wheel, starting up the engine, edging out into traffic. From the moment we leave the house until we arrive at the hospital I feel like I am being guided through the gears of some tight machine. There is a beautiful predictability to the roads, the stoplights, even the other cars. This routine builds such joy that I am close to tears. I don't want my aunt to know how much pleasure I am getting from this.

In the evening, I watch television in a chair covered in plastic. It is his chair. There is a faint smell of Lysol, and feces.

At night, the gray, empty house sags. The huge, walrus-thick carpets collapse toward the center of the room, the hot-air registers shrivel at the thought of heat, the glass figurines and unsteady varnished tables remain upright without the offending hand of my father to scatter them.

There was a hum that followed him as he rambled from room to room, an electric chorus that shook objects within his reach. Now the bungalow was stung with silence, like a heavy engine that sits in the air after an electrical storm. The steeply carpeted stairs that wind up to his room, and the room itself—a mausoleum of window shades, faded spit on wallpaper, linoleum, plastic-protected mattress, and black desk full of finger-length burns—all remain silent, untouched by his weight.

I lie in bed listening to the routine of the house being disturbed by silence, and by the subliminal babble of the tiny radio my aunt constantly plays. I wait for my father to burst through the door, stumble on the sofa, teeter on the edge of the stairs, shatter china and burn cigarettes into the table.

My aunt's friends come by. A symphony of the old. They ask about my father. They are delighted to learn that someone is dying before they are. They trade talk of disease, afflictions, affronts. My aunt is the perfect listener. She loves to talk about disease.

My father liked to drive when he was drunk. I think he dreamed of dying with his family scattered about him, he impaled on the steering mechanism, our heads projected through glass, our chests buried under tons of steel, the upholstery spewed with blood. Once, in a fit of rage, he hurled a typewriter through a plate-glass window. He was forty floors above the street. He motioned me toward the window, and we watched it revolve in the air, scattering its ribbon in long, lazy loops. He liked to hit people with golf clubs and drive golf carts into ponds.

My father enjoyed giving terror.

I once caught him with a pair of scissors at my mother's throat, smiling.

She said nothing.

They were naked at the time.

At the hospital I noticed the two middle fingers of his right hand performing a dance. I thought it may have been Morse code, or some obscure code of his own. There seemed, however, to be no pattern to this drumming. Sometimes the fingers moved in concert with each other, sometimes independently. I asked the nurse about it, and then the doctor. They had no idea what it meant.

Standing at the foot of his bed, watching the green-and-white oscilloscope go up and down, I tried to picture the best time for his death. Should it be in front of me? When I was back at my aunt's house? When I had flown to New York? I would have been embarrassed if he died in front of me. Some part of his body might overflow onto the bed. He might groan or cough or cry, and I didn't want to see him in pain. If he is in pain I don't want to know about it. I wanted to hold him, but he looks so bloated. I don't want to be part of his death. I watch the scope in fear, afraid it will stop. What will I do if it stops? I am afraid to listen to my heartbeat for the same reason, fear that it will stop while I listen to it because I am listening to it. I don't want to be here. I want to receive the news in the mail. Not even over the phone. I don't want anyone to see how I react to my father's death.

Here is what I found in his room: medical texts, microscope, desk lamp with gun-metal-gray swivel base, an illustrated history of pornography, pens, keys, rulers, manuscripts in his curious slanting handwriting, and a closetful of clothes he never wore. I look around the room for more things. I think the more things he has, the more he is. I want to stuff him with things.

I come to the hospital each day poised on the edge of some great discovery. I expect to be enlightened.

I take his hand and lean over the bed.

"Tell me . . ." I begin.

At times no one knew where he lived. He would be gone for months to set up a pharmaceutical laboratory in some hot climate. He detested heat. He would sweat as if he were inventing water. He refused to learn Spanish. I have pictures from Cuba, before the revolution. My father stands with sleek-looking men, glistening, dressed in linens soon to be wrinkled, wearing sharp-pointed, open-mesh shoes. Everybody looks as if he is wearing a shark mask. The pictures were taken in a nightclub, or in front of a Havana pool. The background is dark, obscure, muddy. I have the feeling it was just before, or after, some incredible debauch. My father always came home depressed.

There was not a trace of fire in his room. He must have stood there like a human torch, a giant fleshy wick, and allowed the flames to consume him, saving the furniture. Maybe his shaving lotion caught fire. My aunt shaved him. Aftershave lotions burn easily, though I'm not sure what effect human skin has on them. It's hard to imagine that my aunt would use aftershave lotion on him. He liked shaving. He disliked being shaved. He would quickly turn his head. My aunt would slice a neat ribbon in his face. He bled in drops. He would curse my aunt, who would be too reasonable and explain that the blood was his own doing. But she held the razor, didn't she?

What was it like, burning?

My father must have stood there, surrounded in flames, the mouth and nostrils and trachea and part of the lungs shriveling under the intense heat while the rest of the flame curled about his face and head and hair. He must have been transfixed by this long, brightly colored coil of flame, this searing snake of heat, which wrapped itself around him. It must have happened very quickly, no longer than a few seconds. I can imagine him being enthralled by the vivid energy of the flames; his scientist's mind would marvel at the rapid destruction of his body.

A year before my father set himself on fire, my uncle who wasn't did the same thing. He was laying some cable for my aunt's new washing machine when a live wire grounded and the sparks ignited his shirt. It was one of those synthetic shirts that burn automatically. He lived for three weeks in the hospital, with considerable pain, before he died. My aunt wrote and told me about it. They had been dating for almost forty years. They would drive up to his farm in one of his many Dodges. He would spend the weekend repairing his bulldozers while my aunt memorized all the phone numbers she might ever need to call. Neither of them worked during the week, but they always drove back on Sunday night, stopping for iced frappés.

My aunt lived in that dry, gray house with the knowledge that two human Zippos had gone up in flames there. The house remained untouched. It was a dead zone for flesh.

What if I had been with my father that day, helping him light his cigarette, when the match moved ever so slightly until it caught his sleeve? What would I have done? Embrace him, smothering the flames? Or would I watch?

He must have been drinking. Maybe he found a bottle of rubbing alcohol in the kitchen, alongside the Catholic food, underneath the

Perpetual Novena Calendar with all the saints' birthdays and the dates of retreats and special penances, right next to the telephone that lights up at night with all the possible disaster numbers.

Listen.

My father did what he did because he was in danger of sinking into the earth. He wanted to evaporate in the air.

They brought my father home in a Packard, his face wrapped in bandages. His eyes had reappeared, the huge Ping-Pong balls of flesh around his eye sockets replaced by pupils, which were still surrounded by gray, lumpy-shaped clumps of water-laden tissue. His lips were the size of fingers. His hair had started to grow back.

I wanted to ask my father if he would set himself on fire again, but I was afraid to.

STONES

$3\frac{1}{2}$

LONG AGO, BEFORE HE COULD THINK, HE STOOD ON THE SLANT-
ing porch between his mother and father,
facing the priest. The air on the porch
was gray and cold, even though it was
sunny. To the boy, the air felt huge,
immense, tinged with blue. The priest
was not tall, but because the boy was
so small the priest seemed tall to him.
The priest was dressed in black, dull
black, though parts of the black were
shiny, where he favored the cloth by
rubbing. The priest was wearing his collar and cassock to the racetrack, and he
carried three stones in his pocket. He
wanted the boy to kiss the stones.

He took one of the stones out of his
pocket and told the boy to step forward.
"Kiss the stone," he said to the boy. He
used a high voice, one of several he had.

The boy would not step forward. He did not want to kiss the stone.

"Tell him it's only for luck," the priest said.

"He doesn't know luck," said the boy's father.

"Kiss the stone."

The boy remained between his parents.

"Make him kiss the stone."

The boy's father turned his head in another direction. He did not want to be here, any more than the boy did. The boy's mother was angry with the priest, and with the boy's father, but she said nothing because she wanted the man to do the talking. If she said something, her husband would be angry with her afterward, for a long time, in a way that was not pleasant.

The priest was on his way to the racetrack. He needed to win. All the boy had to do was kiss the stones. That was easy.

"Make him," the priest said.

The father said nothing.

"His lips . . . just touch the stone."

His father turned to him. He was way above him. His father pushed him forward. The priest held out the stone. The boy stepped back, feeling the hand of his father, who pushed him forward. The hand stuck in his back, like bone.

Nann peered through the window. She arched an eyebrow, and the rest of her face, fold after fold, was raised. The priest turned around, as if caught doing something.

"See," he said, "even she wants you to do it."

The boy wanted to go sideways, somewhere else. He did not like the stone. He was afraid that kissing the stone would put something on his lips he could never take off. It would grow on his lips. It was a greasy, gritty thing that would not wear away. The stone would remain stuck to his lips.

The priest looked at Nann and smiled. He turned around and looked at the woman.

"You tell him," he said.

His mother said nothing. She looked at Nann, watching her

through the window. The old woman was thinking about her, about the way she dressed, about her mouth, about her hair. She was angry with her, and looked hard at her, squinting, as if she didn't believe she was there. The old woman's face was a series of quizzical wrinkles that started going somewhere, but suddenly stopped.

"Well, I don't have all day," the priest said.

All day. The boy tried to think what that meant.

"It begins soon, stones or no stones."

He stopped talking, long enough to turn around and look at Nann looking through the window.

"The stones would make it a sure thing."

"Eh huh."

The priest looked at the man.

"You're just like your mother."

The boy turned his head away.

"A little, anyway."

They had come to see his grandparents, not expecting the priest. We should have walked away, his father thought, when we saw the priest on the porch.

"Kiss the stones," the boy's father said. He wanted to get it over with. The woman was already angry at him, and this would just add to it. But he would get back.

Nann came to the door. She said nothing, breathing behind the screen. Her purple dress was white with talcum. Her hair, gray white, iron strong, was pinned in python curls on top of her head. Her belly was part of her chest.

The boy was pushed forward once more and ordered to kiss the stones. He wore very short pants, tan cotton socks, and new leather sandals. They didn't know what Nann would think of the sandals. She stood at the door, watching them. The priest fidgeted. He lifted his head and turned his collar.

"Why does he have to kiss the stones?" his mother asked.

"It's for luck, that's all."

His father kept his hand in his back, his fingers on the edge of one shoulder.

"Put the stones to his lips," his father said.

"He should kiss them."

"It's the same thing."

"It's just for luck. At his age, they've all got the luck."

"He never really kisses. He just touches lips."

"Who ever heard of that?"

"Well, that's just the way he is."

The priest took the stones out of his pocket and held them before the boy.

"If I win, half of it goes in the poor box. That's the way it is."

The stones looked small, pebbles in water, stones used to water running over them. They could be swallowed and hardly missed.

"They're from Europe, the stones. I can't say where."

"I'll bet."

"How come I don't see you at confession? The boy, either."

His father said nothing. Nann stood in the doorway, still saying nothing. The boy expected her to come out and swallow him up. She was a huge thing. She had lots of room in her stomach for him. He had seen her swallow creatures much bigger than himself, many times bigger. They all went to her stomach.

"I don't think I've ever seen you there."

"Try putting the stones to his lips."

The priest held the stones in his hand but didn't move forward.

"Have you been?"

His father pushed him forward so that he was almost touching the priest.

"I can understand her, but you should go."

"I go."

"It's a mortal sin, you know. I suppose you know that."

Nann did not move in the doorway. The boy thought she might have been tied there. Otherwise she would have swept forward and engulfed them, smelling of iron and powder.

"Give me the stones," his father said.

"It's not the same. I can understand her not going."

"He'll kiss one if I tell him."

"She doesn't have to, but the boy does. That was the agreement."

"I know the agreement."

"It's a standard agreement."

"I know."

"She doesn't have to do anything against her faith."

"Uh."

"The agreement is with the boy."

His father reached out to take the stones from the priest, who closed his fingers around them and smiled.

"You understand that. We've got to keep our agreements."

Agreements.

Nann stepped out of the doorway.

"What's happening? Something's happening," she said.

She stood before the boy glowing, like a Bessemer furnace. She melted people with her stomach.

"Something about stones," she said.

"It's nothing."

The boy's mother took off her hat. It was a large hat that looked good when it had plenty of space around it, but here on the porch it crowded everything else.

His father reached out for the stones, but the priest held on to them. His father looked angry. His mother held her hat—a large straw hat with a wide brim and ribbons and flowers—with her two hands in front of her, as if she had forgotten to wear clothes.

"I know it's something."

"Of course it is, but it's not really important."

He put the stones back in his pocket, and then he took them out, quickly, and thrust them under the boy's nose.

"Kiss the stones."

He said it in a way that frightened the boy. His father pushed the boy forward again. He could smell the stones. They smelled damp, full of earth, of death, of dead things underwater. Cupped in the priest's hands, they looked like something the boy was not supposed to see, like some part of a woman, something that happens on the toilet. He put his lips to the stone and gagged.

"Kiss the stones."

He could taste the warm wetness where the stones had been close to the body, close to a place in the body where things came together. Something from the stones got on his lips. He gagged, but did not throw up. The stones smelled of wet darkness. That, and death and the body.

"Did he kiss the stones?"

Nann stepped forward. Her stomach glowed. Where his mother's hands touched the straw hat it was wet. The ribbon was wet, turning a deeper shade of color. His mother turned to his father, who looked at Nann. The boy swallowed. He did not like the taste, but he had to swallow.

"Did he?"

"I think he did," the priest said. "I'm not sure, but I think he did."

The priest turned to his father.

It was his first thought. The boy thought his father wanted to cry.

M A N N

MY GRANDMOTHER LOOKED LIKE BABE RUTH. I DON'T KNOW if Babe Ruth ever had a beard, but my grandmother had a tiny mustache and goatee that she dusted with talcum powder every day of her life. She wore purple dresses that showed the talcum, and her dresses had fringes of lace around the collar and wrists. She always wore a brooch around her neck that looked like it had been pecked by blackbirds.

She hated nature but loved birds. She cemented over her tiny backyard and kept a bird feeder in the middle of the cement right behind the tiny gray house she and my grandfather lived in on the South Side of Chicago, and fed sparrows and shell-shocked robins. She emptied baking pans full of crumbs for the birds and left strychnine for the cats who patrolled her yard looking for birds.

When she was sick she sat up in her room and looked out the window at the birds through a pair of cardboard binoculars and at the same time prayed for cats so she could open the window and pour hot water on them.

But the cats never came while she waited for them. They seemed to know something about her.

My grandmother could fly. The how of it wasn't important. But the why of it was simply that she was my grandmother, that she was at her best terrifying someone, and I knew that she could fly. She had a small dog called Checkers or Spot or some other doglike name, which looked like a rag mop and lived for seventeen years, until it was blind and couldn't walk or get out of the way of its own mess. She would take that dog flying with her. She would sweep the dog up in her arms and they would take off. She and that dog went everywhere, very quickly, before anyone else got there, or even thought of getting there. She liked to hold the dog by the neck, and it would hang limp, content to suffocate, while they flew. She used the dog to wipe things off, grabbing it by the paws and rubbing it upside down on tables and armchairs, brushing the dust off.

I always thought she was made of iron. She swept you into her huge Irish gut, where you would suffocate in old sweat and talcum and stale flowery perfume. When she sat in a chair she looked like she was welded to it. Dust settled about her head and shoulders, tiny iron chips. When she talked I could hear her belly. She had weak arms and legs, like most old ladies, but she had a very powerful middle, like a C-47 cargo plane. When she spoke I thought of a Bessemer furnace, boiling and raging and spewing. Her words came through iron grates, along with showers of sparks. Her words were slab heavy, red hot. Her words were very important.

She would sit and talk to the dog and use it to dust off the lamp stand while she talked. I think the dog was too old to object, or too dumb, or else it thought that this was a very doglike thing to have done to itself.

She didn't fly all the time. She flew on holidays, always on

Christmas or New Year's. Flying in raging storms was her specialty. She would arrive dry as a peacock, the storm outside full of the fury of elves, and she would always arrive hours before my grandfather, who came with my almost-uncle, who dated my maiden aunt, and they came in my almost-uncle's Fluid Drive Dodge.

Flying never seemed to tire her. She arrived with a face streaked in white and red, her national colors, full of Irish hatred and Catholic fury. Actually, I'm not sure if she flew through the air or just sailed through it. I'm not even sure if it wasn't the rag-mop dog that had the knack of flying and she just hung on for the ride. I never asked her. I was afraid to. No one asked her anything, especially children.

Flying wasn't the only thing she could do. She could shut her mouth and talk through her stomach. She was weak, but strong. No arm or shoulder strength to speak of, but she could look at things and they would break. When she came, I would run and hide. I thought if she looked at me too quickly I would break in two, snap, like some dry-as-dust sparrow in her collection of dead birds, which she kept in cardboard shoe boxes in the kitchen pantry.

Most people thought she was a witch. I didn't. She was too thick to be a witch. Most people thought of her that way because of the petrified ham she kept in the china closet and dusted off when company came. The ham was a great-uncle, a famous Civil War general who had his arms and legs blown off by musket shot at the Battle of Bull Run and was now stone hard and preserved for eternity next to the soup tureen and the spoonholders.

She liked to argue. When she wasn't arguing with the Protestants who married her sons, she argued with the petrified ham. I don't know what she argued about. It didn't seem to make any difference what other people thought, even if they agreed with her. It was still wrong.

The aunts plotted to remove the petrified ham from the china closet. They talked to her sons, to priests, to lawyers. But petrified hams seemed to fall under none of their domains, and the huge blackish lump stayed in the china closet, next to the cast-iron 1933 World's Fair Greyhound bus with cab and articulated trailer.

Then one of her sons, one of my uncles, was shaking my hand and squeezed it so hard I cried and afterwards he lay down in a bed and died. She flew to the funeral. I thought that she could make him fly. But he didn't. He went down in the box, in a ditch, filled with dirt, and she stood there looking at the box and shaking her little dog as if she was trying to brush the dirt off the coffin.

One morning she flew down to breakfast and sat across from me at the table. It was early. My parents weren't up. I was eating cornflakes with bananas, and had just poured the cream from the top of the milk bottle. She stared at me with angry iron-ore eyes. I was too startled to be frightened and then too frightened to speak. I wanted to know what I was being accused of and yet I knew she would never tell me. She was bound by some unwritten code not to reveal my crime, not even to speak about it. She just wanted to remind me that I knew what it was. I couldn't tell if she was holding the dog. She had her arms under the table. Finally I spoke, asking her what she wanted. She said nothing. I was afraid that she would take me somewhere, a place I didn't want to go. I wanted to ask her, but didn't. Then I wanted to leave, but couldn't.

I don't think she liked children, though she never told me that. She would have preferred to stretch children into adults, the sooner the better, perhaps over the course of several weeks on some sort of stretching rack. I was sure she knew how to do this. I was sure she knew how to do anything.

At night she flew to our house and sat on the roof, ear next to my ceiling. I could hear her scrambling up there, the yap of the dog, the flutterings and scratchings on the shingles. She was listening, waiting for me to make a move, waiting to pounce. I dove under the covers, threw pillows over me, disguised my breathing. She tried to lift the window. She bored a hole through the roof and dropped the dog through. He was trained to open the window.

When I heard the dog running around in my room I tried to find a hole in the mattress. Sleep was fitful. I slept with one eye, dreaming with the other.

During the day she argued with the Protestant aunts, those that still set foot in the house. The words flew out of her mouth as if they had been hammered in machine shops, as if banners had been designed for their inauguration, as if through long trumpets they had been blown. I ducked, behind cans of white chocolate, behind glass urns of green mints, behind crystal goblets filled with red-and-white ribbon candy. The air, desert dry from the furnace, gray and brown, trailing dust and memories, hissed at the hot-air registers.

She was good at pointing. If I had ever wanted to hire a pointer, someone to call attention to something, I would have hired her. Not that she would rent out. But her finger, index, went straight out, like it came from a bow, and in a flash fixed itself to the offending object, the errant person, lamp, cat, Englishman. She never quickly removed that finger from the air, either, but let it hang there, an object lesson, a monument to error, a signal that someone, something, should mend his ways, or else. *Or else.*

It was that *or else* that terrified me. Anyone who had the power to fly had the power to do other things. Dreadful things. I knew that because she never spoke of them. They remained unspecified, and yet solid, very dangerous, like tanks in the night. Whenever that finger waved in the air I ducked—no, ran, fled screaming, prayed that it wasn't pointed in my direction.

She was called Nann. No one knew why. Sometimes my father called her "The Madam." My grandfather found her one day and married her. She had been waiting for him. I don't know why. He married her the same day he found her. I don't know why. That was in Ireland. I never asked him how they got to this country. She was as old the day she married him as the day she had each one of his seven children. She was old to begin with. She was the Queen of Yesterday, the King of Tomorrow. That's why I was afraid of her. That's why she could fly.

She was not just tall, but huge, and expanded the way a barrel would expand, by adding slats. While she seemed to get bigger, she never seemed to get fatter. Finally she was so huge I thought she would explode. Then she would scatter tiny Nanns across the country. If that ever happened I knew I was doomed.

Once, when the matter seemed important to me and I was able to overcome my terror of her, briefly, I asked her how I came to be, how anyone came to be.

"You were made in heaven," she said. "The Pope made you in heaven."

I could see the Pope busy in heaven, a baker tending to his ovens, checking the temperature. And Nann flying up to help him. She is still wearing her purple dress, but because she doesn't know where heaven is or how cold it will be, she wears a scarf, a red scarf, woolen, and she has Spot/Checkers with her. This is somewhere in a huge stone vault, marble probably, though I am vague on materials.

I hardly imagine her sleeping with my grandfather, but the proof, despite the Pope and his ovens, is there. She was more than female. She was a third sex, a different species, something unaccountable. I don't think she ever let a doctor touch her, not while she was alive. Her children were born at home, in bed. I never saw the outline of her breasts, never knew if she had any, but the evidence suggests that somewhere in that girth lurked a breast or two.

She could fly in the rain without getting wet. She could fly high or low, through clouds or treetops, wearing just about anything. She was always instantly there, wherever she wanted "there" to be. She moved like an elephant, full of heavy grace.

When I was younger, she flew about a lot. She appeared in many places, like frames in a movie. She had errands to run. It was her job to appear behind small children, me among them, and hold us by the neck with that bird-claw hand of hers until we dropped what we held, apologized for something, put back what we had taken. She knew what we were doing, even if we didn't, even if we weren't doing it. Flying was a reinforcement of that knowledge. She could fly because she knew the air. She knew all about air, the places where it would lift you up, the places where it would set you down, the places where the wind blew.

She liked to be right, felt it was her duty to be correct in every instance, and to be instantly obeyed. Being right was an obligation she felt had been bestowed upon her, like wealth or intelligence would be on someone else, and she set about discharging the duties of her office. She made me talk to the priest, made me read the Harvard five-foot shelf of classics, knit me sweaters that itched and sent me silver dollars on my birthday. She gave me a toy truck for Christmas, which I broke in a way that could not be repaired, and the next time she came over I knew she would demand to see "her" truck. I was instantly stricken with debilitating illnesses, all of which required that my jaw be wired shut, that I must not speak, that I must not be questioned. But at best this was a delaying action. She would have me arrested, letting me go only after the truck that couldn't be repaired was repaired.

Nann buys Catholic food. She cooks Catholic meals. It is soft and pale and comes in a variety of colors and shapes—pastels, pliable. It is squeezed out of bags and scooped out of tin cans and dumped out of frozen cardboard containers. It is mixed in bowls and has sugar and eggs and butter and flour added to it, always. It is put in an oven or pan fried on a stove. It is dipped in bread crumbs and fried in oil. It pops out of cardboard containers, the spiraled sides splitting, to be placed like fat, puffy silver dollars on a cookie sheet. It reaches the table pale and steaming: pork chops, string beans, potatoes mashed or boiled or beaten into dumplings, peas, hamburgers that look like abandoned islands, fluffy pies made from sugar and air, compromised cakes whisked to death, huge jungles of cauliflower that threaten to overtake the house, pounds of Jell-O, quivering bowls of tapioca pudding, soft carrots, rings of tomatoes with their edges singed brown, slimy okra, loaves of white bread that can be played like an accordion, cabbage tortured beyond repair, corned beef panting for mercy, waterlogged ham, cornflakes, doughnuts, hot dogs, tomato soup, all served steaming or freezing, broiled or boiled, fried or frozen. It comes to the table overcooked and under glass, sometimes in porcelain or plastic, on china plates, in bowls with huge spoons or scissored scoops.

She can never be too sure about food. It must be thoroughly and completely dead.

She always beat her food to death, whacking it with wood, iron, steel, stone. After many years she had beaten the food out of herself. She looked pale, dreamy. She started to stare at things, afraid they would move, feeling it was only the power of her eyes that kept them in place.

As she got older she got thinner and heavier. She seemed to be weighted down, as if she and gravity were on better terms than they had been before. But more than gravity was involved. It was the Protestants. Her sons had married Lutherans, a race flawed with reason, committed to order, and though on the surface she might seem a natural ally to such logical creatures, underneath she was all puff and magic, a whirlpool of demons. What could the religion of Luther know about this? While they nailed epistles, she purged demons.

She argued with the Protestant aunts about the petrified ham. She invoked the saints, trolls, dragons far and near, charms, garlic, and the sanctity of souls. The aunts, in the wisdom of aunts, would have none of it. They argued with monkish logic, the irredeemable truth. They invoked for her the horror of the Jesuits, the perfidy of Aristotelians. She seemed to collapse in the center, blitzed by this front line of aunts. One evening they arranged to have the ham removed when she was out, and buried.

The removal of the petrified ham, her great-uncle, the armless, legless veteran of Bull Run, seemed to place a great burden on me. I began to question her flying. A hated cousin told me there had been no petrified ham, no great-uncle, and that certainly if there had been, it had not been dusted off.

Nann leaned more. Visions of feathers floated before her eyes. The anointment of birds no longer interested her. She burned her collection of dead birds, sprinkled the ashes in the birdbath. The magic in her reared up, a terrible demon, and threatened to dash her to pieces. I can remember her fussing a room to death, puttering about, moving small useless objects that broke easily from one shelf to another. She made lots of tea, in tiny cups with delicate unrealistic designs. She also made, for no apparent reason, bowls of tuna-fish salad. She fluttered, as if the bird in her was uncomfortable, uneasy about what came next.

"Everything moves," she told me once in the calm of Christmas Eve.

As she got older she seemed to grow upward, become more crystalline. Her skin looked as if it would shatter. Her eyes widened in perpetual amazement. She was eager, intrepid, and yet stunned. She had seen something. Something had opened up. She browsed in bookstores, and moved slowly. I felt she had no right to move so slowly.

The air seemed to press down on her, and I doubted her ability to fly. It was a talent that had left her, flown away. She was cautious. She moved as if objects would crack, as if floors would split open, as if cars would break apart, as if earthquakes would seize her by the throat and pull her deep into the earth. Then she got very dreamy. Gauze had been placed in front of her eyes. The world beneath her feet opened up and she reached out for support, looked for something to hold on to. She had questions about the clothes people wore, and wanted to touch their backs. I felt she was looking for wings, that hers had left her. She sat in a chair and watched the air rise from the register, waiting, as if for the right current.

One day they came to take her to the hospital. She would not go. She stayed in her room and, I am sure, dreamed of birds. The Babe Ruth look in her seemed to fly away.

There is no real evidence, even with her final illness, that she died. I knew no grave, no burial, no headstone. She simply disappeared, and yet she never really left. She is still around. She is waiting.

BOTTLES, HOLES, WATER

5

THE AIR WAS LIGHTER THEN. CLEANER, MORE BUOYANT, AIR
floating in air, air barely holding objects
on the earth, air that couldn't hide the
shape and texture of trees and buildings,
clouds, zeppelins. Taken in, with quick
gulps, it becomes dense, heavy in the
lungs; it becomes a shape, a solid presence. He breathed it quickly, then looked
around to see if anyone was watching.
He continued breathing, gulping it
down, greedy, pumping his lungs, forc-
ing the stars into his eyeballs. Faster,
he pushed it deep into his lungs, as far
as he could, couldn't hold it there, pan-
icked, and let it out in sobs. He got
dizzy, tried to keep breathing as fast as
he could, fell down, and the air rushed,
leaked, out of his lungs. He lay looking
at the sky, dipping, spinning, him or
the sky, he couldn't tell which. That

was the part he liked, the part when he couldn't tell if it was he or the earth that spun quickly around, that bobbed and dipped. He waited until the spinning stopped, until the air stood still and the earth was rigid. Then he began, lungs rising and falling, faster, nose and mouth gulping in gobs of whatever they could suck in. He did it until he got dizzy again and fell down, and would do it over and over until he passed out, until a part of himself shut down and he lay unconscious on the ground, the way his father could, and his mother, if she saw him, would come out of the house screaming, slapping his face. She tried to catch him doing his breathing before he passed out, but he was sly about it, and she couldn't watch him all day. She couldn't even come out every time he passed out. He didn't mind. His passing out, the blackness, the sudden rush of something closing in, didn't bother him. He liked it; he called it going to bed in the daytime. He was looking for a machine that could run on air.

He collected empty bottles and brought them into the backyard. He hid them behind a forsythia bush, until they engulfed the bush, a pile of transparent shells, the thick wavy glass displaying a sea green in the sun, the bottom a sweetly solid residue of ancient alcohol. His mother threw them out as fast as she could. She did not like advertisements. But he would not stop collecting them, despite threats and having the inside of his mouth scoured with Bon Ami. He vaguely thought of filling them with something, something heavy, corrosive. One day he realized he would never fill them with anything. The bottles had to stay empty, in a pile, reminding him of their bottleness, a glassy presence that distorted light and the shape of objects in the background. Bugs crawled in, got stuck, added their compost stink to the residue that clung to the bottom.

This was a thing he set out to do each day, this collecting of bottles. His father never wanted to know why he did it, and he never questioned him about it, but his mother and the priest did, his mother more out of a sense of wanting to know the why of it and the priest just for the excuse of coming by and saving both the boy and his father from eternal damnation, and perhaps saving his mother too, though that was further down in the scale of things, being as the Protestants along with the Jews were heathens unto themselves.

How this questioning about collecting bottles had religious implications quite escaped the boy, as did anything that concerned God, the wearing of suits and ties, or what girls looked like underneath their dresses. Bottles were simple fare, and yet at the same time monumental, possessed of a great depth and resonance the boy could barely grasp and yet knew was there. He pulled wings off flies for the same reason, and liked to mix things—leaves, dog shit, twigs, dirt—in empty tin cans to see if anyone would stick a finger in it. It was a thing he did, this bottle collecting. It possessed a mystery all its own, that began and ended with the collecting, and yet it seemed also to resonate beyond the bottles, as if the shimmering glass was reflecting its own epistemology into the solar system, and beyond.

His father was young, handsome, somewhat athletic, possessed of several negotiable talents, though the boy was too young to be aware of this. His father was quite aware of it, and thought he would make something of himself, indeed already had, but would end up making something quite different than what he expected. The boy existed in the moment. His father had overwhelming power and forced him to do things the boy had no desire to do. For the boy, the world simply *was*. He had no option but to be. Time, and the battle of time within time, had been won. He was not aware of time, and therefore had none to lose. The air was ancient, fresh, timeless.

His mother kept removing the bottles and watched him return each afternoon from his voyage with a bottle on each finger, at least ten in all, sometimes more tucked in pockets or carried in a bag slung over the shoulder. He spent the afternoons breathing, looking at the bottles, measuring the dizziness in his head and the air in his lungs with the space inside the bottles and the air inside that space. He felt as if he could breathe the air inside the bottles into his lungs, suck in the spirit of the bottles. Then he forgot about the bottles and hurried his breathing until he passed out, until his mother came rushing into the yard, wanting to curse but only screaming, a quiet scream that would not waken the neighbors to the double shame of her son's collection and his rapid breathing.

It was a quiet battle, mother against son. His father watched. The bottle pile rose and fell, measuring the industry of the boy against that of his mother, while the rain pushed the bottles and the snow and ice added to the pile, making it grow large, monstrous. A skin of dirt covered the bottles, more filled the crevices where the bottles met, so that a fragile stubble of grass and weeds peppered the dirt. The pile was now glass and dirt and green, now glass and mud, now snow, ice, animal droppings.

Then he went to school, and the mystery seemed to ooze out of things. It evaporated, until things lay still, quiet. He had never said it in so many words, but he could hear things breathe: stones, walls, trees. He matched his breathing to theirs, let his dizziness become their movement. He knew this but did not say it. The words were not there for him to use, but the thought, in some way, was.

For the first time he felt shame at collecting bottles, at breathing too fast. The mystery had not evaporated. It had been taken out of bottles and stones and trees and put into shame. He did not know why he felt shame, but knew only that he felt it. Growing up, feeling a need to grow up, feeling shame at not growing up and then ashamed of that shame, he resolved to end his fascination with bottles and breathing.

One day he came home from school and found that his father had removed all the bottles from the backyard. A spongy yellow vegetation with long tendrils lay in its place, a cramped, pale growth, frantic in its effort to reach sunlight. He did not know this, but his father had saved him from burning. The mystery of bottles and rapid breathing was a dangerous thing. If left uncontrolled it would reach inside him, explode. He could not live with that mystery. He would flame up, blow apart.

He sighed. The air felt heavy, cool. It would not reach as deep into his lungs. The shimmering edges of objects had softened, felt mushy. The world relaxed. It was the beginning of death. He dug holes. He watched the holes fill up with water.

MARGARET'S VAGINA

& THE CATHOLICS

IN CHICAGO, ACROSS THE ALLEY FROM US, THERE WAS A GIRL who would show her vagina. It cost, though it was rumored that for some there was no charge. But I never believed that. She was a long, stringy-looking girl, whose elbows and knees were as big as her hands and feet. Her breasts were the size of lemons, her nipples the size of walnuts, and she had sandy hair that lay in clumps about her neck.

She used to show it in the garage, with the help of a flashlight. It cost extra if you brought your own flashlight.

She didn't have any brothers or sisters, and I don't know what else she did, except this. She never seemed to have to go to school, or study for anything, or work at anything at all. I guess this was her only job.

She was Catholic, in a neighborhood of Protestants.

My friend Nitny was afraid of Catholics. He was small and crawled into tight, dark spaces from which he was pulled kicking and screaming. One day in school he went around and put a dot of bleach on the back of everybody's jacket, uniting us all in a bond of white circles.

When he learned I was baptized he ran away and crawled into a tree trunk, and the only way they could get him out was to call the fire department and cut the tree down.

Nitny played with himself and challenged us to see if we could make "our peckers stand out straight" like he could. He organized pissing contests to see who could piss the farthest, piss the most, or piss the highest. We pissed off roofs, trying to hit people walking by, until we were caught. Nitny said the shape of your penis would determine what you would do in later life. He told me there were some people who pissed through their ass, but I didn't believe him until he told me that's how girls did it, because he had seen his sister squat and make water. Even then I wasn't sure, since Nitny was not reliable on such matters. He said Catholics kidnapped boys and sent them to Rome, where they had to sing in the church choir, and when they started getting hair on their bodies the Pope cut off their wee-wees. You mean their pricks? I said. Whatever you want to call it, he said. A Catholic, he added, had to pledge allegiance to the Pope first, above everything else, and that was why Catholics always crossed their fingers when they said the pledge in school. "They put their hands in their pockets so you won't know," he said. "They always have dirty foreheads because they're not allowed to wash away the holy water the priest puts on them." He told me that nuns had to make water in front of the priests, and the priests could do anything they wanted to the nuns and the nuns couldn't do anything about it because they were forbidden to talk. I told him I had heard nuns talk, and he said that was different, but he never explained why. He said you could buy your way into the Church and if you had enough money become a bishop or an arch-bishop and talk to the Pope anytime you wanted to. He said it cost so many hundreds of dollars to get into heaven, about half that for purgatory, but the Pope was thinking of raising the price soon because he wanted to add to his collection of pornography—the Church had the world's best collection of dirty books and movies. "They got animals doing it with women, guys with three-foot peckers, everything," Nitny said. I asked him how he knew all this. He said he had his sources, which he couldn't reveal at this time. "Jesus," he said, shaking, "how I hate Catholics."

I asked Nitny about Jews and he said he didn't know anything about them, except that they didn't believe in God.

Nitny said you could only trust Protestants. "Just look at Al Capone," he said. "What about Hitler?" I asked. He couldn't hear me, he said.

Surrounded by Catholics, Nitny would shiver. He shivered so hard he shit in his knickers. Then we let him have it and he took his knickers off and started swinging them around and everybody ducked because his shit was flying. Watch out for Nitny's knickers became a common expression.

One day my cousin brought back some wafers from church. He was an altar boy. He asked me if I'd ever tried one and I said no and he said try one, they're different than anything you've ever tasted. It tasted like tightly pressed cotton candy. They're made in heaven, my cousin said. Bullshit, I said. They are, my cousin said, and now that you've eaten one you're a Catholic and bound to the Pope. Bullshit, I said. And anyway, I was already baptized a Catholic when I was a baby, so that makes me a Catholic longer than you, but I'm not bound to anybody. Then we punched each other.

I was surrounded by Catholics. Grandparents, aunts, uncles, cousins, friends: they were all over. I didn't know what I was. I guess I was half Catholic, because I was baptized but didn't go to church or take confession. My friends went to confession on Friday and I went with them, but only to walk into the church. I stayed near the back while they made up things to tell the priest. I wanted to lie on the floor and look up. Everything in the church pointed up: saints' halos and crosses and apses and naves. Candles flickered inside glass tubes, statues of saints and virgins and martyrs, dozens of altars. At first I thought there was a bunch of different religions all going on in the same place, kind of a supermarket of religions. Too many saints, too many candles. Which one should you pray to? Suppose you slighted one? What if you missed a Hail Mary or an Our Father? There'd be hell to pay.

Catholics never owned businesses. They were in civil service or else worked for Protestants and Jews. Once a year they put a big lump of dirt on their forehead. My father didn't like wearing dirt, so he left the Church.

Down the street from us lived a stockbroker, who was so rich he drove a tank that had wheels, and next door to us lived an accountant, who practiced black magic, and next door to him a retired Seabee, who made a fortune in the construction business during the war selling sump pumps. He was always talking to me whenever I walked by, and he always started off by saying, "Do you know what he said? Do you know what he said? Here's what he said. Here's what he said. He said . . ." I could never remember what he said after he said it. Farther down the block lived a drunken milkman, and next to him a fat man, whose son I kept pushing over and whose wife was the thinnest woman I have ever seen. She looked like a hairy straw. She wore wool socks that came up to her knees, slippers that showed off her bony feet, and she smelled of Old Dutch cleanser.

The girl who showed her vagina had a different name, but we called her Margaret. I saw a girl in one of those dog or horse movies whose name was Margaret O'Brien. All she had to show was her face. The Margaret across the alley also let you watch her pee, but that cost extra. We got bored with that, so she tossed it in free. She did it just the way Nitny said.

Across the street from us was a jungle.

It covered a city block and was fenced in. Trees had been growing there for years. Nitny and I scaled the fence and smoked cigarettes we had stolen. A salt and pepper man lived in the jungle. He was an old man with a beard and a gun that shot salt and pepper in your eyes. He lived on dogs and cats and weeds he boiled over his fire. There was an old railroad siding that had rusted away, leaving the boxcar and the rails it rested on. Nitny and I could hear the salt and pepper man inside. After he blinded you with salt and pepper he took you inside his boxcar and made you pee in a jar and keep his place clean for a week. After that he might let you go, though he kept the jar of pee. He had an old dog who was too tough to cook, who ate cats. He kept ants and spiders and he would climb a tree and drop them on your head.

Nitny and I dug a cave deep in the jungle. We sat there and smoked and Nitny told me stories about what priests did to nuns. They all involved nuns having their dresses lifted up. Nuns, he told me, never wore underwear or brassieres. That was in case a priest wanted a good piece and didn't want to spend time undoing hooks or snaps. Nitny told me priests were uncoordinated. He said the nuns exhausted them.

We had wars in the jungle. We put Billy, the blind kid, up in the front line and showed him the direction to toss rocks. He was big and fat and easy to hit and he took most of the attack away from us. Plus, it didn't make any difference if he got hit in the eye. When he was hurt bad he'd sit down and cry, and when he stopped we would take him home. His mother whipped him at home, for no reason at all, and we climbed up on an old tire propped alongside her house to watch him get beaten. Sometimes she would come out and chase us away. We made balsa-wood planes in the backyard. There was powder you mixed with water to make glue. It came in little packets. You mixed it until it looked like pus. With the balsa sticks pinned down on the paper plan, you dropped some glue on the joints. Billy made planes with us. He could do the whole thing by touch. It was beautiful to watch him, the way he could pin a tiny strip of balsa wood and not even see what he was doing but still be able to do it. He was fat and ugly, but he would never know that. He hardly knew he was blind, and if you don't know maybe you're not. Sometimes when we got bored we would pour glue all over his fingers while he was working or make a big mess of his plans. He got upset and went in and complained to his mother who came out and chased us out of the yard. The next day we were back.

In the jungle we sat in the trees and dropped things on people. Rocks and branches and dirt, sometimes tin cans or broken glass. We dug holes and covered them with thin sticks and leaves and watched people fall in them. Then we poured water on them, or if they were girls, peed on them. You could mix dog shit and cat shit together and make a paste and leave it on a footrail or smear it on a handrail someone had nailed to a tree. We smeared it on tree trunks and low branches that grew across the trails, the kind you hold back so the person behind you escapes being lashed.

David was four when he died. Leukemia. I hardly remember him. There is a picture of the three of us, brothers, in the backyard, dressed up. The picture is blurred. My father's hands shook. David was dressed in a sailor suit. I can't tell what my other brother and I were wearing. It was spring. Everything was brown. There were no leaves. Our backyard was full of holes.

I don't know how long before he died we knew he was dying. We knew he was sick. That's all they told us. I don't know what David knew. I don't know what it was possible for him to know. I didn't cry when my parents came back from the hospital. I rode around the block on my scooter. I had this special grace bestowed upon me because my brother died. I didn't miss him. I didn't know what there was to miss.

I can't remember where David slept. We had three bedrooms in our house. My parents slept in one and my brother and I in the others. When David came along there was no bedroom for him.

I think David slept with my other brother, who slept with Fody, who lived in the blanket chest. Fody had no size; that is, he had any size he wanted to have. He wore my brother's clothes, messed up my brother's room. He was the perfect friend. I never saw him, but my brother did. Fody played with him when no one else would. He told him things. They had their own language. Fody played the violin, but you couldn't hear him.

The four of us lived in the house besides my parents. Two got killed before the house was sold.

I don't know what Fody died of. I asked my brother about Fody, but all he said was that he wasn't around anymore. He didn't know where he was, he didn't know *if* he was, nor did he know if he was coming back.

When my parents came from the hospital they told us that David wasn't sick, that he wasn't in pain, that he was in heaven. I asked my mother if that was in the ground. That was where you put dead people. My mother said no. I knew heaven meant dead. My brother and I didn't go to the funeral. Since the casket was smaller and the gravediggers didn't have to dig such a deep hole, I asked my mother if the funeral was cheaper, like getting half fare on the train.

I asked my brother if he was going to have a funeral for Fody. He told me Fody didn't need one.

That was during the war. As soon as you graduated from high school they put you in the army and trained you and shipped you overseas and you either stayed there or came back limping or crippled or came back doing nothing at all. We could hardly wait to fight. The Germans always shot you with pearl-handled Lugers at close range, in the head or in the gut. The Japs bayoneted you in the gut. They liked to stick knives in people. They were perverts. We had to wipe them off the face of the earth. The Germans too. We used bombs a lot. The war came to our block one night.

I was asleep in bed, but I heard the screams. A bus full of navy men was turning the corner into our block. I don't know why. I had a cousin who was in the navy. He hid in a cave for months. When he came back, all he wanted to do was drink milk. The bus came around the corner. Something happened. It caught fire. It hit something, or something exploded, or a Jap bomber dropped a bomb. There was only one door on the bus. They had welded the other one shut to fit extra seats in. The bus caught fire and they all jammed the front door. It happened very quickly, before the fire engines came. I heard screams. The next day we saw burned grass and black plastic buttons with anchors on them. Most of them were melted. I don't think my cousin was on the bus.

I would lie in bed in the morning and listen to the war. They played the war on the radio. They interrupted the war for commercials. To me, hot Ralston will always mean World War II. We knew who was going to win because you always knew who was going to win on the radio. That was how they decided what to put on the radio.

They printed the war too. You could see pictures of bodies. There were big headlines with the numbers killed, wounded, missing. But you never knew who was going to win in the newspapers.

The war in the movies was the best war. We never lost a movie. A lot of movie people fought in the war. None of them got killed.

When the war was over, rolls of toilet paper fell out of the sky. People got drunk. You could do anything you wanted to girls in the street.

I thought a lot about the war. Being brave in the war and killing Germans and Japs was a good thing. But I didn't want anyone to die.

Nitny, Johnny Bregman, Faustio Precept, and I make a boat out of orange crates and dead tree limbs and float across a pond made by a broken fire hydrant. The boat sinks. We leave it there and pile old tires on it and lash poles to the tires and start building a fort. We tie a rope to a tree and make a swinging walkway so we can get in the fort without going through the mud. We sit in the fort and wait for the salt and pepper man. The idea is to throw bricks on him, pee on him, then set him on fire. He's probably a Jap, or a German. That's what the Japs did in *Guadalcanal Diary*, but they didn't show the part where they peed on them. Nitny told me about that.

Margaret found our fort. We let her in.

She walked through the mud, holding up her dress. She never cared about getting her feet dirty because her feet were always dirty, and she never washed because she felt the first layer of dirt protected her from all the other layers.

"What are you waiting for?" she asked.

"Shut up," Nitny said.

"The enemy," Faustio said.

"Who's the enemy?"

We looked at her as if she had rat shit in her hair.

"You really are dumb. They're all around us. They're about to attack, and if you make any more dumb noises they'll cut your tits off."

"I don't see anyone out there."

"We're dealing with concealment. They all look like trees. You've got to be trained to spot them."

She leaned forward and peered through the orange-crate slats.

"Hey, Margaret," Johnny Bregman said, "let's have a look at your cunt."

"You got any money?"

"No."

"No freebies."

"There's nothing the hell to see, anyway," Nitny said.

"There's nothing you're going to see."

"Hey, Margaret," Bregman said, "is that what you're going to do when you're grown up?"

"I am grown up."

"No, I mean taller and bigger breasts and all that. I mean can you make a living doing that?"

"I'll make out."

"No, I mean is there a regular job, like an occupation, you know, showing your thing?"

"Shut up."

We waited. We heard that we were going to be attacked by Nonzio the Armenian. His family were refugees from Albania. They had just come to this country and lived two blocks away. He was thirteen years old but he had hair all over his body, even on his nose. His prick was ten inches long.

"Hey, Margaret, do you know how long Nonzio's prick is?"

"Ten inches, big deal."

Nonzio died in New York years later. He peed on the third rail in the subway and electrocuted himself. His shriveled-up dick is in a jar of formaldehyde in the New York Forensic Museum, but you have to be a doctor to go in and see it.

I watched a trail of ants crawling up one side of the fort. My hobby was ants. Whenever I found them I fed them. I watched them walk single file up to the ceiling to get to work on a Popsicle drop. Don't ask me how a Popsicle drop got on the ceiling. Ants are some of your smartest insects, definitely among the tops, if not the tops, except for your termites. I kept ants at home in our basement. I also kept them in my bedroom, near my window. They climbed all the way up the wall, two stories of brick, to fit in under a crack in my screen and then sunned themselves on my sill. I fed them sugar. The best thing I like about ants is that you can't make pets of them. They don't give a shit about you; they don't care what you do as long as you don't step on them, and to be honest, they hardly care about that. They don't moan and they don't complain, and they all look alike, so you can't pick out any favorites. Ants are really great animals, though I can't say if we all lived like ants the world would be a better place. Also, they don't have anything to teach us, and we don't have anything to teach them, and that's another reason, two reasons, why I like them.

"Nonzio's out there somewhere."

"Probably in a tree, waiting to swing down on us."

"I heard he's got a tail he hides in his leg."

"All Armenians got tails, dummy."

"How the hell can you fight someone who's got a tail?"

"Pin his tail to a trunk, stupid."

We waited for Nonzio.

Whenever we heard a plane we looked up and tried to match it in a plane spotter's manual put out by the Cream of Wheat company. I once thought I saw an Admiral Yamaguchi light attack bomber, but Nitny told me it was only a B-25. Still, one Saturday afternoon I saw a Messerschmitt come out of the clouds, a single cloud, in fact, the only one in the sky. It carried two auxiliary tanks on its wingtips and shot out of the clouds as if it had come into being up there. I hadn't seen it go into the cloud, but it came out like some glorious piece of silver, and did a fantastic series of loops and rolls. There wasn't another plane in the sky. I expected P-38s and P-51 Mustangs to attack it, big sooty puffs of antiaircraft smoke spattering near, and flaming tracers of machine gun bullets. But it remained up there by itself, cutting, riding and gliding on the air as if it owned the currents. Then it hurtled toward the ground, pulling out of its dive at the last minute.

I looked between the slats, expecting to see Nonzio slinking through the jungle, crouched over like a baboon.

"The hell with this," Faustio said. "I'm going out."

He poked his head up through the escape hatch and got hit with an arrow.

"It's Nonzio," he cried.

His earlobe was bleeding. Arrows clattered against the orange crates and a few slipped through the slats. We figured we had a better chance outside the fort, so we jumped off the tower into the mud. Arrows fell, sticking in the mud, in the orange crates, or in us. We started to throw rocks, even though we didn't know where we were throwing them.

"He's got a whole gang of Armenians with him," Nitny said.

"This whole place stinks of Armenians."

"Where the hell is he?"

No one knew.

We watched Margaret climb out of the fort. She climbed out ass first, and Nonzio hit her with an arrow. She took it out and turned around, bleeding.

"Fucking cocksucker!"

"I see him!"

"Stone the bastard!"

We showered him with rocks.

Nonzio yelled and stood up in the tree. He was wearing a banana in his hair. "Balkan wop," Nitny yelled. Nonzio fit an arrow in his bow, but before he could fire it he slipped, turned, grabbed for a tree branch, couldn't hold it, and fell in the mud.

Margaret ran up to him, screaming and shouting.

"You sonofabitch, you bastard, you frozen turd!"

She took off her shoe and kicked him in the back. He didn't move.

"Hey, Margaret, should we look at his prick?"

"You could cut it off for all I care."

Nonzio refused to move. He lay absolutely still, a log in the swamp. He had a peaceful, pained look on his face, with no idea that many years later his dick would be on display in a famous New York museum.

"Why doesn't he move?"

"Let's get the fuck out of here."

"He's dead. I seen dead people before. He's one of them."

"Let me see him," Nitny said.

He leaned over and stuck a finger up Nonzio's nose.

"That's how you can tell if they're dead," he said.

Faustio stared at the body lying in the mud. The year before, his father had died of a heart attack in a huge insurance office, his head falling into the Scotch tape.

"Wait," Margaret said. "Who's gonna fix my ass?"

Nitny got up slowly and started to run.

"Hey," I said.

He ran slowly, taking little steps, barely lifting his feet from the ground. It looked as if he was trying to tamp the earth down as he ran, rocking from side to side. He was drunk, or sick, or maybe just afraid that he had stuck his finger up the nose of a Catholic.

"What is this?" I yelled.

He picked up speed, and I ran after him. It would be useless to yell after him. He would run without hearing, running just to run, like a dog that has it in mind to tear across a street full of traffic. Nothing would stop him.

But the tree that we pissed on people from stopped him. He was standing in front of it, panting. He had taken out his pocket knife and started stabbing the trunk.

"Hey! What?" I said. It was my favorite tree.

He looked at me as if I shouldn't be talking.

"Hey?"

"They'll put us in jail. They'll kill us. We'll be dead," he said. "He fell."

"It won't work that way. That's not the way they do it."

The knife closed on his thumb, drawing a fat slug of blood. He licked his thumb, and then, shouting, stabbed the palm of his hand. I rushed over to him.

"Get away," he said.

He looked at the blood coming from his hand. For some reason I felt his blood should not be red. There was something about Nitny that had to be protected. He was missing something hard over his body, missing a shell.

"It's the Catholics," he said. "When you let them climb trees they fall."

"He's not Catholic. He's a Baltic wop."

"Not Baltic. Baltimore. Baltimore!"

He kept licking the blood that ran slowly out of his hand, as if hand and blood were an ice cream cone. Embarrassed, he looked up. "I got too much of this."

And then he said, "Do you want to trade?"

Before I knew what happened, he cut my hand with his pocket knife. I didn't feel a thing until I looked down and saw what he'd done, and even then I didn't feel anything until I thought about it—the tear in my skin, the knife entering my hand—and having thought about it, felt the pain.

He put his palm against my hand. He had a smile on his face. I could see his teeth, on the bottom, were turning black at the gums.

"We're bonded. We're brothers."

I pulled my hand away from his.

"Now we'll know what the other does, we'll always know."

"Jesus, Nitny, your friggin' blood is probably poison."

He said nothing.

"What a stupid-ass thing to do."

My hand throbbed. I grabbed for the knife.

"Let me look at the blade. What kind of shit is on it?"

He took it out of his pocket and opened it up, running his thumb along the edge. The tip of his tongue curled at the edge of his mouth.

"This is wonderful," he said.

Suddenly I felt he should be exalted, his blood preserved. There was the idiot in him that I loved, a blessed bit of stupidity.

"You see," he said, "I think it's the way we breathe."

It was late afternoon, and I wondered if Nonzio was really dead, and if we should go back and touch his dead body. Nitny said that dead flesh didn't bounce, that it just went in where you pushed it and stayed there and that you had to pull it out and when you did you could see the pinch marks on the flesh. When people died they fell over. I wondered why trees didn't do that. When dogs and cats died they flattened out. I don't know how it is with ants. They must crack.

"I'm trying to figure this out," Nitny said.

"What out?"

"This." He drew a circle with his fingers, the back of his hand level.

"Another thing," he said. "There's this sound that people make, something between a sneeze and a cough; I can't figure it out. They do it when they don't want you around. I think people do it just before they die. You do it in your nose, your throat. You know how it feels when you come out of a swimming pool?"

"The water?"

"Part of it—the part you swallow, the part in the back."

"The water or that part of it?"

"I can't figure it out."

"Do you remember when you hit Faustio with a bat?"

"I can't remember."

Only one side of Faustio's head got bigger, a different color. We thought he had another head growing out of his head, a head that was inside his first head, and Nitny's bash on the skull set it free. People have different heads inside them. That's what I think.

"It's getting late. Let's go touch Nonzio."

We walked back to the fort, dodging upturned rusty nails in boards we had placed on the trail and avoiding the slimy, shit-coated handrails that made climbing easier. The air was filled with an amber fog. The light coming through the leaves yellowed them at the edge. We heard someone sigh.

Nonzio was gone, his body was gone.

Inside the fort, Faustio was dancing with Margaret. His pants were down, her skirt was up. He kept bumping her at the hips. They did a funny little dance across the dirt floor, more like hopping. Faustio seemed to be pushing her somewhere she didn't want to go. He quickly turned to look at us. I remember the way he was breathing.

SMILIN' ED McCONNELL

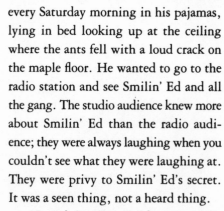

8 ½ - 10

HE HEARD *THE SMILIN' ED MCCONNELL SHOW* OVER THE RADIO
every Saturday morning in his pajamas,
lying in bed looking up at the ceiling
where the ants fell with a loud crack on
the maple floor. He wanted to go to the
radio station and see Smilin' Ed and all
the gang. The studio audience knew more
about Smilin' Ed than the radio audience; they were always laughing when you
couldn't see what they were laughing at.
They were privy to Smilin' Ed's secret.
It was a seen thing, not a heard thing.

   He and the other children were ush-
ered into the studio half an hour before
air time. There were two kinds of air in
a studio: live air and dead air. Air time
was live air: exalted, electric, crammed
with vivid currents. Before the show
was dead air: heavy, turgid, nervous,

people rustling about, kids getting up to pee, engineers testing microphones. During dead air there was no Smilin' Ed and All the Gang, no Midnight the Cat, no Squeakie the Mouse, no Froggie the Gremlin ("Plunk your magic twanger, Froggeee!").

Then the announcer walked onstage, holding the hand of a small boy dressed in blue shorts, a blue jacket, and a yellow shirt. He wore a small beaked cap and had a shock of brown hair that seemed to cup his forehead. The announcer left the boy, who turned around several times with his tongue out and his head tilted upward. The announcer came back onstage with a small wooden chair. The boy's feet would not touch the floor. He kept swinging them, bouncing them off the chair legs. The announcer put his hand out, as if he were *Sieg Heil*ing the audience.

"Boys and girls, let's give a big hand for Ronald the Wonder Boy."

Everybody clapped, though nobody knew what for.

"All right. If everybody's ready, let's have the first question."

The boy on the stage kept looking over the heads of the audience. Who was he looking at?

"Fifty-three times sixty-eight."

"Three thousand, six hundred and four."

The answer came too soon after the question, as if the questioner had answered.

"Make it harder," said the announcer. "Ronald the Wonder Boy can do harder."

"The square root of six thousand, seven hundred and forty-five."

"Eighty-two point one two seven nine."

Seated off to one side of the stage was a man with an adding machine, scribbling furiously on a pad of paper.

Tons of numbers were shouted at Ronald the Wonder Boy, and he quickly reflected the answers back as if he had some kind of special answering prism. The man with the adding machine could barely keep up with him, and made him pause every so often to check the answers.

"Come on," the announcer said, "let's try to stump the Wonder Boy."

More numbers were shouted up, heavier numbers, and barely had the questioner's voice died down than Ronald the Wonder Boy would reflect back the answer. On square roots, the Wonder Boy asked how many places to the right of the decimal point they would like him to carry out the transaction.

The audience became excited, then angry at the Wonder Boy. They wanted him to make a mistake, taunted him, mumbled the numbers, but error was as foreign to him as impermeability was to air. He was not arrogant about his perfection but, rather, indifferent. He slouched in his chair, fingering his cap, his other hand fondling his crotch. His voice carried far for someone his size, someone smallish. The audience became increasingly angry at him, as if their dumbness only served to set off his smartness.

Algebra, geometry, calculus, the erotica of mathematics, were shouted to him from math wizards in the audience, and Ronald the Wonder Boy kept bouncing back answers until one of the questioners questioned his answer, claiming that he had made an error in the fourth number to the right of the decimal point, a ten thousandth, and a blackboard was brought out and the question done slowly on the blackboard, and the Wonder Boy's answer was shown to be correct because he had rounded off a number to the right of that, a one hundred thousandth.

But rather than placate the audience, this only served to infuriate them. A great hum spread through the crowd, an insect buzzing.

"Get him out of here!"

The announcer held up his hands.

"Boys and girls . . ."

"Off the stage!"

"Boys and girls, please . . ."

The Wonder Boy slouched in his chair, his hand furiously rubbing his tiny genitals.

"Ronald only has time for one more question," the announcer said, "before Smilin' Ed and All the Gang . . ."

No one said a word. Someone farted.

The announcer kept wiping something from his mouth.

Suddenly the Wonder Boy jumped up and pulled his hand out of his pants. He started to say something.

"Huh huh, huh huh."

The Wonder Boy walked around the stage, bouncing his head up and down.

"Huh huh, huh huh, huh," he kept saying.

The insect buzz came back from the audience. The announcer ran after the Wonder Boy and dragged him back to the chair.

"All right, boys and girls," the announcer said, "let's have a big cheer for Ronald the Wonder Boy!"

He held the last r of Wonder and then held the oy of Boy.

The audience moaned, growled, buzzed, but refused to clap, and Ronald the Wonder Boy was rushed offstage. Behind the curtains there was a slap, a gargling noise, another slap, and a longer gargle. Then a great stillness settled over the stage, and the audience. People looked around to see who was making the silence, searching for a shape to the quiet, the dead air that weighed down the studio.

There was a boy sitting next to him in short pants, who kept squirming in his seat. He knew the boy wanted to pee, but he was in the middle of the row and didn't want to get up and brush against all the knees and make people push back in their seats. The boy wore knee-length socks and white clip-on suspenders, and his forehead seemed to hang over his nose. The boy also wore Buster Brown Shoes, the sponsors of Smilin' Ed McConnell and All the Gang (Sound of barking. "That's my dog Tide. He lives in the shoe. My name's Buster Brown. Look for me in there too"). Now the boy started to bounce in his seat. It was getting close to airtime, and he knew the boy would not want to miss Smilin' Ed or any of the gang, and if he got up now and started to walk, when he came back his footsteps might be broadcast over the air, and Smilin' Ed would not like that.

Then the announcer came onstage, and everybody laughed and squealed, and the curtains opened and there were several people standing next to a microphone. The biggest one, the one with lots of face, so much face that he had enough face for two or three people, was Smilin' Ed. Smilin' Ed was the first one to talk, and he sounded just like he did over the radio. But his face was huge. It was bigger than any face the boy had ever seen. The boy thought Smilin' Ed was hiding another face inside his, perhaps hiding two separate faces, each one tucked away in a cheek, because his cheeks were so big and had so many folds in them, flesh over flesh, wrinkles that could grip, hold, hide.

"It's Smilin' Ed and All the Gang . . ."

Applause, squeals.

"With Midnight the Cat . . ."

Cheers, applause.

"Squeakie the Mouse . . ."

Applause, squeals.

"Buster the Dog . . ."

Cheers, applause.

"And Froggie the Gremlin!"

Cheers, applause, squeals, laughter.

But where was Froggie? All the other animals were up there, except for Froggie, which was just like him, because he was always pulling tricks on Smilin' Ed and that was naughty, but the kids squealed with glee because they liked him to do that, even though they liked Smilin' Ed too.

"Plunk your magic twanger, Froggeee!"

Boooiiiiinng!

Lots of squeals. There was Froggie. He looked green and long, much like what the boy imagined an oversized cucumber looked like. Froggie talked in a low, gravelly voice. He was about to pull some mean trick on someone, probably Smilin' Ed. Froggie kept hopping around on the piano, as if he was on the end of a string. The boy who had come to see Smilin' Ed and All the Gang looked at the boy seated next to him with the large forehead and saw that he had started to pee his pants. The dribble ran out his shorts and settled on the seat, where it puddled, darkened the covering, and then soaked in. The other boy looked terror-stricken, but delighted with his pee. He was between terror and delight. He couldn't stop the pee from coming. It trickled down the edge of the seat onto the floor. He looked around, expecting someone to notice it, hoping someone would notice it, a combination of the two. Shame reddened his cheeks, and terror froze the shame.

Froggie did something mean to Smilin' Ed. Midnight the Cat was stuck up a tree and Smilin' Ed had to climb the tree and rescue Midnight. Froggie had put him there. "Yes I did yes I did oh boy oh boy oh boy!" Smilin' Ed climbed the tree on the radio, huffing and puffing, but when he got to the top of the radio tree, Midnight was gone. On the radio, he was on the ground. It was another one of Froggie's tricks. "I did that too I did that too oh boy oh boy oh boy!" Huffing and puffing, Smilin' Ed had to climb down again. But he only did this on the radio. On the stage, Smilin' Ed never moved. He huffed and puffed into the microphone and made noises that sounded as if he were climbing. And yet if he were home listening to the radio, he knew Smilin' Ed was climbing. He was there, but he wasn't there. There was a world, the boy knew, somewhere between the studio where the sounds were made and the radio where he could hear the sounds that the *real* Smilin' Ed did climb the tree, and Midnight the Cat really was up the tree, conjured there by Froggie the Gremlin, and then conjured back down again on the ground, and that world was not something he made up in his mind. It was real. It was a place, he knew, not just in his mind but in a real space, a space that he thought might be between the studio and all the radios listening to Smilin' Ed.

When Smilin' Ed came to get Froggie, angry at being tricked, there was an explosion, the kids squealed, and Froggie disappeared. "Where did that darn gremlin go?" asked Smilin' Ed. The kids shouted and squealed. The boy thought that Froggie had disappeared into the world where Smilin' Ed had climbed the tree. That world, between seeing and hearing, was the real world. It was the world of air.

"Well, boys and girls, Smilin' Ed wants to remind each and every one of you to pour yourself a big glass of milk every day—"

"And pour it on your head!"

"Yes, and pour it on your head—no no no. . . . Darn that gremlin."

Shouts, squeals, shrieks.

"And be sure every night before you go to bed—"

"To pee in your pants!"

"Yes, to pee in your pants—no no no. . . ."

More shouts, shrieks, squeals.

"To say your prayers and brush your teeth."

Kids still laughing.

"Now, you be quiet, Froggie. And listen to your mother and father, and do what they say, and—"

"Dump ketchup on the table!"

Laughter, squeals.

"Now you're not going to trick me anymore, Froggie. I just won't listen to what you say. I'll put my fingers—"

"In my mouth and vomit!"

"Yes, I'll put my fingers in my mouth and vomit—no no no. . . ."

Shrieks, prolonged screams.

Then Midnight the Cat played his violin and Squeakie the Mouse and Buster the Dog sang a song and Smilin' Ed sang too and the show was over.

When the boy left the studio, Ronald the Wonder Boy was sitting in the back seat of a car by himself, picking his nose. His skin looked too white to be human. The more he picked his nose, the more the boy wanted to ask him about Smilin' Ed's secret and what went on behind the curtain and if Smilin' Ed was really one or several people, heads inside heads. But the whiteness of Ronald the Wonder Boy's skin frightened him, and he suddenly realized that the Wonder Boy knew less than he did, much less, and that he would never know much more.

TIME

I AM TEN YEARS OLD AND FRANKLIN ROOSEVELT HAS JUST DIED.

I don't know who he is, but I know who Mickey Mouse and Bugs Bunny and Sid Luckman are. Some people cry because he died, but I don't and my father doesn't. Shortly after that the war ended. I knew it was over because toilet paper fell from the sky.

I am ten years old, wishing desperately to be twelve. I want to leap across eleven, jump directly into twelve. Twelve is a number so exalted it has its own name.

I am ten years old and have seen large amounts of my own blood, seen a man get on top of a woman, had the idea that eternity doesn't have so much to do with time as with space, held a tiny bird in my hands that died because I breathed on it, tried to hear the sound of pure wind, built all the major American fighter planes out of balsa wood, cut open a snake and taken out a frog that was still alive, been bitten three times by the same wasp, eaten grass, wondered where all the shit goes, tried to get ants to fight, drunk old beer, and made plans to put my hand on a woman's breast. I am rude when I can be, sneaky when I must be, a mind on the verge of foul thoughts, an expert pusher, a stamper of toes, someone who collects pictures of big women wearing tiny clothes.

Now that the war is over, Nann is disappearing. She lies in a big bed in the back room, the one at the end of the hall where my aunt sleeps. I walk in the room and the bed looks like a fortress—huge posts at the corners. Nann hides under layers of comforters. She looks like a pile of peeled potatoes. She doesn't speak. I can barely see her. The room tilts toward the bed. China madonnas, paperweights, and macramé quilts threaten to tumble into her bed. Linen is piled high in one corner of the room. The shades are drawn. There is only one window in the room. I feel like I am inside a tornado. My father leans over to speak to her. I can't hear what they are saying. Her gray hair tumbles over the pillow, powders like rust. Her eyes are soggy marshmallows. She has a bulbous nose and her throat sags in many places. When she speaks, little patches of her face speak with her. Her throat mimics her lips. She lies deep in the bed, as if its pillowness will wrap itself around her head.

She says something about "the boy" and turns toward me. My father nods, almost smiling. She looks loose to me, as if parts of her will die at different times. My grandfather has died several years before, but I don't know what room he died in. The room that Nann is dying in is the room that my father and his brothers and sister were conceived in. It has four layers of wallpaper, the last yellowed and bubbling. The varnish on the doorframe is black and lined with cracks, like drought-stricken land. A light bulb hangs from a soft velvet cord; when you turn the switch, it feels like it turns in heavy cotton.

I don't want to be in that room with Nann. My father knows this and rarely brings me up there.

I sit downstairs with my cousins while aunts and uncles climb the spiral staircase to see Nann. My aunt has white linen over the hot-air registers to catch the soot, and every time the furnace goes on, the linen does a little dance, hopping and skipping to the tune of the heat. I put my foot down on the linen flap over the register next to me, pushing the heat back into the furnace, back into the air where it came from.

I still rock myself to sleep every night by turning my head from side to side while I lie in bed. I make a pact with myself that when I become twelve I will no longer do this. I will fall asleep from sheer boredom, like an adult. Boredom is a sign of maturity to me.

My father wears a double-breasted suit whenever he goes to see Nann. It is dark blue and accentuates his belly. I watch him climb the stairs, stepping dangerously close to the narrow center part of the staircase. I expect him to come bumping down on his ass, with a businesslike expression on his face.

It takes Nann a long time to die. Wherever you go when you die, she doesn't want to go. Even when she does die she will not go there. She doesn't like people telling her where to go. She won't let God tell her where to go.

She doesn't die. She disappears.

BEING

10 ½

IT FELT FUNNY TO BE. HE KEPT PINCHING HIS FINGERS, HANDS, punching himself in the arm.

What if there were different me's? he thought.

He was struck by the way things just were. He was struck by the willed being of things, by their urgent necessity.

He could see the air. The air had a secret message. He could decode the message on his Captain Midnight Secret Decoder. He was a Secret Squadron member. After every program Captain Midnight broadcast a secret message in code. You could not reveal the message on pain of death, or worse. As a Secret Squadron member, you had taken a sworn oath. Here is what one of the messages said:

Never cut down trees.

Trees are the fingers of the soul reaching for air, grabbing for air. Air is the home of the soul. The soul wants to go home. The soul is tiny. It rises in the air. Wind is the noise the soul makes rising in the air.

He would open his skin. He would cut himself. He would burn. He would rise in the air.

WAR

LET ME TELL YOU HOW NITNY SHITS. HE LOWERS HIS PANTS and sits on the toilet seat. Then he jumps up. There may be something swimming in there that bites. Then he shits. He wipes himself standing up.

He is standing up now. He is leaning forward so the dirt will fall off. He has dug himself out of the hole he had dug himself into. But Nitny does not belong in dirt. He buried himself in the ground because they were after him for putting circles of bleach on everybody's jacket.

Nitny has united us in a bond of white circles, tied us together in a circle of white circles. He has a curse on us. He makes us do things. The bleach is like pigeon shit, like the white in pigeon shit.

We have decided to punish some

kids on another block. It is one of the things we do. Their block smelled funny. No one knew why, but as soon as you walked on that block you were hit with this odor, like socks or lasagna, or old people's dress clothes. Things drip on that block: trees, buildings, people. It bothers us that all the houses on that particular block had been built on a slant. They looked cracked, though they were larger and grander than those on our block.

Nitny explained to us why we were better. "We have white circles," he said. "What do they have?" It was a good question. I couldn't think of an answer. We planned to go over and start the war on their block, but before we could, they beat up Nitny. He stumbled back to our block, his face roughed over. He had bruises on his neck and a yellow stain on the back of his shirt.

"Why did they do that?" Higby said. "We didn't do anything."

Nitny looked dull, as if he had twenty or thirty IQ points punched out of him.

"It's no fucking fair," Vernon said.

"What does Nitny have to say about it?" Charney said.

But Nitny had nothing to say. Speech had been sucked from him. We drag out our engines of violence. Slingshots, rocks, rubber-band guns made from sliced sections of inner tubes, bows and arrows, blowguns, and garbage can lids. This brightens him up. He finds some cone-shaped paper cups. We fill them with mud and throw them like footballs, hoping the spinning point of the cup will lodge in someone's eye. To add ballast, we put rocks in the cups, and when we run out of cups plan to throw rocks.

But their technology is superior: nails, gravel and rocks, railroad spikes, broken shards of mirror, chains. We spend most of our time ducking. Even blind Billy, our point man, runs home crying, almost getting hit by a car as he crosses the street. Nitny has us form a circle. "The power of the white circle is supreme," he says. I like the way he says it, as if he were dipping a diseased foot in a tub of bleach. They dump hot nails and oil over our heads. It is bad. Starting at Seventy-fourth and Jeffery, they push us back to Seventy-fifth and Jeffery, where the breastless lady runs the candy store.

Nitny suggests a counterattack through old man Taschnitz's basement, but they are waiting for us at the rear door and bombard us with rocks, two-by-fours, and dog shit, the last item outlawed by the Geneva Convention. Nitny is hit in the head with a rock, and we drag him to safety behind some garbage cans.

"Where are the elephants?" he asks.

A beautiful sort of purple blood is streaming from his head.

"Feed the elephants," he says. Then he starts to vomit.

Leaving Nitny to puke, we come out swinging two-by-fours and charge their positions. They only have time to throw a few rocks before we overrun their garbage cans. I catch one kid going over the fence and get him in the shoulder. There is a funny look on his face. His arm hangs limp from the fence, but I don't see any blood or even a hole in his shoulder. I am about to hit him again, but he puts his good hand up and then kicks me in the stomach. Kneeling over and wishing I could puke, I watch him stumble off, his one arm swinging like a pendulum as he ape-motions his way across the yard.

A bucket of tar flies off the roof. The bucket misses Jorgensen, but not the tar.

"What's it like over there?" Nitny asks.

He is leaning against a set of garbage cans. His head is wrapped in a deeply stained T-shirt.

"You got hit with a rock."

"Huh?"

"The bleeding's stopped."

"Huh?"

Jorgensen is trying to pull tar from his hair, but all he does is get it on his hands, which he wipes on his pants. Other things come off the roof: milk boxes, bottles, tire irons that twirl in the air, and chicken wire that seems to float down.

"When it stops we can rush him. He won't have anything left."

"Rush him now. The stairway is hidden from the roof."

"Sure. And run across the open yard?"

"He stopped. Rush him, Charney, rush him."

Charney is a small kid whose face looks like a quilt. Bits of his mouth are spread all over his face. He runs bowlegged.

But he is fast. It is about one hundred feet to the stairway, and another sixty up to the roof. Charney runs along a back sidewalk, pumping his arms, rocking from side to side. As he runs, I see something coming down from the roof. I can't see what it is, only that it is long and flat and seems to twirl or go end over end as it rushes toward Charney. He doesn't see it. Both he and the thing are in a race to see who can make the stairway first. We shout at him, but he is hard of hearing. When he was younger, five or six, he spent several months stuffing vegetables into his ears. Just as he reaches the stairway, the thing, or part of the thing, lands on him. We hear the sound in the alley, sort of a watermelon-falling sound. Charney is under the thing.

"Jeez, someone pull him back."

"What the hell hit him?"

"C'mon, someone pull him back."

Charney sits up. He looks like he has just swallowed a Ping-Pong ball. He is half Irish and half Polish, though nobody knows which half is which. Even his parents aren't sure. His father is a milkman who drinks Southern Comfort and his mother takes in ironing and they both take turns beating Charney, one on one side of the head and one on the other, which is why he is hard of hearing, though he also has a few teeth missing, and most of your important hearing comes through your teeth.

Charney starts to crawl for the stairway. As he does, I notice someone on the roof edging a huge object over the side. It is a mattress. It falls like sin, pinning Charney to the ground. Another mattress floats down, followed by another and another, the revenge of sleep. It is raining mattresses. Higby and Vernon rush the stairs and start for the roof. By now there are five, six mattresses, all overlapping, on the ground. They look very peaceful, as if they had grown there overnight. When Higby and Vernon reach the third floor, a figure appears on the edge of the roof. He looks older than it is possible for any kid to look. He is tall and wears a cape that floats behind him in the wind. He has something stuck in his hair. It looks like a pineapple, or five squirrels tied together by their tails. He puts one foot on the edge of the roof and waves something in his hand. It looks like a sword, or the radio antenna from a car.

Then he starts to yell.

Spysmasher, he yells. He keeps yelling it.

As Higby and Vernon reach the roof, he salutes them and steps into the air. I had never seen anyone fall before. He did it as if he were stepping into an elevator. There was something saintly about his falling, as if he expected to go in the opposite direction. But he dropped, very quickly, followed by his cape. Landing on the mattresses, he got up as if nothing had happened. There was a board nailed to his foot. He walked off skiing with one foot.

I felt that I was in the presence of an authentic hero. The air around him was charged, jammed with an extra measure of life. He had a sense of sadness, of resignation, as if he had no control over his heroism.

Vernon dragged Charney back to the alley. Charney had a carrot stuck in his ear. His eyes were open, but his head seemed to be hanging from a place above his shoulders. The tattoo above his left eyebrow, put there by his father, who was taking mail order tattoo lessons, was darker than I had ever seen it.

"I'm OK," Charney said.

"What did they hit you with?"

"Yes."

"No, what was it?"

"That's right," he said.

We moved Charney next to Nitny.

"He never knew what hit him," Vernon said.

"He still doesn't," Higby said.

I liked Vernon. He was tall and had an Adam's apple that looked like a chicken claw. He was born in April. My mother always cleaned house on his birthday. He had a way of throwing a baseball that stung your hands when you caught it, no matter what glove you wore. Higby hung around with Vernon. You couldn't describe Higby's face. He was just there, like he belonged in an ad for station wagons.

The war moved into a vegetable garden. We left Nitny and Charney against the garbage cans and crawled among the corn and tomatoes, arming ourselves with rotten tomatoes and corncobs. Higby wanted to find peas. He loved peas. He smelled like peas.

"How the hell can you throw a pea at someone?" Vernon asked.

"If you rub a pea in someone's eye they can't see."

We didn't find peas, but we did find melons that looked like discarded breasts from German opera singers. Vernon picked one by the nipple and heaved it. He had a great arm. What a joy to watch him throw! Vernon's melon skimmed the corn tassels and hit a brick wall in the other yard. It spread itself along a small perimeter on the brick and then quickly flew out, leaving gobs of vegetable mucus hanging on the brick.

As heads peered out, Vernon let fly again.

"Après moi le déluge," he said.

A barrage of melons tumbled through the air. Some came straight in, bowling over the corn, others dropped unexpectedly from the sky. Broken shards of melon were draped over heads, bits of glutinous vegetable mush and strings of seeds hung from ears.

"Now we can rub peas in their eyes," Higby said.

"Sit down."

"It's OK; I've got my briefcase."

He stood up and held a cracked leather briefcase before his face and started walking forward.

"Come back," Vernon yelled.

When Higby was about fifteen feet from the other side, they opened up with a tomato barrage. It was a red attack. He looked like pizza. A green tomato in the groin dropped him. His peas spilled on the ground. He tried to gather them in. Tomato goo crawled over his head, tomatoes bounced off his arms, a gushing red tide began to grow around his beloved peas.

Vernon counterattacked with melons, and I managed to pull Higby back.

Following this salad, we dragged our wounded off. Higby was too heavy to carry; he wanted a stretcher, which we didn't have, so Vernon and I pulled him by the arms until they hurt more than his groin. We propped him against a fence and went back to Nitny and Charney.

Charney's eyes were the size of marbles.

"I think you better see about Charney," Nitny said.

"How are you?"

"The bleeding stopped."

"Can he talk?"

"Ask him."

"Can you talk, Charney?"

He said nothing. His eyes rolled, and he gurgled, as if he were trying to swallow them.

"Where's Hig?"

"We left him by the fence. He's too heavy to carry."

"Did he find the peas?"

"He found them."

"He's got these special peas."

"I know."

"He tell you?" Charney looked up. "He told you?" Charney looked down and tried to swallow his eyes.

"He said something before that made sense," Nitny said.

"What was it?"

"I forgot. But at the time, it made a lot of sense."

Higby's briefcase had our battle plans, and we'd left that back with the tomatoes. Someone had to go back and get the plans.

"I'll go," I said to no one, responding to a question that was never asked.

I walked back to where Higby was. He hadn't moved. He was just the way we had left him, his arms over the fence and his knees sagging and his head resting on his chest, with dribble from his nose running down the zipper on his jacket. As I walked by, he followed me with his eyes. I stopped to look at him. There was nothing I especially wanted to say. He looked at my hands, which were stained tomato red. I put them in my pockets.

"There's something I want to say," he said.

"Spit it out."

"I know there's something I wanted to say."

I waited. The sky turned lushly red, then purple and brown. It seemed to change faster than I could think about it changing. Air hit me in the face; not wind, but a block of air, something solid, heavy.

"I'm tired," he said.

There were purple and red marks on his face, as if someone had put colored decals there. His jacket was ripped, and his mouth was bloody and pushed over to one side. The nose looked indistinct, not quite deciding where it should appear. They had come on him when we had left, and worked him over. I had the strange feeling that it was done without malice.

WOOD

11

"LOOK AT THIS PEN," HIS FATHER SAID. IT WAS A LONG PEN, longer than any the boy had ever seen.

"The first pen that writes underwater. It also writes on the top of mountains. The ink is dry; it won't smudge. Thirteen dollars."

The pen looked like a steel tube with something heavy inside. His father wrote on paper. The ink skipped, the pen seemed to bounce over the paper.

"It takes getting used to. The ink is dry."

He rubbed his finger over it. Where the pen wrote, the ink was heavy, pasty, small ridges of greasy blue.

"It writes on steel, wood, glass. It has a ball point."

He bought anything new. Things that coupled to other things and turned them in a different direction, things that twisted lids off, things with hooks and claws that grabbed odd-shaped objects; things that focused immense amounts of energy in tiny spaces, cut through steel, snipped off glass; large handle-shaped things that fastened two pieces of wood with one handshake; things that plugged in and turned sets of gears that meshed with a complaining whine; things that let one see longer, closer, wider, narrower, deeper, through doors, around corners; waxes, pastes, and polishes that promised freedom from waxing, pasting, and polishing; things with long handles that put leverage in small places, glues that held elephants, knives that cut steel, pots and pans that never needed to be cleaned . . . He swept them all into the house, believing that to waste time or energy was a sin against science, a smirch on the rational mind.

Then having been used once they seemed to frighten him, rationality run amok, and he put them in drawers or hung them on hooks, inert reminders of a perfection he detested.

The boy watched him work in the basement in his undershirt, sweating heavily, using hand tools to construct an endless supply of tables. The tables filled the house with their clean, flat surfaces, begging for objects; they were tables with a flaw, a slight tilt, geometry askew, a pair of legs shorter or fastened off-level at the corners. They were small, high tables, long-legged, whose ends bent inward like deer hooves. The center of his undershirt was deeply wet. Bubbles of perspiration hung from his nose and chin. He smelled like honey, like old shoes, like bandages.

He seemed to be storing up, protecting, nurturing a great anger. He grunted as he worked, inaudibly swearing, furious at split wood and bent nails, throwing gouged-out ends of screws the length of the basement, where they would bounce off the wood floor and onto the cement of the boiler room, sometimes pinging against the furnace. The boy remembered the moan of the saw as his father knelt over the wood, his face turned toward the cut, moisture falling on the wood, sawdust sprinkled on his hands and forearms. His chest was wet, hairless, crowded with freckles. He had thick hair, at first red, then brown, finally graying into a golden white. His arms, though thin, were backed up by a powerful chest, which was able to project a terrible strength that opened bottles and twisted off the ends of branches. It was not, however, a finger strength. It ended at the palms, worked when he could get his shoulder into the thing but quickly played itself out if only the effort of fingers was called for.

Open jars of paint were scattered about, and dozens of paint-brushes, their bristles frozen in place by ancient paint, lay wrapped in sandless sandpaper. And the empty jars of turpentine, their contents long ago ascending to paint-thinner heaven.

Sometimes blood: a knuckle too close to the hammer's arc, fingers catching a run of saw teeth, a needle of wood slipping into the skin. The blood was bright, dark, it bubbled, oozed, spurted. He barely registered the hurt. It was his blood, it exposed the insides of the machine, it had made real what was hidden. The blood was his communion, bleeding appeased the wood and showed its mercy. Blood softened the wood, made it more palpable, a fake clay. Blood lavished on wood strengthened it, like Damascus steel, forged and reforged again and again until it would bend but never break.

"Look here," he said to the boy, "look at this joint."

It was beyond movement, that joint. The head of the screw, gouged out so the slot was now a half circle, lay deep beneath the surface of the wood, his father's anger pushing the steel deep, making it impervious to change. The joint would stay, transfixed, establishing a relationship between the wood as unchanging as the speed of light. Eternal lovers: the wood was hugged to death. The corpse of a right angle.

He would use his new ballpoint pen, the thirteen-dollar pen already on sale at some places for ten ninety-eight, to mark where the saw should cut, the screw hole drilled, the nail driven. The pen, having made its claim to write on wood, would belie that claim and skip, gouging bits of pine and depositing a trail of ink scat, intermittent blobs pointing in the same ominous direction, like termites half buried in the wood, a dashed highway divider that signals an area of passing. There is where the saw would cut, along that partially inked, gouged-out groove, that almost-straight line.

"Look at this line," he said to the boy, trembling.

The wonder being that the boy could see it, and seeing it, held his breath, wondering what else about the line he would be asked, if length, width, other dimensions would be part of the quiz. The boy waited.

His father placed his thumb on the invisible line and put the blade of the saw against it. He drew the blade back as gently as a cello bow, lightly scoring the wood with the saw teeth. A whisper of sawdust, an insect antenna of shavings, fell forward. Now a plume, a spray of wood at both edges of the cut, front and back, each heavier as the saw dragged its teeth across more wood, shook the offending bits of timber free from the piece that held it and scattered it on the floor. The saw blade sang, became hot, sometimes binding when the tilt of the blade wavered.

A duo: the saw moaned; he hummed, swore.

The sweat bubbled up from his skin, coating the hairless sides of his cheek and the stubble of the beard that grew on his chin and upper lip. He smelled of honey, something sweet, then something sour. Heavy breathing, that saw, heavy moaning.

A clatter: falling to the floor, a sliver sticking out at the edge where the wood broke and fell before the saw could complete its cut.

Then he clamped the wood in the vise and, leaning over the wood with a hand drill, shoulder in the handle, dripping on the wood, began to turn the drill and watched the tiny springs of shavings that sprouted from the wood and the hole that remained in their place. The drill bit got hot, the tip browning the wood. The boy could smell it: toast, leaves in a bonfire, old shoe leather. The drill broke through the wood with a jar, the bit resting on the surface of the workbench, his father's cheek on the handle, still bouncing.

Amazed: his father's eye wondering, trembling, held true by the wood.

"This is it," he told the boy.

The object of that pronoun lay hidden, and the boy brought forward in quick succession: furniture, baseball games, the look in his mother's eyes when his father came home at night, his dead brother, the stars, hope that tomorrow would be different.

His father grabbed him by the shoulders.

"You see," he said, "I have to do this."

The boy didn't see it at all.

"I mean I don't have to do this, but I do. You see that."

Of course he did. Now he did. Now he saw everything.

"It's not what you think. I mean this wood, the furniture, these tables."

What did he think?

"A table, well, how can I explain a table?"

Still sweating, but now with excitement.

"Something to put something on. A resting place. The reason for all these tables."

He took two pieces of wood, recently drilled through, and clamped them together, pressed them into each other, like lost lovers, and began driving the screws that would eternally bind them.

He looked up from his connecting, grunting.

"The wood," he huffed, "has been waiting for this, just waiting."

The boy walked over to a wood box and began idly pawing through pieces of scrap wood. He felt like driving a nail into one of them.

"Take any one."

As soon as his father said it, he felt that he didn't want to take it, the saying that allowed it prohibiting the taking of it. His hand felt for oddly shaped pieces, something less than a right angle.

"Nailing," his father said, "gives a man a great deal of satisfaction. Driving the steel deep into the wood is a very positive feeling."

His father stepped back from his creation, shaking the table on its off-kilter legs.

"I am very brave in wood," he said. "I soar, I fly."

The boy found two pieces of wood that he wanted to nail together. His father continued talking.

"But nailing won't hold a damn. The only way to hold wood is to screw it."

The boy had hammered three nails into the wood, none of them going through, all of them bent at some point in their journey in different directions.

"You can't hesitate when you nail. You see what happens. The nail knows when you're not sure of yourself."

The boy took the hammer and buried the nailheads in the wood. He drove them in deep, leaving an indentation of the hammerhead in the wood.

"I'll help you," the boy's father said.

"No," the boy said.

"It's OK."

"No. That's what I wanted to do. I want them like that."

"You can't connect the wood that way."

"I want them like that."

CHRISTMAS

MY UNCLE WHO ISN'T MY UNCLE AND HIS GIRLFRIEND, MY aunt, are coming over for dinner. It is Christmas Day. It's been snowing for hours, and the city is muffled in white. Everything sharp and separate is smooth and joined, soft and deceptive. We wallow in snowdrifts, breath clouds as big as get-well cards billowing in our wake as we pull Flexible Flyers up hills and turn creaking snowballs into magnificent baby-crushing boulders.

We is Nitny, Johnny Bregman, Faustio Precept, and myself. We are cold, bored, secretly lonely. The day is stiff and slow, like amber candy. We watch cars floating in the snow, wheels churning a froth of ice and powder. Bregman says if it gets any colder it won't snow. He says the clouds will freeze into sheets of ice and hang in the air so you can land a plane on them. We look up but see no planes.

We prop a tire against the house next door to mine and stand on it so we can look in the window and watch blind Billy. We take turns watching him do nothing, sitting in a chair. Sometimes he stands up to do nothing. Then his mother comes out and chases us away, embarrassed because we caught him doing nothing.

At the street corner, two cars hit each other. A lady sits in one car, a Nash Ambassador, with her head on her chest. She has quarter-size spots of rouge on her cheeks, and there is a spiderweb of broken glass on the windshield. A man is trying to pull her out of the car.

"Come on, Alice, for chrissakes."

Her knee is bloody. The blood seeps through the stocking and runs around the knee and onto the seat.

"Come on, Alice, you're all right."

He tries to pull her out of the car.

She lifts her head up.

"Leave me alone. Go away."

"Come inside where it's warm," he says.

"Just leave me the hell alone."

The other car is a Packard Patrician, two-tone green.

"Holy shit," the other driver says. "Holy shit."

He keeps saying Holy shit even after the police and the ambulance come. He tries to straighten the chrome strips on the side of his car, then starts kicking the grille.

"Holy shit, holy shit."

"Let's go," Nitny says.

"Is she dead, Nitny?"

"How should I know?"

"If she is, I wanna see her, because I never saw a dead woman before."

"How can she be dead if she's talking?"

"Who said she was talking?"

"Who said she was dead?"

"I've seen lots of dead people before," Nitny says.

"Your mother's ass you have."

"What I want to see is a nude dead woman."

"You wouldn't know what to do with it."

"Eat a pound . . . off the ground."

We blitz cars. Faustio throws snowballs with an overhand hook. He stands sideways to his target and gets an amazing amount of speed from his hook-thrown balls. He packs tight, hard, bony-looking snowballs that always look dirty. They spin in the air, the lump points searching for flesh. He likes snow that is near gutters or on car hoods, snow that is partially melted but will quickly freeze again. He wants it rock-hard in the air, throws his snowballs glove-less, his hands bony chicken claws, impervious to the cold. Standing behind walls, he throws with just his eye and arm exposed. He hopes for massive internal bleeding or, failing that, a long, jagged, hard-to-sew-up gash.

Bregman's are soft and grapefruit heavy. They disintegrate before they hit the target. He scoops them up on the run, giving the snow a few quick pats as he throws. He wants to startle, amaze with his snow showers, so he can rush in and clip you at the knees, hoping the body above will snap forward, like dry spaghetti in the hands of an insistent cook.

Nitny's specialty is ice. He wants to commit the perfect murder with an icicle. He breaks off jagged, skull-piercing chunks of ice from underneath car fenders, throws at anything that moves, wiping his nose afterward on the arm of his jacket until there is a clear, stiff shield of frozen mucus coating the wool.

I throw a snowball and it hits a car door, banging like a snare drum. The driver slams his brakes, skidding sideways in the snow so that he blocks the street.

Faustio hops back fences while I go through the alley. I can hear Nitny and Bregman behind me, their soft galoshes puddling the wet snow. Cutting across a yard, I leave widely spaced, frightened steps in the snow, as if I were advertising myself. The footprints look lonely, and bigger than they have any right to be. My trail is too easy to follow.

Jumping two steps at a time, I run up a wooden stairway at the back of an apartment building, turning around on the second floor to see the driver of the car bouncing after me. He is an older man, with unbuckled galoshes flapping in the snow. His black overcoat is unbuttoned, and a silk scarf around his pudgy neck tries to hold in a sack of fat. He has no hat, and little hair. Fat weighs him down; it seems to come from within: fat bones, fat feet, thighs the size of pig bellies. It is a great effort for him to run, and he does it badly, puffing through unused lungs.

There is a garage just below the stairs; I jump from the stairs to the garage roof. He follows my tracks into the alley and then stops when he reaches the backyard, looking around, somewhat contented, dreaming. I am afraid he will follow my tracks, but he doesn't. His mind is set on not finding someone, and when it doesn't, he unzips his pants and takes out his penis. The steaming yellow urine hisses off the snow, putting a series of little holes in the ice. When he is finished, he keeps holding his penis, afraid he will lose it, and rubs it. He looks around again, still holding, still rubbing, and growls. He spurts, shivers, and starts to moan. I am afraid he will see me, but he does not. He moans again, plaintively, as if he were trying to entice someone. Then he grunts and lets go of his penis. Arms hanging down from his shoulders, like shovels hanging from a peg, he lets out a long sigh. Then he raises his arms and begins to flap them. He starts to cry.

I step back from the edge of the garage roof. Nitny and Bregman are on the roof behind me. We watch the fat man plod back to his car, still sideways in the street. The air is heavy and wet, with the clearness of water. Objects seem to give off heat in the snow, as if they are steaming in ice. I feel that I have been pumped up with some sort of sadness.

"What I want," Nitny says, "right now, is to see a dead man."

He jumps down from the roof. "We've got to go to the police station."

We run after him. He runs as if there is no snow, his shoes slideproof in the ice and slush. We try to keep up, but he puts distance between us. Nitny is small and frightened, a perfect recipe for speed. We finally see him in front of the police station, being pushed out the door.

"They won't show me a dead man. I pleaded with them, the bastards. They're all goddamn Catholics."

"Nitny," I say, "why . . . ?"

"It's Christmas," he says, "that's why."

"What does that have to do with it?"

"Everything . . . just everything."

Huge, wet snowflakes the size of licked postage stamps begin to fall. They linger on wool, drape over Nitny's cap, slowly losing their designs to water.

"It's fucking stupid, if you ask me," says Faustio Precept.

He puts his hands on Nitny's shoulders and pushes him down. "Fucking stupid is what I say."

He stuffs a dirty snowball in Nitny's mouth. Nitny kicks him and gets up.

"You don't understand. You're a jerk. You're all jerks."

I can see tears in his eyes, and then he is running. His run is all business. We must move fast to keep up. He runs hard, runs well. There is a persistence to his running. I am afraid he will find a dead man.

"For chrissake! That bastard!"

"Jesus, follow him."

We run past crèches and Christmas trees, houses with lights strung on the roof and plaster Santas with leery lips about to descend into tiny chimneys. Nitny is all heels and elbows. He is running for his life, running after death.

The air is massed and heavy, loaded with pressure. Cars, trees, buildings, look wet under the snow, waterlogged, threaten to puff up and explode. The water on windows makes them look shattered, and I expect something depressing, inexplicably depressing, to come through those cracks. A water explosion. Ice and steam. The wrecked steel of cars caught in Christmas, falling buildings that force bricks through skulls. Blood in bodies reversing itself, backward osmosis, spurting through nostrils and ears.

Now he is being pushed out of a funeral parlor. The man pushing him is dressed in black, has a face the size and color of two pumpkins, a large belly, and hands that look like catchers' mitts. He seems to flick Nitny out of the funeral home, pushing him with underhanded scoops the way one might accelerate a box turtle. He is anxious not to have his suit snowed on, so he flicks Nitny under the canopy that extends from the front door to the curb, and when he has reached the edge of the canopy he turns around and walks inside, placing vast amounts of weight (he is big, fat, dense) on the sidewalk. Nitny stands in the rainy snow, his hands jammed in his pockets. I wonder what he is dreaming about, what kind of beast has entered his mind.

"They're all fucking Catholics. I asked to see a dead man."

He turned to me, almost pleading.

"It's a funeral parlor, isn't it? Dead people are there."

"Nitny, go home."

"I don't want to go to fucking home."

Faustio wants to push Nitny down and I grab Faustio and we give each other a hard look. We know how much we hate the other. It is a moment of great relief, this hating, lifting something between us. Someday we shall fight and do much damage. It will not be pleasant, but it will be a great relief to hurt each other.

". . . won't go to fucking home," Nitny shouts, and again he is running, and again we are after him, and now I want to find a dead man so we won't have to chase him, so we can continue to do what we were doing before, which was stand around getting cold and lonely and bored and feeling depressed the way everyone else feels this Christmas Day.

"I want to look at the air around dead people," he shouts, panting.

Breathing heavily, we run past streetlamps, a muffled cottony yellow shining through the white, the snow plastered to the poles. Warped shapes loom in the swirling snow, the softened grotesques of cars and mailboxes and bushes and trash cans slathered with thickened, frozen air. Sounds have disappeared. I hear nothing, or almost nothing, only the faint crunch of tires in the damp-softened snow. Though I am not crying, my breath comes in sobs, hurting, the water-tinged air banging against my lungs. I carry a bubble here, a weight in my lungs, and try to spit it out. I fall down in the slush and snow and get up again, dizzy, hurt. Something is moving inside.

"Where are they when they are dead? When they are just dead?" he shouts, running and shouting, running toward himself, toward the mysterious Nitny who looms ahead, who is also running in front of the Nitny who is trying to catch up to this ghost Nitny, this phantom Nitny.

We run by the liquor store, still open, the icy glare of bottles barely visible through the translucent window, and continue by a Chinese laundry with dusty bundles of shirts, *Sands of Iwo Jima* at the Avalon movie house, a newsstand selling the Chicago *Herald-American* and my favorite comic strip, Maggie and Jiggs, Our Lady of Peace Church, where most days at three o'clock the nuns turn loose whipped Catholic schoolboys lusting for revenge. We rush by my almost-uncle's garage that holds his two bulldozers and his two-and-a-half-ton dump truck, three of the five pieces of heavy earth-moving equipment he bought for a five-acre farm he owns in Crown Point, Indiana; past a Childs restaurant with glass-topped tables and old men warming their hands over steaming mugs of coffee, watching the chilling slowness of the Regulator clock as it ticks off the agonizing minutes.

Nitny runs head up, back forward, knees reaching for his chest. Then he is in front of a hospital, inside a hospital, and finally, at almost the same time, being pushed out of the hospital. I am the first to reach him. He is crying.

"Why do they always think they can push me? Why?"

There is a dead cat in the gutter, belly popped open.

"You look like someone to be pushed."

He looks at me, frightened.

"Why?"

"You can tell by the hands."

For the first time he seems preoccupied with something else. He is searching for a word.

"Where is the air?" he says.

"Nitny?"

He looks shocked.

"There's magic in dead people. I realized that today."

He blows his nose into his cuff. "No; only the new dead. Only the fresh dead."

"You're crazy."

"No; they have this air, like lightning."

"What air?"

"I have to run."

"No."

"They're telling me." He nods his head, smiles.

"Wait."

"That's what all this is about."

"All what?"

"This!" He waves his blue hands through the chill of wet and ice. His fingers look small, lonely, frightened, about to fall off.

"Watch your fingers."

"I don't have to," he says.

"Put them in your pocket. Put them in your fly, for chrissakes."

He looked like he wanted to sing. Then he ran.

"Where is the morgue?" he shouted over his shoulder.

"Downtown," I said. "The Loop."

He stopped, and licked his fingers as if he wanted to taste the air.

"That's too far," he said. "I need to find an accident."

He sat down on the curb and started to blow on his fingers. Somewhere deep in his hands there was a fire he was trying to blow life into.

"I need a dead accident."

"It's Christmas."

"Christmas is no accident."

Faustio and Bregman caught up with us. Bregman had a sickly smile on his face. He poked Faustio, who poked him back. I looked on enviously.

"A car wreck, twisted steel, dead bodies strewn about."

"Look," Faustio said, "no one dies on Christmas."

"Really?"

"It's a mortal sin."

"But what's this?" he said.

"This what?"

"This." Nitny waved his hand around. "What we do."

"Eh?"

It was less of a word and more of a sound, but it was enough to set him off running again. He seemed resigned. He ran more slowly, almost plodded, perhaps wanting us to catch up. We were growing tired of Nitny and dead bodies. He turned around as he ran, and shouted something over his shoulder. No one could make out the words. He shouted again.

"What's he saying?"

"He doesn't want to be crucified."

He shouted again.

"No . . . something crucifixion, something something."

He turned a corner and we lost him. We were at Seventy-fourth and Oglesby, blocks of gray four-story apartment buildings, hushed and muffled in white. Each block had a back alley with wooden stairs that ran up the rear of the apartments. A small yard was in front of each apartment building, with a low pipe-iron fence. The snow hung from the fence like thick glue, dripping in bunches where the pipe irons crossed.

The apartment buildings looked grayer against the darkening sky and the soft white of the snow. It was colder. The wind frothed the snow and whipped up drifts it blew against the buildings, filling courtyards and sunken sidewalks in thigh-deep waves. A crust was beginning to form on the snow. As we trudged through, it crackled, like crinkled cellophane. No one ran. We plodded, waded, forced our way through a white swamp. We had it on faith, though no one knew whose, that Nitny was ahead. He was probably crouched in an alleyway, deep in white, waiting to fall on us.

Bitter wind, cold, dark. It felt like we were inside something, that we were being shaken about, blown on, bumped around. Wherever Nitny was, now he was lost, buried in drifts, frozen, having become what he was looking for. The buildings became part of the sky, no longer earth doomed but huge, a great damned presence, as if heaven and hell had switched places. Faustio and Bregman were silent. I walked behind them, worn by wind and snow. Shouts filtered through the wind, like someone whistling.

"I think he's ahead," Bregman shouted.

"This is it," Faustio said. "This is the end."

We plowed through the alley, stumbling over snow-hidden rocks and garbage cans. The alley was deep, endless, and dark beyond black.

Faustio ran ahead. I could hear the funny popping his boots made when they punched through the crust. He seemed to bounce off the snow, halting momentarily at the crust, then his weight taking him through the crust and into the depths of the snow.

"Oh, sweet Jesus," he said.

He was still ahead of us.

"Oh my God. Oh damn."

Bregman and I ran to catch up, the snow momentarily hard and then soft. The wind had died down. The alley was bathed in light.

Nitny was up against a wooden fence. I wasn't close enough to see what was holding him up. His back was across the upper part of the fence, his arms outstretched, imploring us to do something. But he refused to talk.

A light fell on him from a second-floor landing. It made him look yellow, almost golden. Then I saw a single nail through both his feet. There was another nail through the palm of his right hand. A rock, a bloody hand-size rock, was under him in the snow. His shoes and socks had absorbed most of the blood from his feet. But the blood from his hand spurted, as if he held a tiny engine to help pump it out.

Hours later, when I got home, my uncle in his 1947 green Dodge business coupe had arrived with my aunt. His nose and chin were red, and his voice came from the bottom of his throat: gruff, bubbling up through his thick neck. It was immensely comforting to be here. The warm light was tinted with reds and greens from the tree, which seemed to sparkle in the corner. The smell of pine, sherry, and mincemeat filled the house. I could see the snow raging against the windowpanes, melting when it hit the glass. My uncle does not wear a suit but always manages to look as if he is wearing one; he is almost wearing one, which befits his status of almost-uncle. He has a quarter or an eighth of a fortune. He celebrates Christmas by burning money, though this Christmas there are rumors that my father and another uncle, Patrick, who wears bow ties and holds people by the elbows, plan to burn more money than he.

My mother serves the turkey. She brings it out, and the streetlights shine through a murky fog of snow and steam. The turkey looks shiny and hard, as if it had been eternalized in porcelain. My father hates to cut turkey, so my mother cuts and serves with slow, majestic strokes, the blade dancing lightly in turkey flesh. My uncle who isn't grinds his cigar into a small plate of used cranberry sauce. He winks at me. His eyes are as blue as snow, driven by Hungarian dreams. He chews on turkey as if it were a transmission gear. My mother pours him wine and he drinks, his Adam's apple bobbing up and down. He looks out the window to see if his car is on fire. All cars, sooner or later, catch fire, he believes.

After dinner, after the dollar, five-dollar, and ten-dollar bills have gone up in flames, the men go down to look at the furnace. When they come back, my father has to hold on to the tree for support, almost pulling it over.

My uncle leans to one side.

"How would you like to drive my car?" he asks.

The dashboard is a Wurlitzer of buttons, lights, knobs, dials. Wet blobs of snow fall on the windshield. We turn left on Seventy-seventh Street and head east for the lake. The night is a sloshy white. I can barely see over the huge plastic steering wheel with the molded finger indentations, but it makes little difference because the night is a murky porridge—a fog of flakes that hovers around thirty-two degrees. Like everything about the day and the evening, the snow is almost: almost frozen, indecisively frozen, wetly frozen. The big Dodge slides slowly on the mush, its rear end swinging like a pendulum. My uncle stares straight ahead, benevolence in his hair and eyebrows. I skid to a halt at Jeffery Boulevard, halfway across the street. We continue, up the hill over the railroad tracks, across Oglesby, and past my grandmother's house.

The car slides and sloshes down the street. I must do something with my uncle's calmness, but I do not know what to do. We are nearing the lake. I can't stop the car. It goes just as fast with my foot off the accelerator. Panic makes its home in my stomach. I do not steer the Dodge; it steers itself. My uncle has fallen asleep, his head thrown back over the seat, a tiny river of spittle draining from the side of his mouth. I can feel the Dodge becoming angry with me.

We take a final slide. For a moment, my world, and the world of the car, is balanced on an edge that is neither real nor unreal. It is the world between the two, the world just before falling, just before hitting, the world just before dying, when air separates and the dead scream.

PRAYING IN THE BATHTUB

11½- 12

THE BOY FOUND HIS FATHER PRAYING IN THE BATHTUB. HE had never seen his father praying in water before, never knew that he could pray. He was down on his hands and knees in the tub, hands clasped together, head below the water, his tight, well-shaped old man's ass sticking up in the air. What could he be praying for? Bubbles escaped slowly from his mouth. The boy stood at the door, afraid to move, wondering if he should do anything. Why was the bathroom door open?

He thought: He doesn't want me to do anything; he wants me to stand here.

He thought: This is his way of teaching me how to feel.

He thought: How long will he stay down there?

Then his head broke the surface, bringing with it slathers of foam and an exhausted groan. His eyes opened wide, looking wild, the water rushing to rid itself of his face. He farted, a rippling fart like strings of tiny firecrackers. Another groan, eyes wider yet, and he plunged back into the water.

Why is he going down in the water? What does he expect to find? Who does he want to take with him? What if someone sees him like this?

(The bathtub was his cathedral, his Chartres, his holy place of water worship. Doubled up, doubled over, submersed in water, he looked less like a fish than an archaeological find, a sunken cannon, still half cocked, crusted but ready to go off as soon as it was lifted to the surface. There was something sparkling about him down there, something gleaming. He was too glistening to be a fish, too sunken, too leaden. He was a fixture of the bathtub. It was his pew, his ecclesiastical excess, his synagogue of suffering.)

There is something he wants, the boy thought. He will not say it directly. That would violate some vow, some secret promise, barely thought about.

The boy was annoyed, angry, partly ashamed. He is doing this to get back at me. For what?

He thought: He wants me to translate for him, he thinks I am the only one who knows his languages, the language we speak and the language he pursues down there in that watery world.

His wet pew. Let him bump his head on the sides of that theology, let him bang noggins with that minister. His hair floated in the water, waved at him, a chorus of keratin. There was nothing he could do in that position except open his eyes and stare through water at the white of the porcelain tub, signal for help with farts and bubbles. He refuses to talk; he prays, he looks, he waits for the boy to translate for him.

He plays stubborn. He does it to annoy, to enhance himself. The boy will watch him. He expected his father to find some opening at the bottom of the tub, to be sucked through it, to appear miraculously at the kitchen table, glistening and supreme.

He thought: Is this an endurance test, is there something here I know nothing about?

The bathroom was on a landing halfway up the stairs. The stairs went up from the living room, paused at the landing, then turned back on themselves and continued up to a bedroom over the living room. The stairs were carpeted. He had seen his father come down the stairs on his feet, on his ass, on his back, shoulders, legs (rolling), but never on his head.

On either side of the landing was a bedroom, where the boy and his brother slept. A third brother died before he was old enough to have his own bedroom, and the boy thought he had died because the house had run out of bedrooms.

The living room was shaped like a hand reaching for a tiny hold on a rock ledge. The fingertips were the front door, the palm of the hand the dining room. This was the dining room where the boy's aunt had invited a suitor to supper. The man, a captain (first mate perhaps), had fallen asleep in a bowl of soup, cream of spinach with bacon bits, having passed out from joy at seeing the boy's aunt. It surprised everyone, because the soup had been served steaming hot, and the captain (though perhaps only a sailor) did not wake when his head hit the soup, and had to be saved from drowning by soup, had to be pulled out of the soup, nostrils clogged with spinach, bacon bits (painstakingly hand cooked and dried by his aunt at the boy's house) clinging to his gray hair.

Behind the dining room was the kitchen, with the sink where the boy had his mouth washed out with soap when he said something his mother preferred not to hear and, detecting no repentance from the boy, decided to dislodge these prurient parts of the body, errant theology, slurs on lineage, and other bits of doggerel. She was a firm believer in the power of metaphor: a clean mouth.

Bubbles were coming up from his father's mouth, sprinkling the surface of the water before they popped.

He thought: How shiny, how white, his ass looks.

Behind the kitchen, down a few stairs, were the furnace and the laundry room, where the boy's almost-uncle would burn money.

That was the room with the two big mud sinks, two feet deep, where the boy was dragged from the backyard, stripped of clothes, plunged into gallons of steaming water, and scrubbed with a cake of Bon Ami, dunked, scrubbed, dunked, and scrubbed again. His mother could not get him clean enough. Just to the right of the laundry room (coming down the stairs) was the playroom, with its splintery wooden floor, where his father worked on wood projects and late at night set up a card table with a typewriter and yellow paper and spent sober hours writing. Between the playroom and the laundry room was a small bathroom, space only for a toilet and small sink, where the boy sat with his pants down and dreamed.

Behind all this was the backyard, where he dug holes and built orange-crate forts and where he and his friends battled with Christmas trees, where he collected whiskey bottles, and where he rolled on the grass with a girl whose father made ball bearings for Chryslers. The backyard was where the boy collected air, where he softened the air, where it felt like velvet, where some nights it was so wet and smooth he thought he could gouge some out, leaving a hole where he had taken the air, and take it with him, feeling comforted by the look and shape of it. More, it was a place where the boy lay on his back late at night and looked up at the sky, trying to figure out what and how he should feel, thinking there was some lesson in human emotions he hadn't been taught.

The boy's father came up for air, his hands still clasped together; the water in the tub shook violently, a bathroom tsunami. He shook his head, flinging water in a wide arc around the room. His mouth opened, but no sound came out; he plunged his head back into the water.

Behind the backyard was the alley and the garage where Margaret showed her vagina, and farther down the block, across the alley, a friend of his lived with his father, who was a cripple, who looked as if he had been compressed, his shoulders and chest put in a vise and crumpled up so that his chest stuck out in the center and his shoulders looked abnormally flat; he wore huge Nazi shoes with soles twelve inches thick and braces that let him walk with crutches, and the boy happened to be in the apartment when the cripple, who didn't like to talk to anyone, was unstrapping himself from his pants and shoes and braces and the boy saw his legs, or what was left of his legs, and his feet, like twisted bird claws, and the cripple caught him looking at him and rushed to slam the door shut, falling over because his unbraced legs would not support his weight, and the boy thought: Where was God when those legs were made?

Underwater, his hair floating, eyes open and magnified, the boy's father was trying to talk. He talked bubbles.

He thought: If someone comes and sees him like this I will be ashamed—for him and for myself. But he also thought: if I walk away I won't have to be ashamed for myself. He would reduce the shame by one half. He couldn't leave. He didn't know why.

Across the street where his friend lived was the high school he didn't go to yet. He wanted to be older and yet not older, to be in a place where time moved and stood still, like in a movie with a happy ending where the same story could be played over and over again until it got worn into your being like a groove and you could approach the happiness again and again, getting more excited each time, until the thrill became continuous and, ultimately, exhaustive, explosive.

Around the corner was the gas station that advertised itself with a picture of a dinosaur, run by a veteran who kept a bayonet with Japanese blood hanging from the wall. The gas station was next to railroad tracks, whose fine rust was rubbed off once a day by an empty freight train so that the company could still claim right-of-way on the tracks.

He emerged from the water as blunt and smooth as a seal, heavy as stone, teal yellow, his hair painted on his head, his eyes wide, unblinking, rapacious, his mouth open, revealing recent dental work, his hands curled into fists, with the knuckles resting on the bottom of the tub, his butt no longer elevated but lowered on his haunches, settled into the water. He took a deep breath of air and screamed.

THE BREASTLESS LADY

& THE MUSEUM

THE CANDY STORE WAS RUN BY AN OLD GERMAN WOMAN WHO had her breasts cut off. She had been trapped in China when the Japanese invaded and was caught in a plot to smuggle Hitler to Argentina. A Japanese swordsman sliced off her breasts.

Then again, maybe she was one of those German women who had no breasts. A lot of German women are like that, doing penance for being German.

Her front was as flat as a washboard. She wore round-necked cotton print dresses that seemed to hang from huge collarbones. She had the biggest collarbones I ever saw. She was good at making mayonnaise sandwiches on white bread. I liked the way she spread it with a knife, and I liked the way she cut cheese, as if she were circumcising it.

I don't remember her name. It

sounded German. We spoke in low whispers around her. She always looked as if she were about to be provoked. I thought her skull was outside her skin, because her face was the color of bleached flour. She had no lips. Her hair was pulled back in a bun, welded into a hand grenade.

She was quiet, stern, and kind of soft. She rarely reprimanded us. She always seemed to be looking over our heads, at something in the distance. She rarely spoke, and when she did, her English was so soft and clipped and precise it was impossible to tell if she had an accent. The breath for her voice came from her collarbones, which rode up and down, cresting on a wave, as she spoke. We knew she was German because she looked German. Faustio thought she had a shortwave set in the back of the store and beamed messages back to Nazi Germany about munitions factories and troop movements. She learned things from us. No matter what we said, she could deduce troop movements and munitions factories from our conversations. Germans were clever that way; they were trained in it from birth.

The candy store had a back room separated from the rest of the store by a beach towel sewn around a brass rod and suspended in the doorway. One day when she was down in the cellar bringing up a case of Nehi, I pulled back the towel and looked in. I didn't see any shortwave set, just a bed and some chairs and dishes drying in a drainer that rested on a towel. Next to the bed was a dresser and on the dresser a picture of somebody in uniform: high collar, puttees, and a saucer-shaped helmet. He had something sewn on his lapel. His face was scratched out. I wanted to take a closer look at the picture, but I could hear her labored breath as she dragged the soda pop up the steps. Then she appeared at the top of the steps, panting, a case of Nehi at her feet.

We tried to listen to how she talked and what she said, so we could deduce troop movements, but this didn't work because she rarely spoke. One day we decided to throw rocks at her for being German and starting the war. She chased us down the block, shouting at us in a language that was neither German nor English.

But we came back because we wanted to watch her make cheese and mayonnaise sandwiches, and she didn't seem to mind. We seemed to be the only ones who came into her store. She didn't seem to mind this, either. Then the boy in the picture came.

She had gone down in the cellar for more soda pop, and as soon as I heard her on the stairs I ran for the beach towel and swept it away. Rushing in, I bumped into him. He was in a wheelchair. At first he didn't look up, though I had jarred the wheelchair, even knocked his arm. But he wasn't as frightened as I was. I jumped back. He was bigger than in the picture. In the picture he wasn't in a wheelchair. His chin was on his chest, and his thin arms were on the arms of the wheelchair with the wrists bent, turned inward. His pants flopped around his legs so that the wonder was this: How much leg is in there? How much hip? How much knee? He looked up, turning his head to look at me. I could see nothing on his lapel. He seemed to want to tilt his head to look at me, as if he couldn't trust himself to look at me straight ahead. Then I thought: He has to turn his head to see anything. There is something wrong with his eyes. They're not in the same place in his head. He has to squint and turn his head to see anything. *They've done something to his eyes.*

"He won't speak to you," she said.

It was the softness of her speaking that startled me. The words seemed to come from her skull. Bone words.

"He can speak, but he won't speak to you."

Why? If he could speak, why wouldn't he speak to me?

She had lugged another case of Nehi up the steps. I could never figure out who was drinking all the Nehi. We weren't. She carried it out to the front of the store, leaving me with him. She didn't seem upset that I had gone in the back, that she had caught me there, that I had discovered him. He was sitting on a towel that was doubled over. There was another towel behind his legs, pinned to the wheelchair.

"Who are you?" I asked.

He turned his head, opening his mouth slightly. Something

metal was inside his mouth, something dark and metallic, that shined. An eyebrow lifted up.

I put my hands on the gray rubber handles of the wheelchair. He made an effort to turn around, to see what I was doing behind him. He wasn't able to turn his head very far, and tried to move his position in the wheelchair. His hands pawed at his legs, trying to move them sideways so that his body could turn, so he could see behind himself. But he had difficulty moving his legs. His hands were curled over, and this made it difficult to grip or push his legs. His hands kept slipping off, and when they finally managed to push, the legs quickly slid back. His legs seemed to have their own memory. They kept returning to their original position, as if spring loaded, out of his control. He began to get frantic when he couldn't turn around to see me. I heard a little hum, high-pitched, like some long-necked animal whimpering. He twisted his shoulders, trying to look up and over his forehead, trying to look behind. I felt thrilled at his efforts, felt that I was torturing him in some small, insignificant way. And yet only he and I knew what I was doing to him.

"Wheel him out in the air."

I hadn't noticed her in the back room. The beach towel hadn't moved. How long had she been standing there, watching us?

She held open the beach towel and I pushed him through the store, maneuvering carefully around the red metal Coca-Cola cooler. His leg hit a wooden counter, jerking his body around. I backed up and wheeled him through the door, setting him so that he faced the street, his back against the plate-glass window. There was a lock that kept the wheels from turning, which I stepped on so he wouldn't roll into the street. I wondered what he would do if he rolled into traffic. I wanted to let him roll into traffic, then save him at the last minute. I wanted to do it again and again, saving him later and later, letting the traffic get closer and closer to the wheelchair. I wanted to see the look on his face when this happened, and I wanted to see the look on the old German woman's face. I didn't want him to get killed. If this happened I couldn't roll him into traffic anymore. But I wanted him to get partly killed. (Was he wounded now? What was he wounded with?)

"Let's go," Faustio said.

He kicked off the lock on the wheelchair and began pushing it down the street.

"Mush," he said, to no one in particular.

"Wait a minute," Charney said, running alongside, bowlegged, trying to keep up with Faustio's long strides.

"Wait just a fucking minute," he said again.

Faustio ignored him. We all ran to keep up with him.

"It's OK," he said. "She said it was OK."

Faustio gave him a push and we watched him roll along the sidewalk, unattended, the wheelchair bouncing when it hit the cracks.

"Watch out!"

"Watch out for what, birdbrain?"

His arms and head bounced when he rode over the cracks, but his legs seemed to be tied to the wheelchair. What was he thinking?

"He needs air. We're giving him air."

"I wonder if he has a pecker. Let's take his pants off."

We pushed him down to the Illinois Central tracks, and then over the tracks, bouncing, his head bobbing off his chest, his neck bent so that his cheek rested on his shoulder. The air was speckled. Egg-size pieces of soot fell on the sidewalk, disintegrating, invisible.

"I don't think he's got anything inside his head," Bregman said. "He's got a hole where his brains should be."

"He's got brains," Faustio said. "He's smarter than you."

"Rat's ass he is."

"Let's push him to the museum."

The museum was built hundreds of years ago to celebrate stone. In front of the museum was a pool and in the pool was a man-eating shark and every month the guards at Cook County jail threw a condemned man to the shark, late at night, when no one could see. But Charney said that was all bullshit. He said it wasn't a shark but a twelve-foot crocodile that lived off children's feet. The museum also had a submarine on its front lawn that could torpedo buildings.

We rolled down Sixty-ninth Street, Sixty-eighth, Sixty-seventh. Three-story red-brick apartment buildings with leaded casement windows lined the streets. Many had interior courtyards with waterless fountains and huge bushes whose shiny leaves were the size of fingernails. An old man whose face was lower on one side watched us rolling the wheelchair down the sidewalk. He clucked at us as we went by, shaking his leg, trying to get rid of a turtle that had attached itself to his pants.

We reached the park and sat down on a bench. Faustio set the lock on the wheelchair. I looked up in the sky and watched the clouds passing and felt dizzy. Did clouds know they made us dizzy? I wondered what it would be like to be a bird, and if birds ever got dizzy looking down, and if they ever aimed their bird shit at anyone when they flew by. Birds could tell us a lot, if we'd listen.

"Hey, look."

Bregman pointed to a guy several benches away. He was alternately feeding pigeons and pissing on them. He seemed to have an inexhaustible supply of pigeon food and piss. The pigeons didn't seem to mind the piss falling on them, as long as they could eat. He used one hand to do two things, an amazing feat when you think about it, and he didn't seem to care who watched him.

More clouds; it was getting colder.

We roll the wheelchair down to the Japanese Gardens, a huge one-story wood building that stands on stilts. A wide porch runs the length and width of the building, and a slanted tile roof has a giant carved devil at each end. We couldn't pull the wheelchair up the stairs, so we left it on the gravel that surrounded the building.

Bregman looks up at the sky. He has incredibly bad breath and farts all the time. He blows it out at both ends. He walks like a marionette, jerky and floppy. You have to remind him where he's walking to, and sometimes when he's standing still and starts walking you have to remind him he isn't going anyplace. His favorite thing is to stick a knife in wood. He'd rather do that than whack off or stare at Sonja Shankman's boobs.

Where is Charney? Probably hanging up in the eaves like a damn bat. All that blood rushing to his head is dangerous. He doesn't care. He spits on us as we walk by, and when we look up he's gone. He's found a crack he can fall through, thin as ice, but he slides by. Charney's a genius in cracks.

Bregman will never find him. He'll walk into a post and fall on the ground and sit there counting his feet. I'd be surprised if the number comes up two. I'd be surprised if Bregman can count that high.

Watch Faustio. He's a fox, a chicken, a scrambler. He goes sideways, cocking his ear to the ground, listening for someone breathing. We will fight one day.

Bregman's father has a store. I don't know what kind it is, but I know it's the kind that makes a lot of money. People go in his store, leave some money, get what they want very quickly, and then leave, followed by new people, who do more of the same. Faustio's father is a painter. He is between jobs. He's always been between jobs.

It starts to rain.

"Let's bring him up the steps, out of the rain."

But we can't pull the wheelchair up; the wheels keep catching on the stairs. We leave him down in the gravel. A wind comes up. Thunder.

"Jeez, look at the rain!"

I watch drops form on the end of his nose. His nose seems the strongest part of his body. It is big, solid, and it makes the rest of his body look pale, breakable. The harder it rains, the quicker the drops form on the end of his nose and fall into his lap.

"Maybe we can lift him out of the wheelchair and carry him inside."

"You don't lift cripples out of wheelchairs," Faustio says. "It breaks their bones."

Inside the Japanese House, the light comes in slim bars, strips of yellow that splash along the floor. The wood is dark red, brown, black, and it smells like a urinal. Initials are carved on the walls. In one corner someone has built a fire, charring floor timbers and sooting the roof rafters. Shivering, I watch the wind blow candy-bar wrappers and popcorn boxes along the floor.

Faustio catches flies and throws them into a glass jar. Then he shakes the jar, stunning the flies, and picks them out one by one, taking a piece of chewed gum and sticking it to the fly's back and sticking the other side to a piece of paper. He has twenty flies stuck to a sheet of paper.

"Take your average housefly," Faustio says. "He's thirty-five percent protein."

"I don't eat flies," Bregman said.

"No one said you did, Johnny boy."

"You eat flies, Faustio?"

"When the occasion demands, one can eat anything."

By now he has filled the paper with over two dozen flies.

"What do flies eat?"

"Anything. But they're partial to shit, human or otherwise."

It rained harder. It sounded as if someone was dropping pebbles on the roof.

"Shouldn't we wheel him back?"

"All we'd do is get wet. And he's wet already."

I watched him from underneath the roof, shivering in the rain. His shoulders twitched. Why didn't he talk? I had the feeling that he was used to this kind of thing, that it happened to him all the time. He struck me as a person some people liked to mistreat for no reason, simply because he offended them by his being. But he didn't bother me.

Slender rods of water hung from the roof, inside and out. I remember what Nitny once told me. If you stick a long hatpin in someone's head, in just the right spot, above the ear, you'll either kill him instantly or he'll be your slave for life. But if you inad-vertently twist the hatpin slightly while you're pushing, at the first opportunity that arises he'll kill you. It is, Nitny said, a risky business. Because before he kills you, his behavior will be no different from that of the slave.

We talked about Bobby Brasho. Bobby would do anything. He once got hit by a car to see what it felt like. One day when his parents were at work he stayed home from school and tied a rope around a second-floor banister. He tied the other end around his neck. His foot was still in a cast from the time he had been in the hospital. His mother came home first. She got off the Illinois Central at Seventy-first and Jeffery. She was a fast walker. She was the first one in the front door. The stairway was right in front of the door. A chair he had been standing on was kicked over. His face hadn't changed color yet. Bobby Brasho greeted her hanging from the rope, his tongue sticking out. His pants were wet. When his father got home, his mother was in the kitchen throwing up. That was the end of Bobby Brasho.

Someone *was* throwing pebbles on the tile roof. They clattered down to the gutter.

"He's not looking good out there."

"As long as he's still shivering."

"He ain't shivering; he's just twisting."

The treetops flattened out in the wind. Layers of clouds raced over each other. Nuts, seeds, and pods from the trees were scattered on the gravel.

"I feel funny, him out there."

Faustio went out and put his jacket around his shoulders. He buttoned it up, without putting his arms in the sleeves, so that the jacket pinned his arms to his sides.

He came back in dripping wet.

"I saw this movie once," Faustio said, "where this guy comes back from the war—"

"Which war?"

"He comes back from the war and he's got this hole in his head, and the place where he remembers is where this hole is, and everybody has to fill up this hole in his head for him."

"What do they fill it up with?"

"Memories, dummy."

"Anyway, this guy comes back, see, I think it was John Agar or somebody like that, only what they don't know is that he's really a spy, and the stuff they're telling him is stuff he wants to know, and every night he goes out into the woods and sets up this radio set and broadcasts to the Nazis, like the old lady that runs the candy store, only someone knows he's doing this, see, a little kid, who tags along because he likes him only he doesn't know exactly what this guy is doing, so this guy kidnaps the kid and feeds him and all and the little kid's dog finds him and he's got to kidnap the dog too and it turns out the guy likes the kid, you see, he didn't have any brothers or sisters where he grew up, only what he doesn't know is that he really does have a hole in his head, and the doctors give him only a week to live but he doesn't know this except his girlfriend does—"

"Who's the girlfriend?"

"June Allyson."

"So how did it end?"

"I don't know; I got lost in a box of popcorn. When I got my head out of the popcorn the picture was over and the lights were coming on and I'd already seen the cartoon."

"How could you get lost in a box of popcorn?"

"I was sitting in the movie with Jorgensen."

"Never go to a movie with Jorgensen."

Everybody was quiet. The park lay around us like a wet glove, with the fingers slowly moving. I could hear footsteps on the gravel, and vague, buttery shapes flitted in and out among the trees.

"I think we ought to wheel him home. I really do."

"And get wet?"

"Why? Wet is wet. He can't get any wetter."

"I don't like him sitting there."

"Let's wait until night, when the devil comes out," Charney said.

"That's a lot of bullshit."

"Why night?"

"Sunlight burns him up."

"That's more bullshit."

"What does he look like?"

"Whatever. Sometimes he looks like a goat with a man's head and a big pecker that he sticks in women. You can smell him. He sets things on fire and cuts legs with knives and he can drag you down to hell through a sewer."

"What does he want?"

"He wants you to sign your name in blood and then he owns you. You've got to do what he says. He makes you do all kinds of things with coffins and skeletons and bats and chicken hearts and dog livers."

"That's so much crap, just boiled crap."

"People who've got their blood sucked out of them get up at midnight and go around spitting curses on people and curing warts. When you're asleep they can sit on your head and pour themselves through your ear and get in your dreams and jump around and make you do things you're ashamed of and they're happy because they got you doing something you wouldn't want to do and in the morning they turn into a fog and come out through your asshole when you fart and spend the day sleeping and when night comes they're at it again."

"I don't fart, and when I do you can be damn sure it ain't no devil coming out."

"When the devil is running around, where's God?"

"I don't know."

"What's your religion?"

"I don't know. It used to be Catholic, but lately my parents haven't been making the payments so I don't know what we are."

"I'm Jewish," Bregman says. "At least my father is, and my mother I don't know."

"We're Italian," Faustio says.

"Is that a religion?"

"In our house it is."

Suddenly the rain stopped, and so did our talking. Faustio had turned him around a little so he was partially facing us. Even so, he kept twisting his neck and smirking with his mouth, looking over his shoulder to try to see us. I would have preferred to have him facing away from us so I wouldn't have to see the way his mouth went down on one side, and the way he lowered the bottoms of his eyes, as if his eyeballs were going to fall out, and the way he twisted that huge nose of his. It looked like something was trying to escape from his mouth and that he held it closed only with the greatest effort. Something was bothering the side of his face. It was getting darker; even so, he looked very pale, almost blue. Then he opened and closed his mouth, and I saw flashes of the silver thing in his mouth. And his foot started shaking. I'd never seen that before. His right foot bounced up and down, as if he was trying to stamp something into the ground.

I started to shiver. I didn't want him to look at me. I couldn't stand to have him look at me. Even out of the corner of his eyes, the only way he could look, even with his head down and his mouth dancing, jerked around by wires inside his gums. I couldn't stand to have him look at me. It wasn't that he was accusing me of something. He saw something. He could look at me without talking. He could look into me. He could look into anyone. *That was why they did the thing to his eyes.*

"Turn him back again, for chrissakes."

"Let's wheel him home."

"He looks blue."

"That's his normal color."

"He's drooling."

"He always drools."

"Do you think he hates us?"

"He doesn't think, stupid."

"Rat's ass you say."

He was somewhere else. He was used to being cold. He knew all about cold. He couldn't control what happened to him when he got cold. His body ran amok. He started shaking. People who were around him got upset.

"What about you, Charney?"

"What about me, what?"

"Religion."

"I ain't nothing."

"He's probably a Protestant. That's what you get if you don't know what you are."

"Rat's ass."

"What will they say when they find out we left him in the rain?"

"How they gonna know?"

"How do you feel, leaving him out in the rain and all?"

"I don't know. How do you feel?"

"The same."

"Me too."

The room darkened; waves of blackness swept across the floor. My head was nodding. I looked up, to see the pigeon-pisser dancing around the room. He was nude. His clothes were piled in one corner. He wore a raincoat snapped at his throat like a cape. He had a smile on his face and there was a pin stuck in his ear. I am afraid to find out if I am dreaming. I am not dreaming, but I am afraid to tell myself that.

"He said something!"

"What?"

"A word."

It was almost dark. A lower strip of the sky was burning: oranges, purples, magentas swirling, burning the clouds. He was facing us. Someone had turned him around. His hands gripped the sides of the wheelchair. I didn't know his hands could grip anything. His mouth was open, displaying the silver thing. It sounded like he was gagging on something.

"I think he wants us to take him back."

"He's probably hungry."

"I'm cold."

He was trying to stand up! My God.

"Look at him."

His face was twisted with great effort. The wind kept flapping his hair, first on one side and then on the other. His eyes seemed to change color. His skin looked translucent, creamy. I could see through to his bones, see his heart beating, the veins surging. He opened his mouth wider. The silver thing was clear, sharp. It hurt to look at it. It looked like a bullet or some kind of knife. He was going to speak, but he first had to twist his mouth around to one side of his face. I wanted to cry. I didn't know why. I felt awful. I wasn't afraid of him, or for him. It was something else. He reminded me of someone else. Someone wounded. I started to cry. He reminded me of my father. "Help," he said. "Please help."

D O N K E Y

B A S E B A L L

1 2

THE DONKEYS DIDN'T PLAY BASEBALL. BUT THE BILLBOARDS advertising the game made it sound as if they could, as if a special breed of donkey had been brought up from Argentina or Chile, around Cape Horn and through the great locks at Panama. No expense, of course, had been spared. The men seated awkwardly on these highly trained creatures played baseball, which might have confused the donkeys had the donkeys been capable of confusion. As it was, the donkeys were only capable of stubbornness, or what passed for stubbornness but was in fact merely a reluctance to do anything that didn't originate in their own pea brains. The men played what, minus the donkeys, would have been at best a barely passable game of baseball.

warped, crooked, and grainy, had many hidden recesses, like cupped hands, where pants were unbuttoned and dresses pulled up. On the field the men cursed and spit, sometimes slipping off one of the animals to lie in the manure-enriched grass. The donkeys were generally unwilling to move, especially when the players wanted them to move. The only thing they wanted to do was to chew on the grass in the outfield or wait patiently for the huge erections that seemed to be forever blossoming out of their groins: one foot, two feet, two and a half feet of something that looked like a large stiff hose with a shiny, glistening tennis ball at the end. If this came at an inconvenient time, when the player had, for some reason, hit the ball and needed the donkey to run to first base, the batter would lean over and tap the elongated donkey prick with his bat, hard enough so that the annoyed animal would want to retrieve his sex. Those without a bat, however, were forced to endure the animal's pleasure.

The boy wasn't sure why he watched this. He disliked baseball. But there was something funny about what the men did, and he liked to listen to the words they used when they came out of the locker room, words he never heard at home, words that dealt with the triumphs and failures of the groin, the trials and tribulations the players and their personal bats suffered under the yoke of women, sometimes young, wild, more often old, nasty.

The owner sold popcorn, soda, and, though he had no license, beer and whiskey at inflated prices to anyone with the money to buy it. He always looked disheveled; clothes were uncomfortable on his frame, shirts could never cover his bulbous middle, could never stay tucked in his pants, and the zipper and top button of his pants forever malfunctioned, so that he was half zipped, half buttoned, on the verge of bursting forth from his clothes. He looked as if he had jaws within jaws and cheeks within cheeks. A wild, maniacal light filled his eyes. The boy was sure he ate wood; normal food was not enough to sustain him; he wanted more. He was beyond greed, had exceeded gluttony. He needed to devour

With the donkeys it became something else: a s\
humiliation.

The boy, along with his friends, got in free to \
he had promised the owner he would collect the cushi\
of the game. They were rented by those who could \
sit on) the wooden planks that served for bleachers. \
the ballpark was a large fat man who underfed the \
overfed himself, running the hot-dog concession and co\
leftover franks at the end of the game, then herding t\
beasts into tiny stalls while he pulled strings of frank\
his hip pocket and stuffed them into his mouth. The anin\
balked, refused to move, or moved at inconvenient time\
manure where it was not needed which the owner steppe\
he pitted his considerable bulk against that of the donkey\
them into darkened, cramped stalls with his shoulders and \
bullying the beasts as much as they could be bullied, w\
not as much as the ballplayers could be bullied. In fact, h\
the donkeys better than he did the players. At least the\
had no fear of the owner and were immune to his promis\
the players it was just the opposite. For many of them, \
baseball was something they had done so long that to s\
unthinkable. Not playing had simply ceased to be an option\
of them had been minor-league players, a few had played t\
ball. Here they had dropped to the bottom of the alphab\
below: no letter could represent the depths that stood for d\
baseball. It was no longer baseball, hardly even a circus, cer\
not a sideshow. It was a form of ritualized degradation. The o\
realized that if people would pay to see someone abase himself, \
certainly would pay to see a group of people do it. The ho\
catcalls, and braying that greeted the men on toy horses when \
trotted out on the field seemed to wrench the spirit out of the\
to put them in a place that was beyond demoralization.

Games were played in the evening. The ballpark had a vagu\
erotic look and smell to it; the green wood bleachers and fenc\

117

whatever it was he could touch, so that he could say: I eat, therefore I am.

The donkeys managed to slow down a game that already verged on boredom, and as the boy watched in the growing darkness, and the sky was charged with dark light, a glowing orange with streaks of purple at its edges and vast muddied lakes of blue, the game seemed to fall apart, as if what was happening in the outfield was something separate, a continent away. The men, seated on sway-backed donkeys, looked like sentinels, keeping vigil over a ritual that had lost its meaning. The boy felt as if he were waiting for a signal, something divine, a thing that came not from the game or the park but from somewhere else, perhaps the city or the sky, a sign of sorts that this humiliation was not in vain, that it must be endured, that its very uselessness served some grander purpose.

Sometimes the men in the outfield gave up any pretense at being part of the game. When a ball came, lazily plopping in the grass, they would pretend not to notice. The humiliation of leaning over to pick it up without falling off their donkeys was simply too strong to be endured. They had ceased being players; they were watchers, waiters. And the boy knew that he too was watching, waiting for something, some grand event he had no knowledge of, something mesmerizing.

The owner, furious, would shout from the sidelines and throw bagfuls of popcorn at the outfielders, which the donkeys would eat. The motion of the donkeys seemed to shake the outfielders out of their lethargy, and they would prod their asses over to the ball, and then, in defiance of the regulations of donkey baseball, dismount and retrieve it, throwing it to the nearest infielder before mounting. The owner, apoplectic, shouting and screaming from the sidelines, an enraged sack of flesh, what passed for a stomach protruding from his shirt, would wave a baseball bat in the air, as if he were signaling the audience, which assumed he was and showered the field with whatever debris was at hand. This included hot dogs, beer, marsh-mallows, seat cushions, wire milk cases, cigars, barstools, light people who lost arguments, and bags of donkey manure prepared for the occasion.

What happened next depended upon how much was tossed on the field, and the mood of the players. If most of the objects were small, and the players had consumed enough beer, it usually continued. If other conditions prevailed, the players would charge the stands, eighteen Don Quixotes in search of windmills, swinging bats, throwing softballs, urging their dim-witted and recalcitrant asses to climb the shaky wooden bleachers in pursuit of a fan to club. The donkeys were reluctant to ascend this shaky ziggurat, and when they did, frequently managed to poke their legs through the gaps in the bleacher boards, throwing the players, and then wedging themselves between the boards. They did this, the owner thought, not out of caprice but on purpose, preferring to be wedged in by boards.

"Asses," the owner shouted, "my asses, get them out of there."

But unwedging a donkey out of the bleachers was not easy. They seemed to develop, once stuck, an affinity for the boards that trapped them, held them so tight their circulation was threatened, and indeed they were able to puff up their bodies to make extraction, never an easy prospect, even more difficult. The bleachers were stuffed with donkeys, like a plum pudding with raisins. The donkeys' eyes glazed over, as if in the throes of sexual passion. Most managed erections while trapped. Far from frantic, the beasts seemed to exude a sort of unconscious contentment, as if freedom from use of their limbs enabled them to withdraw from the hurly-burly of donkey baseball and contemplate their donkeyhood, the very essence of assness. They seemed relieved, as if a great burden had been lifted from their backs, as if the mystery of the colors of the night was about to be explained to them in ass language. The owner used pry bars, food, axle grease, block and tackle, and as a last resort simply sawed a few out, letting them drop to the ground. There was one animal he could not remove; it remained there until the end of donkey baseball season, alternately starving and being fed hot dogs and popcorn. When the cold weather came, the owner abandoned the beast, and it was fed by kids who scaled the fence during late fall and early winter. It died in midwinter, and when spring came, it looked not like a dead animal in the stands but like some sort of sparsely furred robe thrown over a pile of sticks, vacant pigeon-pecked eyes staring blankly into yet another season of donkey baseball.

The dead donkey in the stands became an unofficial mascot of the new season, and visiting teams took note of his long since rotted carcass. The boy wondered if people realized how much effort it had taken for the donkey to climb as high as it did without slipping through the boards, until finally, reaching almost the top of the bleachers, it took that fatal plunge of several inches, and remained to brood over the new season. He could not imagine why donkeys wanted to trap themselves, until he thought of his father. One evening the owner climbed the bleachers to the dead donkey and poked it through the boards, letting it drop. Everyone in the stadium felt as if he had violated some unspoken trust. It was the last season of donkey baseball.

BOOZE

MY FATHER IS THROWING A PARTY. ALL HIS FRIENDS ARE COM-
ing. His friends are alcoholics. There is
plenty of booze. They will drink until
they throw up or pass out or are carried
home.

We live in a Protestant neighborhood, but the people who come to our
parties don't live in the neighborhood.
For the most part they are doctors, athe-
ists, and, for some reason, Scandinavian.

Some of them were Catholic athe-
ists, like my father (who believed in the
saints but not in God), while others,
lacking that faith, were agnostics.

I always thought a party meant you
were honoring something, or celebrating someone, but my father's parties
meant neither, and I'm not sure why
they were called parties, except that I

didn't know what else to call them. That's what he called them, and in some way he may have been celebrating something I knew nothing about. Nobody played what a sane person would call games at his parties. Nobody received any awards. As far as I could tell, there was only one thing people did.

My father's favorite trick was to imitate a sober man. He would greet guests at the door with the measured gait of the slow walker. The first syllable was voiced with great effort, slowly, as if he had to break duct tape that held his lips together. He smiled, struck an agreeable pose, was eager to please—a thoroughly unnatural posture for him. (No, he could be eager to please. But these bits of eagerness came to him at random moments, unexpected.) He mixed drinks, handed them out with great flourish. He spoke with a serious eagerness that was spurred by alcohol. Booze made him earnest, believable, intense. I see him arguing anginas and carcinomas with his drinker's face well hidden, his stiff, artery-heavy arms waving in the air.

In my father's graduating class at medical school there was a Dane named Thorvaldsen. I never knew his first name, or maybe never learned his last name. He learned how to drink in Copenhagen: beer with schnapps. My father detested beer, so Thorvaldsen always brought a case to his parties, along with a bottle of schnapps, which he put in the freezer. Thorvaldsen was tall, brown-haired, had a long nose that looked like a shoulder blade and an Adam's apple that looked like a nose, played chess with my father, had a terrible temper, bad breath, and a wife who couldn't seem to grow anything with his sperm.

"God knows we've screwed enough, John, but it doesn't seem to take hold."

(I sit on an upstairs landing, hidden by a banister, listening.)

His wife looked like what his daughter would have looked like if he had one. While he had that ruddy, open-sea look Danes get, his wife's skin was smooth and pale, as if she had contracted one of those diseases that ensure long life.

Thorvaldsen didn't talk, he babbled—about screwing, chess, diseases, and mistakes he made on the operating table. He hated Walker another classmate, who always came to parties with him.

Walker was known as J&B.

"How do you screw?" he asked Walker.

"With my right hand, Thorvaldsen."

Walker looked like a handsome mole. His forehead continued halfway up his head, refusing to stop at a decent interval, and his hair looked like a receding glacier. It was brown and glossy. He wore brown suits with open-mesh shoes and specialized in nose and throat.

"The uterus should be tilted downward," Walker said.

"How the hell do you know?"

"The body temperature should be ninety-eight point six. The female should be between periods."

Thorvaldsen froze him with a schnapps-chilled stare. Schnapps always went right to his eyeballs. Walker was one of those people who made everyone else look badly dressed. His suits never wrinkled. They seemed to bend, like soft metal, around his body.

My mother was helping someone throw up in the bathroom. Out came the tiny sandwiches she had spent so much time making. She flushed the toilet. Down it went. It didn't make any difference. The toilet would get it sooner or later.

My father is talking with DeKuntz. He was a red-haired Dutch gynecologist who liked to wake his wife up in the middle of the night and strangle her. In the morning he would tell her it was just a nightmare she had. She went on a bender twice a year, slept with anything that wore pants, and then checked into an asylum. They had one child, a boy, who made tropical poisons.

Thorvaldsen came over and asked DeKuntz what was the right way to screw.

"With the penis," DeKuntz said.

"What's best for conception . . . every other night? Once a week?"

"Why don't you ask Walker?"

"The trouble is," Thorvaldsen said, "he already knows."

Thorvaldsen turned toward DeKuntz's wife. He placed his hands on her hips.

"Should the pelvis be pointed up or down?"

"Any way you like to point it," DeKuntz said. "Personally, I don't like it pointed at all."

Thorvaldsen turned DeKuntz's wife around.

"What about from the rear?"

"It's entirely a matter of taste," DeKuntz said.

A golf ball came in through the window, knocking over a bottle of Dewar's. Simonsen went down on his knees to catch the cascading Scotch in an empty bottle. He poured himself another drink before he set the bottle back on the table. Simonsen was in practice with Walker. He did eyes and ears, leaving nose and throat to Walker. He had a ten-thousand-dollar hi-fi set, over which he played recordings of steam engines through a dozen time-delayed speakers spread over his house.

Thorvaldsen walked over to Simonsen.

"Look," Simonsen said, "I don't want to talk about screwing."

"Neither do I," Thorvaldsen said.

Huber came in, looking for his golf ball.

"Look," Simonsen said, "you almost killed a bottle of Scotch."

Huber didn't talk at parties. He liked to drink, play golf, and deliver babies, in reverse order. He had delivered me, and my brother, and was the one who advised my mother to have a hysterectomy after David was born. He drank as if drinking came natural to him and alcohol a vital fluid his body needed. There was a gloss on his skin that was replenished by Scotch. He never made an abrupt movement, or move, in his life. He was unmarried. His classmates had thought he'd flunk out of medical school because there was a softness in him most doctors lacked. But my father said he had a healing sense very few doctors had. He never startled with his diagnostic skill, or seemed overly brilliant or imaginative, but there was something in him that glowed, and he was able to transfer that glow.

My father had on his golf shoes, and he and Huber were out on the front lawn putting when Thorvaldsen came rolling out the front door, wrapped in a rug. He had a dopey gleam in his eye, the moment before madness, as he rolled across the temporary putting green and out into the street, oblivious to a car bearing down on him. Huber and my father looked up, golf clubs in hand. For a moment there was a mixture of personal terror and professional anxiety, and then the two emotions blended as they calculated the places in Thorvaldsen's body where bones would be broken, blood vessels ruptured, organs smashed and spread about the street. The car jammed on its brakes. Thorvaldsen, from the safety of his rolled rug, waved to the driver and continued rolling until he was across the street and up on someone's lawn. The owner of the lawn came out to stare at him, and Thorvaldsen stared back, the two men, one horizontal and the other vertical, locked in an eye dance. Finally the lawn owner, embarrassed at what he thought must have been a purely private moment of Thorvaldsen's, turned off his porch light and stepped back into his house, leaving Thorvaldsen in control of the lawn—the general of grass. Thorvaldsen rolled back to our house, apologizing for dirtying the rug.

"I don't drink alcohol," my father once told me. "Alcohol is too polite. I drink booze. Booze is like alcohol, except it has no veneer. I hate the veneer. I hate things that come wrapped up."

He hated the taste?

"Oh God, yes."

Was it the idea of it?

"There is no idea to it. Booze is merely an invitation."

As a social custom?

"Sure. But I drink booze because I want to fly."

One night he was convinced people could fly if they held each other tightly. He squeezed my mother's arm until it bruised.

"It's the lightness of it."

Isn't that an idea?

"Lightness is not an idea. Any more than air is."

You intellectualize too much. You like to drink so you can tell people to fuck off. So you can tell yourself to fuck off.

"I just drink. You don't have to understand it."

I make up my understanding. He makes up his misunderstanding. My fear is that it amounts to the same thing.

Are you happy?

"I'm not happy. But I have joy."

What do you find in booze?

"I'm not looking for anything."

He lies. He is looking for the center. He told me so. He told me the center hid itself in the center. He said booze burned away the fat that covered the center. He said booze was the only thing that had no surface.

"The joy is burning through me."

He was pissing in his pants when he said this. I see no joy. Or do I?

More drinks appeared: Scotch, rye, bourbon. There were women's drinks and men's drinks. Drinks with sugar, salt, onion, lemon, a twist of this, a sprinkle of that, mixtures, drinks that looked cloudy, any unnatural colors (greens, oranges, pinks), things that had to be stirred, frosted, heated, singed, that required a swizzle stick, sounded unfamiliar, cute, or foreign—these were women's drinks. The men's drinks were what the women's drinks started life as, before adulteration. As the night wore on, old drinks, used drinks, became burial grounds for cigarettes. An alcoholic slurry of gray-brown began to grow in glasses with lipstick smudges and oiled etchings of pheasants and golden retrievers. When the booze started to run out, the truly needy surreptitiously filtered this sludge through cocktail napkins, cautiously sipping, in some cases gulping, what remained.

My father stood in the center of the living room, tilting, his imitation of sobriety no longer convincing. Something seemed to leak out of him; parts of his face, his legs, deflated; he was unsure what to do with their collapse. His conversation was abrupt, his tongue a foreign object in his mouth. The room and the occupants of the room began to take on the colors of hostility. Booze had cleared away the haze that covered his perception, and he saw the environment for what it was. Politeness had fled; even the veneer of politeness had vanished. Beneath the skin he saw the unspoken words still forming in people's mouths. He could see the way chairs and tables edged their sharp corners closer to where he would walk, the shelves jiggling as they began preparations for falling, scattering papers, books, fragile things that would shatter, sharp edge up, into nearly perfect foot-piercing size. And then thoughts came to him: what people were thinking, what they would soon be thinking, what they would say and what they really meant.

DeKuntz's wife was doing a striptease. Thorvaldsen had soaked her in beer, celebrating, he said, her extraordinary charm and grace under pleasure. She took off her clothes, stood on the top of a coffee table, and put two cream-cheese crackers (with chives) on her nipples and a spear of broccoli somewhere else. She kept on her high-heel shoes. DeKuntz had passed out in the kitchen, his head in the goldfish bowl. The next morning all my brother's goldfish were dead.

The food left was olives, pickles, a few crackers. There were no clean glasses; the guests held on to theirs, or wiped out the slurried remains of a dead glass with a cocktail napkin and refilled their drink. Conversations centered around unreasonable hopes or unreasonable despair.

"What's the use . . . ?"

"Valium dreams . . . we had to use a pliers . . ."

"Sinking fast, until they brought in the medicine man . . ."

"They never count the petty cash . . . head of the clinic is catatonic."

"Olfactory sex . . ."

Ashtrays were used as hockey pucks. They flew across the floor, skimming the top hairs of the wool rug. My father stood in the middle of this activity, not sure if the ashtrays were aimed at him or around him (but beginning to think the former). Someone had taken DeKuntz's head out of the goldfish bowl and emptied it into the sink, goldfish still alive at this point, to use the bowl for a goal. The other goal was a loaf of white bread that had been found behind the sofa and had been pierced, for some reason, with toothpicks.

The women were suddenly told to go to one side of the room and sit down, crossing their legs. All the doctor's wives, except one, obeyed. Then the crossed-legs game was played, which seemed to have no point to it other than the men walking over to the women, and with their hands, crossing or uncrossing their legs.

Cigarette smoke obscured the ceiling. A quiet viciousness seemed to descend upon the party. I could hear grunts and groans from people who did not look as if they were undergoing pain. People began to slip out of focus, hidden from view. As if by prearranged signal, everybody started to circle the room. My father stood in the center, turning to their motion. They were silent, the shuffling of their feet masked by the rug. My father opened his mouth, as if to speak. Nothing came out. My mother was watching from the kitchen, horrified.

I fell asleep on the stairs.

And then woke up to a loud argument. Our door was kicked several times, punches were thrown, someone's wife was insulted, clothing ripped, and before the windows were broken but after the bottles were thrown, there was a wrestling match. No, it was more like a dance, an embrace with grunts. Two doctors were rolling across the rug, locked in each other's arms. They were drunk, vicious, and incapable of any damage. They seemed to be trying to find out who could squeeze harder or pull each other's arms the farthest. I couldn't tell if my father was one of them. Chairs, tables, lamps, were knocked over. They held each other in a pile of magazines, afraid of drowning in paper.

Then from my window I watched everyone drive home. For those who were able to find their cars there was the added burden of finding the street.

My father is sitting in a chair that has been pushed to the middle of the room. He has no drink in his hand, no cigarette. His eyes are wide open but far away, blurred by regret. The living room looks as if someone had opened several very full vacuum cleaner bags and scattered them about, making sure the debris was evenly distributed.

Now his eyes are focusing on something. He knows something, but he doesn't know what to do with this knowledge. It is a burden to him, a terrible joy. He crosses his legs and taps his knees. My mother is watching from the kitchen. She is afraid he will get up. She does not want him to get up, because if he does he will fall and she does not know if she can pick him up. She is too embarrassed to ask one of her neighbors to come over and pick him up. If she leaves him there, sleeping, he will be furious the next morning. She would never ask me to help lift him. She wants to hide his falling from me. She knows that I know, but she wants to hide his falling.

He hasn't fallen. He is still sitting in the chair. She does not know what he is going to do, and this almost frightens her more than his falling, should he get up, should he fall if he gets up.

He knows we are looking at him and he knows what we are thinking and he wants to spite us by not getting up and not not getting up; he wants to hover between the two, have the choice of getting up or not getting up, he wants to forever have that choice, but he knows that having that choice will soon mean that he does not have that choice; by not picking the one, getting up, he will have picked the other, not getting up. It may be this knowledge that bothers him.

No. It is something else. Something has happened at the party, something I don't know. It is a great joy to him. But it is more joy than he can bear. It is too much joy to expect any man to bear.

CHURCH

1 2 ¼

"ARE YOU READY?" HIS FATHER ASKED. HE WORE HIS GRAY Robert Hall suit and a wide flowered tie. For some reason he had forgotten how old he was. He was around eight, or twelve, or somewhere in between. It wasn't terribly important how old he was, but it was strange to have forgotten his age. He was very conscious of age. It stuck to him, hard, like new teeth. He was always aware of just how old he was, in years and months, but there was something about the day that seemed to have pushed the age out of him, or pushed the consciousness of his age out of him. He had two aunts who always argued his age, one pushing for a year younger than he was, the other for a year older. His parents had set them right, but their saying never seemed to hold, and the aunts slid back into how old they thought he should be. They made him think that his real age was a blot on his moral character, that by being the age he was he had done something intolerably wrong, as if an evil had been allowed to come into being, which they must correct.

"Let's go then," his father said.

They were going to church. It was the boy's idea. He insisted that his father take him to a real church. A real church was a Catholic church, not a Protestant church. He wasn't sure why he wanted to go. He felt that the air inside a Catholic church was different. He wanted to see what it looked like, to see how it was different. Perhaps it was richer, more pungent, perhaps there was a color to the air that warmed objects, made them glow, vibrate.

He might be guilty of something. He didn't know what that could be, but perhaps the air inside a church could ease this. He need not know what caused the guilt, only knew it could be slid off him, like soiled clothes. He didn't even know what guilt was, but he thought he had it because he had heard people speak of it, hardly criticizing it, making it seem some sort of healthy disease, a thing that he wanted to be rid of in the way that one got rid of a cold. He had no idea how you caught it, but that made no difference. The thing to do was to get rid of it. There was someone in the church who could do that. He attracted guilt. He was a sort of guilt magnet.

"Hurry up," his father said.

He knew his father was not anxious to go to church; he hadn't been to church in years and the priest had long ago stopped coming by. He knew this because his father was horribly sober, eyes wide, startled. His face seemed to stand at attention. The wrinkles around his nose and mouth looked as if they were about to break up into new wrinkles. His father's shirt was starched so stiffly the boy could hear it creak when he moved. The suit he wore was dark, double-breasted, and the shoes and tie were also dark. His father seemed afraid of something, and the boy knew that his father was doing this thing for his sake, that he much preferred to lie in bed and drink coffee, that the thought of going to church terrified him. The boy did not feel guilty about this. The boy also knew that his father was not terrified out of guilt. He was immune from guilt. It was something else, a terror that sprang from a different source.

"Ride in the front."

It was more command than suggestion, not that the boy needed it, since he preferred to ride in the front anyway. The green Ford had a grille that looked like the prow of a ship, and the boy imagined the Ford slicing through invisible waves of air, rising and gently falling with the bumps in the road as if they were waves in the water, as if the road had frozen the long swells of an ocean. On the ceiling of the Ford, as if spray from a wave, was a long arc of sputum, which had discolored the gray sackcloth fabric that covered the interior. It had appeared there mysteriously one day, like a trail of mushrooms.

His father lit a cigarette and inhaled deeply. It would be the last cigarette before church. It would be one hour until the next one. He drove with both hands on the wheel, the cigarette between two fingers.

No, he did know what guilt was. That is, he did and he didn't. He knew the feeling that it produced; he didn't know precisely what it was. For example, now he felt guilty about going to church, about wanting to go to church; he felt guilty about feeling guilty. He wasn't sure if he should do this, wasn't sure if he should have asked his father to do this, but having had some sort of desire to do it, he had acted upon it before he could feel guilty about it. He confused guilt with not knowing what one felt, a thing that existed on the surface, that sprang from something murky underneath. It was something that made you want to squirm, an itch where nothing itched.

"When we get inside, just do what I do."

He would. It was an order, a definite act. He had been waiting for this. He had been waiting for something to follow. Not some*one* to follow, some*thing* to follow. He felt relieved.

His father took a huge suck on the cigarette. He seemed to
inhale forever, as if he were sucking the very air from the car, as if

he were drawing the contents of the car into his lungs. It seemed
to remain in his lungs forever, and then slowly, like flowers growing,
come out. He opened a side vent to free the smoke from the car.
The air came rushing in, swirling the smoke about and pushing it
out. The boy had eaten no breakfast. He had lost his appetite, just
as he had lost his age.

The church, situated on a hill, built on a foundation that seemed
inordinately tall, and then the church itself taller yet, gave the
impression of something that would continue on forever, that its
spires and steeple would pierce whatever it was that was up there.
There were long stairs at the front, but his father made him go in
by the side. Unlike the front doors, the side doors had to be opened.
They were tall, made of heavy wood, pieces strapped together by
fingers of black iron.

"Watch me," his father said.

Going in, he caught his breath, tried to hold it forever. He had
the feeling he was disturbing something; what was going on was
vast, immense, and he was a speck, a mote in the eye of this
machinery. It seemed as if the church were tilted on one end. He
wanted to lean back, to look up, to look at an *up* that seemed to
go on and on, statue climbing on top of statue, angel above angel,
fluted column above gargoyled flying buttress, air above earth. The
ceiling, if there was one, was lost in an immensity of altitude,
somewhere at the upper end of height.

His father dipped down on one knee and then pointed to his
chest. Then he sat in one of the benches. The boy did the same
thing, and was about to sit down.

"No," his father said.

He grabbed his finger. It hurt. He wanted him to touch his
heart with his finger. He wanted him to make a sign over his heart.
The boy wanted to, he tried, but his father's hand, large, veined,
too white, got in the way. They fumbled over his chest—his hand,
his finger, his father's hand trying to guide the finger and the boy
moving the finger against the guidance, thinking that one had to
do it oneself, that doing it voluntarily was the whole point. His

father wrenched his finger across his chest, pushing his finger into his chest, drawing it along the collarbone. The boy turned aside, ashamed. He tried to sit down. There were tears in his eyes. He couldn't see the bench. He reached out with his hand, feeling for the back of the bench. His father was down on his knees, hands clasped in front of him. The boy wanted to apologize. He didn't know what to do. His father was kneeling the same way he had in the bathtub. Still standing, he said, "I'm sorry."

His father said nothing.

He sat down. He saw his father's hand shake. He thought he wanted a cigarette. He looked at the fat on his neck that doubled over his collar and the bristles of hair that stuck out from the skin. The collar was a knife of white at his neck, a guillotine of cotton and starch. His father's jacket was drawn tight across his shoulders and back, his elbows pushed forward and pressed in. When he tilted his head forward, the fat on his neck was swallowed up. Except for his stomach, it was the only place on his body where he had fat.

The priest raised his arms and everyone stood up. The boy's father looked straight ahead, eyes wide, as if he were watching something that frightened him.

Everyone sang. The priest's robe glimmered, gold and cream. Standing in front of the altar, he looked as if he were in a spiderweb, shaking, being shook, dazed. He, the priest, his father, were caught in the immensity of the church.

Everyone sat down. A bird, trapped in the church, flew just under the ceiling. It was a large bird, large enough so that its flying was not a frantic affair but controlled, leisurely, sure in its movements. It seemed to have a regular route it flew, back and forth, circling from cherubim to angel to gargoyle. As the priest spoke, it flew overhead, and the boy wondered whether anyone else noticed it. The ceiling was a soot gray, and so was the bird; the only time he could see it was when it flew in front of a dusty window and a gleam of sooty light fell on its wing, glimmering briefly in the shadows below. Then the boy thought it might be something else:

a balloon, a leaf, a piece of paper. It disappeared into the air, into the sacramental air, a bit of dust, of nothing.

"Did you see that?" he turned to his father, saying.

His father looked at him in terror. His eyes were wide in wonder, full of ghosts. "No," he said. "No!"

He stood up, stumbled over the boy's feet, and ran toward the side door, pushing it open with difficulty. The boy sat on the bench, not daring to move, waiting for the signal when he, along with the rest, would get up. The priest seemed to speak for hours, and when everyone did get up, the boy forgot to dip down on one knee and make the sign over his chest. He was swept to the back of the church, the front entrance, where he ducked under the hand of the priest, who was shaking someone's hand, and stumbled down the long row of steps. The sunlight made him blink, made his eyes teary, made him confused, angry in some unknown way. The small priest at the top of the steps, shaking people's hands as they left the church, was the same priest who years before had asked him to kiss the stones. He looked wobbly, shaky. He was not the priest who had stood in front of the altar. The boy thought that this priest, this tiny priest, would never be allowed to wear such magnificent robes. He was forever doomed to dress in black, with a small slit to show off a turned-around collar.

The boy thought that forgetting to dip, forgetting to make the sign over his chest, would go against him in some way. His father was sitting in the Ford, ashen, distracted, vaguely annoyed. The boy opened the car door.

"Get in," his father said. It seemed to the boy the two most unnecessary words he had heard all day.

He sat in the passenger's seat and watched the heat rise off the hood, distracting the air beyond, making a kind of wavering reality of the church.

"Why did we have to come?"

"I don't . . ."

"Why did I have to come?"

"I . . ."

"I could have left you off. I could have come by to pick you up."

The boy sighed.

"Didn't you see what was in there?"

"What?"

"It's tight in there. It's always tight in there. I can't breathe."

It came in waves, like the distracted air off the car hood.

"Why did you do this? Why did you make me do this?"

"I didn . . ."

His father shucked it off, sighing.

"I hope you got what you wanted," he said. He started up the car and drove out of the lot. He drove slowly, cautiously, testing the tires, the road, the traffic lights.

"I certainly hope you got what you wanted."

His hands shook, but his driving was steady, controlled, planned. The boy looked out the window. The roads were filled with cars, the sidewalks with people. The trees seemed greener than he had remembered. He could hear a clattering, a raucousness that filled the air, made it sharp, stinging, made of it something hard.

"I don't know what I wanted," the boy said.

"Don't tell me what you wanted," the boy's father said.

The car slowed for a stop. The air was filled with Sunday morning. His father turned to him.

"You don't know what you want."

And when they were moving again:

"You don't know *want*."

MY FATHER GOT DRUNK EVERY NIGHT OF HIS LIFE AND MOST
days, except Thursday, when he sobered
up for the AA meeting. I could tell
when he had been drinking because his
skin stunk. It smelled like he had bathed
in honey and rinsed off with formaldehyde. When he sweated, it was worse.

He was very stiff when he drank.
His bones and muscles turned into gears
and levers. He moved with a vertical
motion, very sure of himself. Walking
made him look serious. Sitting made
him look silly. He would lower his eyes,
and the bottom half of his face would
fall asleep. I wished the rest of his face
would too, but it rarely did. He looked
like his head was wrapped in transparent
gauze that pulled lumps of his face into
odd places.

I was afraid to talk to him then, but my mother wasn't. She kept asking him questions when he was drunk, and it would take hours for him to answer; he would slowly turn his head, slowly move the lumps around his face, drop his jaw, and then begin to speak, the words fighting their way through the self-ingested slur he kept in his mouth. My mother turned to me, feigning shock while insinuating outrage. He's drunk, I told her; what do you expect?

He hated alcohol. It made him throw up. But he loved to drink. He drank until he got drunk, which was just before or just after he threw up. If just after, he'd drink again until he got drunk, hoping he wouldn't throw up again.

The AA meetings were a small circle of Irish alcoholics: a missionary priest from China who drank the communion wine before the parishioners could, a hot-fudge salesman, a man who ran a whaling museum in Kansas, and several doctors. The meetings were at our house. The strain of sobering up for the meeting was a traumatic event. My father's face underwent a series of lumpy explosions, as if knotted ropes were being dragged across his forehead. His nose got red, he picked it; he seemed to have a rash on his neck, which he had to scratch.

My mother made lots of coffee. There is something very serious about coffee, something godlike; it's communion wine for alcoholics.

The hot-fudge salesman always showed up first. When I answered the door he always said the same thing: "Th-th-th-that's all, folks!"

He looked like a piece of pale white chocolate, and on some Thursdays I could smell a familiar sweet sickness on his skin and knew that he hadn't quite made it through the day. He knew I knew, and he spent the rest of the evening trying to figure out if anyone else did. He consumed quarts of coffee, chain-smoked, did a lot of running to the bathroom and agreeing with whatever was said, his face a ball of amber perspiration. He took off his jacket, put on his jacket, loosened his tie, tightened it, shuffled his feet, kept rubbing the tops of his shoes on the back of his pants legs.

The priest had electrified eyebrows. They looked like a row of pine needles stuck into his forehead. He had a long, thin nose you could see through, gray eyeballs that reflected color, and long fingernails.

They spent most of their time talking about when they were drunk. They loved to talk about their drunks; it was the only thing they got drunk on. "A drunk" did not only refer to a person; it also referred to a specific place, a state of being, something you went to or a ride you got on. Being sober was hell; they knew it. They were in awe of drunks who could stay drunk. Drunkenness they could stand. It was the sobriety between their "drunks" they couldn't stand. Sobriety pressed on their veins, strangling them, until they had to renounce it. They were willing to remain sober as long as the paradise of drunkenness was not held out to them. They could only view the land of alcohol from afar; they were envious, bitter, sober soldiers of coffee and tea and plenty of fruit juice laced with lots of sugar.

People envy drunks. AAs envy them most of all. When I see a drunk I hear bones snap, knees crunch, I hear air sucked out of lungs. I hate the smugness of drunks, their surety, their smiling impetuosity, their superiority. I once bit my father's arm, leaving blood and teethmarks. He had to clean it up with the remains of a bottle of J&B, as if to prove to me how serious a bite from the human mouth was.

I grew up around drunks: drunk drunks and sober drunks. I saw them sober on Thursdays, drunk on Saturdays, and at various stages on other days. I was alternately ashamed, enraged, happy, bitter, perplexed, and passive about this parade that floated by. I collected money from the neighborhood children in return for showing them a drunk. In our neighborhood one rarely saw drunks. I had a flourishing business. But when the parents of the children learned about it, my business suffered. When my father learned about it, his only comment was that I hadn't charged enough. When the parents complained to my father, he asked them how much they thought I should charge.

I was fascinated by sober drunks.

When they came to our house on Thursday night I kept looking for small signs of drunkenness, some escaping steam of liquor that would slur a syllable or cause a foot to catch on a rug. I was sure that last Saturday's drunk had filled the house with an incredible stench which would make itself known to this group. They would find out and kick us out of our house. As a child, I was always afraid of someone coming along and kicking us out of our house. It is a persistent fear that sticks with me.

I don't know why alcoholics wish to be anonymous. My father never was. He went to great pains to make sure everyone knew he was drunk. At times I thought he wanted to send out announcements.

When he was brought home drunk, helpless, puke stains on his shirt, he dared me to be angry. I could see it in his eyes, clouded, barely open, shot through with red. "You are not a polite drunk," I say, "you are not a witty drunk, you are not a charming drunk." And he will say, finishing it for me, "I am a sloppy drunk, maudlin, a puking vomit drunk." He refuses to accept my pity. I refuse to give it to him. I will keep it for myself. He claims superiority by spurning self-pity. I claim it by indulging in it, like expensive chocolate, bite by bite. I never gobble. What does it mean to gloat over one's misfortune? To feel superior because of it? (But how can one feel superior as a consequence of self-pity?)

Sobriety insults him. It is a lid, a mantle over his mind. If he could stay perpetually drunk he would be safe. He would be free. He cannot. Alcohol is an enemy to his system, and he embraces his enemies, he tortures them to love him, knowing that they never will, knowing that their embrace is deadly. But he does not wish to die. He might have done so long ago, but he has no wish to die. Whatever it is he does, he wishes to continue doing.

Booze liberates his spirit.

Booze gives him wings.

Booze is something that cannot be breathed. Booze is a lack of air.

Booze is the sound the body makes when it is crying for the soul, the noise it makes when it looks for the soul. When the soul is too heavy, booze tears it from the body. Then the body must look for its soul.

NIGHT RIDE

1 2 ½

"I WANT TO TALK," HE SAID. IT WAS A STRANGE TIME TO talk, the boy thought, driving at night, the air immense and dark, a cavern with hidden walls, the largest part of the mind. The boy was crumpled in the back seat of the green Ford. Outside, Gary and East Chicago rolled by, huge belching cities, their fires muted in the night fog.

"I want to explain something," the boy's father said.

These were Bessemer cities that shook the car as they drove by, iron and steel cities with blasts of furnace air, oxygen hot to the touch, searing, hurricane strong. The night air was sly, slick, close to fog, and yet hugely powerful, locomotive quick.

"It's night. I can talk better at night."

The boy knew about night. Every night he died. He took off his clothes and put on his pajamas and went to bed and died. At night the nursery figures came off the walls, pushed out, as if some giant thumb was working at them from behind the wallpaper. They fell on the floor and rolled about: the three men in a tub, the candle-stickmaker, the butcher, the baker, the rub-a-dub-dub man. Every night while he lay in bed they rolled around the room, chattering in toy language. The moon came out and went back in and the trees blew around his windows and the night air, black velvet, thick as water, heavier than fog, swirled in. Nann was in the room. He couldn't see her. He died. He came to life in the morning.

"There's a thickness to the air at night," his father said. "You can taste it."

The boy waited, huddling.

"You have to understand something."

Then he stopped talking, concentrating on working the car around a series of wide bends.

"No, wait a minute . . . no, I take that back."

The boy couldn't remember what his father was taking back.

"You won't be able to understand. You can't understand."

He didn't want to understand. People always wanted him to "understand."

Through the mist he saw taverns, behind them rows of houses. That and the Bessemer furnaces made up Gary.

"All you have to do is listen. You don't have to understand a thing."

The boy didn't want to listen. He was always being told to listen, to be quiet, to pay attention. He wanted to do none of these things.

He saw flocks of birds in front of the car, diving and wheeling, disappearing into and coming from the fog, keeping pace with the car, racing ahead. The birds reminded him of hands, and the hands, of hats, and that reminded him of the brown Borsalino hat his father wore, a hat that looked as if it were about to explode.

"I've tried to talk before," his father said.

The boy waited, but his father said nothing. The boy sat up

straight in the back seat, head against a spot where the fabric was ripped and worn and yellowed from seven years of sunny afternoons. The car throbbed, bounced and shook, the tires hummed, the squinted instruments clicked off their soundings on the dashboard. Now they were leaving the furnaces, running along the grit-flecked sand dunes, past hastily built taverns sinking in the soil, crumbling cement bungalows with galvanized roofs whose rust stained the walls, making them look as if arrows had been pitched at their sides, through fog and blinking yellow lights.

"When we get there," his father said, "all your aunts will be there, and all your uncles too."

The air was heavy, stiff, resisting the motion of objects that passed through it, like a machine that creaked.

"They all want to talk to me," he said.

They drove by a faded billboard that said THE LAST BIRD, the paint peeling, lit by stray bulbs, and the boy wondered not at the meaning of the sign but at his lack of wonderment at the meaning of the sign. For some reason that he could not explain, it seemed perfectly reasonable that the sign was there, displaying its "signness." It reminded him of a time in northern Michigan when he had gone out very early one morning to a windswept baseball field, the air clean and hard after a night rain, to come upon a group of nuns playing baseball. The wonder of it struck him as something immense. The majesty of their black robes flapping in the wind, the way they held their habits up to run the bases or go after a ball, the calm joy with which they batted, as if giving birth or cutting flowers, struck him as miraculous. The sparkling blackness of their clothing, a gift of God, flapping about on the white baseball field in the early-morning sun, the little swirls of dust they stirred up with their sensible nuns' pumps, the way they stood over a base, as if they were about to pull something deep from within the ground, held him in awe. This is air, he thought. This is the lightness of air.

"They have this idea that they need to instruct me."

The boy believed, though he did not see it, that his father winked.

"They have this idea that I am instructible."

He paused.

"It is, of course, a mistaken idea."

The boy noticed a man closing up a fruit stand by the side of the road. Under each arm he carried a flat of blueberries, which he put on a tractor-pulled wagon.

"People enjoy holding on to their mistakes. Especially your aunts. They love to instruct. They think the world exists so they can teach it something. That is the German mentality, the Lutheran mentality."

The boy saw the man had padlocked wooden shutters on the sides of the stand.

"They don't believe that I know more than they do. Their minds are closed to that."

The car sped up, and then suddenly braked to a stop, the rear end skidding on the sandy road. His father started to back up; the boy looked out the rear window, terrified that a car would come speeding around the corner and ram them in the fog.

"We need blueberries. We need to bring them blueberries, something to disarm them."

The car kept backing up, and the boy grimaced, thinking of tires skidding, metal smashed and crumpled, glass broken, his body pressed inside the Ford like an ill-prepared sandwich. Finally the car stopped, his father pulling off the road.

"Blueberries."

It was a command that he get out of the car along with his father, that he march to the stand with him, side by side if necessary, behind if need be, and be there to help carry back the crates of blueberries his father would buy.

A small man with a mustache was loading crates of blueberries on the back of a wagon that was pulled by a tractor. He looked rumpled, soiled from something other than dirt. As they approached, he loaded the last of the blueberries on the wagon. His father reached into his pocket. The man spit into the sand, making a small crater of brown liquid.

"We'd like some blueberries."

The man spit again.

His father waited, wondering if the man had heard him, wondering if he could hear, if he was mentally defective. The boy could smell the water from Lake Michigan. He hadn't realized they were this close to the water. It would explain the dampness in the air, the fog.

"We want blueberries."

The man looked up. He tilted his head to one side, a sudden movement that frightened the boy. The boy heard a dog barking, then growling.

"Closed up."

"I can see that," his father said, "but you can sell me these blueberries."

The man took a pipe out of his pocket and put it in his mouth. The boy noticed large, gouged-out pieces on the stem that were filled with something yellow and brown. The dog growled again, and the man took the pipe out of his mouth to spit. Each time he spit, before and after, he made a retching sound in his throat. It was a sound that made his eyes go yellow.

"Goin' home."

"That's obvious. I'll save you hauling those blueberries."

The man pondered what his father had said, the words needing to travel to some distant outpost, where they were decoded, made intelligible to him. The boy felt uneasy, as if he were in the presence of sin.

"Can't." He put his pipe back in his mouth.

"Don't be stupid. Of course you can."

The dog barked again, and the man started to walk around to the tractor. The boy's father stood in the way. The boy wanted to tug at his suit, to say, come, let's go, let's get away from here, but he was afraid to do that, as afraid as he was of the man.

"Look out."

"You can sell me some blueberries."

"Look out."

Now his father was blocking the step to the tractor seat. The man reached into his pocket.

"Get out."

"I want blueberries."

"Get out!"

The man quickly took something out of his pocket. The boy could not see what it was, but it looked like something small and shiny, something cold, almost blue, and the boy had the feeling that it had something to do with earth or water, with the soil or the sea.

His father reached for a crate of blueberries. With the hand that had nothing in it, the man reached up for his father, as if to hold him or to find a part of him that was soft, something that would crumple.

The boy tried to shout. He wanted to say No! he wanted to scream it at both of them, but he could not, or felt that he could not, and then was ashamed that he would not. He became terrified. Something seemed to slip within his knees, tendons came loose from bone. He was afraid. He was ashamed of this fear, and began to walk away, then started to run, to cry, then stopped, feeling that he had betrayed his father, that he had let himself be turned into something shameful, one of those creatures that hide from the light. He walked back to the car. His pants were wet. He tried to stop crying. He looked back at his father and the man. They seemed to be pulling at each other, pushing; arms moved quickly and it became a blur. The boy crawled in the back seat of the car. He could hear a shout, a cry. Then there was another shout, louder, and a cry that was either pain or something else. Then silence. The boy sobbed. He blubbered, knowing he was too old to do it but unable to help himself, feeling a shame he knew would be permanent, indelible, that would live with him.

His father came back to the car. There was sand on his suit. His face was heavily flushed, red, as if it had expanded into regions it had never been in before. The boy stopped crying. He huddled in the back seat, thinking that in the silence he would go unnoticed, that he could will himself to disappear, that by an incredible effort of mind he could erase the last few moments of his life, or through sheer force compress his brain so that he would forget what had just happened.

They drove off. The boy was puzzled by how slowly his father drove, almost shocked by his cautious driving. He associated careful driving with his shame, and wished his father would speed up, go racing around curves.

Nothing was said. The volubility of the evening had evaporated. The night slid by, and the air, formerly warm, humid, was sharp and wet, stretched with a smell that etched, cut, seared. The only things on the road were trees, cabins, and taverns. Chunks of tires and rusted hubcaps littered the sides of the road. Every so often the car moaned and shuddered when it hit a pothole. The boy was wet and cold. His father drove with the window down, and the air came not just at his head but up from the floorboards, shaking his groin.

His father lit a cigarette, the wind fanning the glow and blowing the ashes into the back seat. The boy hoped that he would feel pricks from the glowing embers.

His father braked to a halt in front of a tavern. He got out of the car and before closing the door looked back at the boy huddled in the rear seat. With one hand he held the door open, waiting. He slowly lifted his hand off the door and ran his fingers through his hair, smoothing it down. Then he slammed the door shut and walked into the tavern.

The force rocked the car, and long after the door had shut and his father had gone into the tavern he could feel the rocking in the car, by now turned into something else, an electric current, or a small clicking or tapping that made its way around the metal part of the car.

You are a terrible thing, the boy thought. *You stand several feet over me and you wear white shirts and dark suits.* He could taste the shame in his mouth, salty, metallic, bitter, like a filling in his tooth. *You never slouch in your seat.* His mouth was dry. He was thirsty. He hoped his father would bring him back a soda, but he didn't expect it. There were many things he hoped for, didn't expect, and then was angry he didn't get.

No, he thought again. *You are not a terrible thing. But you will always stand several feet over me, and though you may not be a terrible thing, you are a terror thing.* He wanted to go asleep, was afraid to fall asleep, was afraid of his father coming back, afraid of what he would be like when he drove. The road was not wide enough for his driving, the car not strong enough, the air not soft enough.

He heard some singing, some shouting, and his father was propelled from the tavern door, walking swiftly toward the car as if his legs were sticks, hardly bending his knees, so that he bounced off the ground. It didn't take him long to reach the car. He opened the door and slid into the front seat. When he turned around, the boy was amazed at how frightened he looked.

"I had," he said, "my fingers around his throat."

He put his hand up to his face as if he wanted to support something inside his head.

"I was choking him. He pushed me down."

The boy was terrified, and yet relieved. Terrified of his father's driving, and yet relieved that the conversation did not encompass his shame, that the running away had been forgotten about, that it hardly existed. And then he realized that his father had not even noticed it, that it had simply ceased to exist in his father's mind. For that he was relieved, and then: *I barely exist for him. He talks to me, and yet I am not here. There is a space where I should be.*

"I had my fingers around his throat."

He was merely an attendant in his father's drama. At most, at best, he had a walk-on part.

"I could feel his pulse in my fingers."

The car had gathered its own music, the creak of springs, the click of relays, and combined it with the beach insects that buzzed about: mosquitoes, June bugs, horseflies, cicadas. The boy was part of that music, that background. There was an ease to that. He was no longer an individual. He was scenery, backdrop. There was no longer a body and a will. He simply was a body willed.

The night was black, calm, and terrible. There was the lake, the sand, the insects, and with hardly any exertion he could smell one, and then the other, hear one, and then the other. They entered into his body like lightning, as bold as a rock, as quiet as a wave. The water and the air were deep in black, restful, with the cadence of death.

"It was so easy. I could have killed him."

MICHIGAN

WE ARE FISHING. HE HAS SOMETHING IMPORTANT TO TELL ME about fishing. "The greatest danger in fishing," he says, "is the temptation to catch a fish."

He sits absolutely still in the back of the wooden boat; he seems to extend below the boat and deep into the water. I lean on the rotten oars. The afternoon is quiet, unmoved, a thing apart from time.

He has buttoned up his shirt, rolled down his sleeves, and put on his hat. He has the kind of Irish-red blotchy skin that turns lobster pink, lobster red in the sun. Even his fingernails burn.

Accompanying us in the boat is one rod, one reel, some line, leader, sinker, bobber, hook, and one worm. It is a tired worm, well used. My father refused to fish with a new worm.

He baits the single hook with the worm and drops it in the water. I row. The plan is that the worm and hook will never come out of the water until we are back on the dock.

I row out to the middle of the lake, drop the cement coffee can into the water, and start bailing. The water near the top of the water is hot. The sun takes up too much space in the sky. The water feels like melted butter. I have the idea that fish in the water make it slimy.

My father fished as if he were discussing love. There was no plop when the hook and sinker hit the water, just a clean entry. It is scary. I should correct him in his fishing, but he won't take directions. That is why we ended up on the lawn with the plaster-of-paris flamingos and a trail of mud that was used to skid two tons of dead sycamore. He loved that log. He loves wood, but I can't take it anymore. I can't look at that log and think of love anymore. I refuse to do it. I refuse to fish with my glasses on, dreaming of being underwater, thinking of how birds swim and the way he looks with his glasses on, puts them down on his nose and then up on his forehead, over his forehead when he types, and how he types as if he were fishing, just as he fishes as if he were discussing love. I can't take that anymore.

The water is like soil, like the mud the sycamore was skidded on. It comes in different colors, rises and falls in long hills and valleys. It does not obey the laws of gravity or follow the tides. It uses some other arcane law, some exception to the general rule about things that fall. The fish have myopia because of the water. Their eyes bulge out of their heads. They are not fish one can digest, but gray, leathery things that glide or fly in the water. Some have fins, some scales, most have whiskers and huge bloated heads with large, rheumy-looking eyes. (One summer the lake disappeared. In its place was a huge hole with gray muck. The fishermen put on hip boots and dragged their boats through the muck. The next summer the lake was back, as if it had taken a vacation.)

My father is dressed in accordance with his personal vendetta against fresh air and sunlight. He is boarded up with clothes. Nevertheless, I sweat while he sits. His hair leaves his head in all directions, trying to bat away the sun. I gently rock the boat, dream of drowning. My father would do better as a fish. He must know this. He dreams of water, whenever he dreams. He is a good swimmer. Air gives him a hard time. It is the dust in the air, the way air dries things out, that bothers him, gets him angry. He is happy in mist.

What he wanted to do was skid the sycamore on mud until he could get it into the water. Then he wanted to carve it in the water. That's not what gets me, that's not what bothers me, any more than his vacuuming his typewriter. Those are reasonable acts from an unreasonable man. I applaud them. He wanted to make a totem pole. That's not what bothers me. He wanted to hollow out the totem pole and make a boat of it, fill it with supplies, paddle to some island and set the totem pole up. That's not what bothers me, either. My father had the idea that the totem pole would serve as a beacon for errant canoers. He felt that people who canoed were dreamers, visionaries in the worst sense of the word, who needed help in rooting themselves to the world. He had it all planned out, knew when the tides came, though I didn't think they worked in this water, had the supplies ordered, sent away for catalogues of carving knives, researched what water does to wood. He set up tanks in our backyard, dropped logs in them. None of that bothers me. All of that is very real; you can put your hand on that.

But confusing wood for love: I can't take that anymore. It does something to me. I can barely follow my dreams now, have no idea where they are going.

As he fishes, I look at him and reach out to touch him. He is surprised, and somewhat shocked. So am I. I have no idea why I do this. He does not ask me why, but just looks at me, guessing, pulling me into his eyes. I shrug my shoulders and try to smile. It is a moment of closeness that shows how far apart we are, creatures on different planets. That distance is me, that reaching out my coldness, that touching my wariness. There had been no act or moment of drama that had called forth this response from me, so I sit mute, full of shame.

The wind came up, and he reeled his line in. When the hook broke water it was shiny and wormless. I started to row. Bass Lake was bent in half like a pair of saddlebags, and we were a bag away from the cottage. There was a promontory around which we had to row, and the closer we got to it, the more vicious the wind. Small froths of waves broke against the boat, hitting the bow as if to chastise us. The bow jumped up and down on the water with a heavy slap. I could barely row forward. The sky was dark gray. There were waves of a size I had never seen before. When we reached the point, I couldn't row around it. The boat seemed to be tied to the shore. My father took off his shoes and socks and rolled up his pants. He put one foot over the side, and a long, skinny, veined calf disappeared in the water, discovering the bottom; the other foot joined the first. He stood in the water, testing the waves, tilting. Then he motioned for the bow rope, and I handed it to him. He put it over his shoulder, leaned forward, and took the boat in tow. The water played at his legs, darkening his pants. Slowly he pulled us around the point. He does not look as if he is in water. Leaning into the rope, he looks resigned, as if he were pulling the world behind him, as if it were reluctant to come.

Once we were around the point, the wind eased off, and I thought he would climb in and let me row to the dock. But he pulled the boat all the way to the dock, his mouth now set in some grim fury. He glared at the boatkeeper.

We walked back to the cabin and he lay down in bed to sleep.

Rain fell for ten minutes in huge, grape-size hunks. The screens over the windows were clouded with a liquid glaze, the topsoil directly under the edge of the roof washed away to reveal sand, and when the rain finally stopped, there was a sad stillness, as if life itself were between breaths. I walked out to the boats. The sky was a dazzling white, clouded over but somehow brighter than the sun. I got in a boat and rowed. The rain had washed the lake clean. I could look through the water and see the bottom, full of twisted, tubular pieces of green that grew tangled, waving at me. There was a convertible resting on the bottom, with a doll's head in the back seat. I could not imagine how it got to the middle of the lake. I kept rowing and reached the other side, skirting the rushes that crowded the water's edge.

There were few cabins on this side of the lake. Mostly pine trees and mosquitoes. I could hear summer rushing away. The trees were full of wind, and dragonflies lay low under bushes that were bent to the ground. Waterlogged worms rested on the soil, sodden, bloated. I was swept with a wave of sudden nostalgia for memories I was yet to have. Whole chunks of future summers seemed to flit before my eyes; months, years, were compressed into minutes, seconds. They left a taste in my mouth.

THE GOOD FATHER,

THE BAD FATHER

· 1 3

HE LIVED WITH TWO FATHERS. HIS MOTHER HAD REMARRIED,

but for some reason had kept his old father, her old husband, along with the new husband, his new father. The two fathers lived in the same household, though they rarely, if ever, appeared in the same room together. They disliked each other, but in some way were disposed to put up with this queer sort of cohabitation. They even looked alike, and it made one wonder why his mother bothered to marry a man who looked like her former husband. They even had the same occupation and knew the same friends, which was responsible for no small amount of friction. But since they generally stayed out of each other's way, had indeed an almost psychic sense of where the other was and made sure not

to intrude on the other's ground, there was little danger of one bumping into the other.

The boy never saw them together, or if he did, confused them to the point where one blurred into the other, where they were not merely congruent but perfectly equal, so that the features of one offered a precise fit for the features of the other. In time, the boy came to distinguish them. He called one the "good father" and the other the "bad father."

The boy suspected his mother was sleeping with both of them, not at the same time, of course, but alternately, like the most advanced form of electrical current, which goes back and forth between one's house and the power plant many times a second. These fathers were not that quick, and where the other slept when his mother was sleeping with the one, the boy had no idea. Not that it presented much of a problem. The house was big enough so there was no lack of sleeping places.

The boy thought about the house as the Kingdom of His Father. There was something about the presence of his father, fathers, that seemed to hover about the house, waiting for something. His father, fathers, had no knickknacks, no doodads, no briar pipes, no heavily shellacked beer steins. There was nothing particularly masculine about the furniture. It was furniture shaped for Germans, made in Michigan, patterned after British and New England antiques. It was sturdy, but not overly sturdy, made for overweight people and amply cushioned, without the excessive "thickness" a piece of furniture needs for those who are famously heavy. He thought it might be the smell.

There was no leather furniture, yet there was the faintest smell of leather, along with a whiff of penicillin, a dry yeasty mold, the kind of thing one smells when opening a vacuum cleaner bag: old hair, dust, scraps of fabric and bits of wood, slivers of steel, pins, thread ends, pieces of leaf, and tiny indiscriminate leavings of the body. Though the house was over a thousand miles from the ocean, there was a saltwater smell, along with the smell of glass, freshly washed, which smelled like a bump on the nose.

Every morning the good father appeared, freshly starched, with steel-scraped face, wrinkle-free clothes, benign wonderment about him, a man who believed that excesses of goodness were at best an inconvenience. There was an air of duty about him. His actions were quick and precise, the starch folds on his shirt were replicated in his face, which was calm and turgid at the same time. His skin had a mottled clearness to it, and his eyes, while heavy and puffy, looked as if they had been shaved, wiped clean of the night's excess. He was attentive, eager, chock-full of answers to questions not even asked. It was too early in the morning for the world to be an affront. He remembered the real names of imaginary things. He waited for the first in a long series of apologies.

He ate breakfast without malice. Objects were not party to any vendetta. Bacon and eggs held no terror for him, toast was simply unparanoid but overcooked bread. He let the coffee swirl around in his mouth, awash in false teeth, waves of caffeine dashing against the gums.

He was severe. Yes, the good father was severe, and a bit frightening. This was not excess baggage; just a storm warning. He was hearty, enthusiastic, a chucker of chins, a straightener of ties. Talking seemed to have been invented for him. But the severity showed through in the gruffness, as if the edges of this good morning cheer were a bit rancid, spoiling at the corners.

The boy associated the good father with three things: morning, going to work, and not being there. The latter was an absence that felt like a presence, that imbued the house with a smell of here-I-was-so-here-I-am. The boy wanted the good father to stay, and the good father's sin lay in his going to work, and also in his being there by leaving behind "eyes" that watched and commented on what the boy did. Almost leaving them. The sin of his seeming to not go lay precisely in that *almost*. The boy had expected to be guided and then let loose. By being held, he was free, precisely because he knew when he was not free, and it was this knowledge that signaled freedom. But when the good father left he wouldn't quite leave, he left part of himself behind, the part that *almost* instructed. He left behind an observer. The boy operated out of anxiety, out of a sense that he almost, but not quite, knew what was happening.

The bad father showed up in the evening. He slept late, probably didn't go to work, or if he did, something went horribly wrong at work, the result of stupid people. His shirts were excessively wrinkled, and something had been put over his eyes, a clear mud, a distracting fluid, a glue that held the eyelids down and stiffened the joints. He moved with difficulty, choosing usually not to move. He sat. He looked. His sin lay in the fact that he would not leave, and was compounded with another sin, the sin of already having left. He had vacated his body hours before, in some secret fashion that was unknown to the boy, a sort of transmigration of souls. He was slow, slurred his speech, talked in a kind of shorthand composed of clipped, cryptic sentences. He was a paradigm of paranoia, had names, dates, and places of people who plotted against him. He spent most of the evening sitting in his chair, a cigarette burning between his fingers until it burned his fingers and was dropped on the carpet. In that enigmatic position, he expected the boy to do something. Or so the boy thought, until he realized finally that this father expected him to do nothing, that nothing would ever be asked of him, and that the bad father also expected nothing for himself, that he was simply waiting, dazed, for some unknown event of unperceived magnitude to occur, like cracked china on the plate of existence. The boy was free to do whatever he wanted (in that lay the tyranny), as long as he understood that his father was emperor of the chair (in that lay his freedom) and would remain so, and that he was too dazed to fall asleep.

When he was younger he was hoisted onto his father's shoulders, and from this position, legs draped around his father's neck, he would put his chin on his father's head and hold his father's chin with his hands, fingers clasped tightly together. He could feel the stubble on the chin. The roughness of the skin thrilled him, made him want to pee. The huge head, which he had always seen from below, was now below him, safely wrapped in his arms and legs.

Being this close to his father's head, a head the size of his own body, he could hear and feel the source of its great power. The boy had separated from the ground, the world, and was now dependent upon that head.

As he grew older, his father's shoulders became more inaccessible, and the boy blamed himself for that, for the distance he was putting between the two of them as the more nearly equal their physical dimensions became.

He was thrown into a panic one afternoon when a father appeared and he could not tell if it was the good father or the bad. The father that appeared seemed somewhere between the two. The boy wondered if his mother had gotten married once more, wondered if he would have to put up with three of them, two of them always on the outs. Were more to come?

This father was starched, and yet he did not move with his customary speed. He seemed, like an engine in danger of overrevving, to have had a governor placed on his motions. He was somewhere between talkative and quiet. He had a glow, as if something were bubbling underneath, and it could reach the surface only with great difficulty. He widened his eyes until the boy thought they would fall out of his head.

"What's this?" this father asked, holding him by the arm.

The boy looked around.

"Oh no," he said, "it wasn't you. Oh no."

It was an old-fashioned speech, almost charming, the words quaint. The boy was uneasy. He had a sense that the questions had no reference to solid objects, that they reflected clouds, dust, thoughts.

The father kept holding on to his arm, as if the message hadn't reached the fingers, as if part of the brain were reluctant to obey.

"Do you know who I am?"

The boy was frightened. For a moment he did not, and when the familiar appeared once again, the familiar face, the familiar smell, something strange came along with it, as if the familiar had always brought with it an unrecognized oddity.

"I . . . know . . ."

He felt that the two fathers had been squeezed into one, that this was the original father, the Ur-father, which somehow separated to form the other two. He was happy to be back with the original, yet sad at losing the extremes of the others. Somehow it seemed as if the very definition of the father had been lost.

"I don't know . . ." he started to say, and then stopped.

"I once saw a man on crutches beating another man," his father said. "He leaned against a wall and swung his crutch around, beating the other man to the ground. Then he began poking him with his crutch, as if the man lying on the ground were a snake, or something vile that he wanted to inspect."

His father paused.

"I have always felt I should be on crutches. I don't know why. I don't think I would like them. I'm glad I'm not. Do you understand this?"

The boy nodded, not understanding.

His father looked at him. "Why don't you talk to me?"

"I'm afraid to talk to you."

"Of course."

"I never told you before because I was afraid."

"Are you afraid now?"

"Yes."

"That's good. You should be afraid."

SAGINAW

WE WENT TO MICHIGAN BECAUSE THAT WAS WHERE THE UNCLES were. Michigan was full of uncles. Saginaw was dense with them. It was a city of uncles, older men with cigars and no bellies or swollen bellies and small pointed shoes that looked dainty on fat legs. They walked by stepping over imaginary logs, tiptoeing down the street, doing the uncle dance. They wore their hair slicked back, had forward-looking backward views, and were good at folding papers, which they put in their left front shirt pocket, picket-fenced by ballpoint pens with advertising writing on the sides. Uncles always had something to do with cars. They sold them, repaired them, washed them, got parts for them, insured them, repaired the bodies that came out of them, stole them, or sometimes just watched them.

They were sedentary creatures, but they liked to watch things that moved fast, powerful machines connected to the ground through gears and wheels. Words of warning, advice, passed through their mouths, but these words were easily ignored, meant to be part of the background conversation, words on wallpaper. Uncles frequently talked to the air.

My cheese uncle lived there, defying general rules about uncles. He garaged his cheese. He was a tall, sallow-faced man with extremely large hands and a face that seemed to exist for his nose. Everything with him was "shucks" and "gee," his chin parroted his upturned mouth, which perpetually clamped and then chomped on a large, soggy cigar. He had a comic's face, was a born laugher, and had an Adam's apple that looked like an arrowhead. He also had the largest feet of any man I have ever seen.

My aunt came up to his armpits. Her face was the reverse of his, as was her body. Where he was lean and lanky, she was short and dumpy, where he was all knees and elbows, she was all breasts and hips: a petite boxer with an upturned pug nose, flyweight to his welterweight.

Everything in their house was painted many times over until it had a shiny white sheen, diamond hard, finger thick. Glass sparkled from cabinets, silver shone from chests, tables looked like they were glazed with thin, clear water. There were lamps with huge cream-colored lampshades covered in clear plastic and taffeta. And bright, confection-colored pillows that added frosting to sofas and chairs.

In part of the house, and yet not part of it, lived my stepgrandmother, a turtle-shaped woman waiting to go crazy. She had a small apartment built against my uncle's house. There was a door between the two, which could have been opened if my uncle hadn't barred it. Sometimes, when the noise from her apartment got too loud, he would remove the steel bar that kept the door shut and go in. On rare occasions, my uncle would invite her into the house. She would walk in slowly, carefully, stepping as if the carpet were alive with caterpillars. Her son by a previous marriage kept hunting rifles in her apartment. He claimed he never left any ammunition with her, but one day we found her playing with a box of 30-06's, trying to crack them open with a hammer.

My cousin liked to go in and tease her. She was forbidden to, but she did, anyway. Each worked up a good hate for the other, and then coated it over with cloying sweetness. The old lady invited her in, glinting at her with rheumy eyes. She would insist on fixing food for my cousin. The old lady kept squares of food embedded with dirt fuzzballs in her kitchen.

The old lady invited boys in from the street and plied them with candy and lemonade. They felt the leathery caresses of her wrinkled hand under their chins as she petted and patted them like molds of butter. She stroked and combed and tugged and straightened and sent all the boys back to their mothers cleaner and neater than when they started out, their hair matted down with her spittle. She gave new pennies and strings of licorice and was adored by all the mothers on the block, while she waited, with razors and poisons, for my cousin's next visit.

At night when everybody had left the living room I lay on the floor with my ear to her door. I don't know what I expected to hear, but crazy people had a way of talking that could tell you things. She didn't talk much, but I heard a lot of bumping and dragging, as if she were moving furniture.

The house talked in the wind, creaking and groaning. Each room had its own voice, its own shout and whisper, and when they joined together the house sounded like a banshee.

Sunday afternoon.

Saginaw lay inert. The dust from the unpaved streets refused to rise, dreaming of mud. My uncle was in the cooler, checking cheese. My aunt was upstairs, taking a headache nap. My parents and brother were somewhere else. That left my cousin and me.

She knocked on the door.

"Yes?" said the voice behind the door.

"May I come in?" my cousin asked.

"Of course."

The bar on our side was lifted. The door on her side was unlocked. The door opened.

"Please," she said, with a sweeping motion of her hand. She looked nothing like Nann. Small, wispy, with a sly smile that tugged down the frowns in her forehead, she waved us in.

"I was just moving some furniture for you," she said.

I stood in the doorway, rats nibbling at my knees. I could feel the pee rising in my bladder.

"Who's the boy?" she asked.

"My cousin."

"He's welcome too."

"I don't know if he wants to come in."

"He can if he wants to."

"Maybe he doesn't."

"Whatever you wish. But I must shut the door."

She walked over briskly and with the hook end of her cane pulled the door shut. I managed to step inside.

"There," said the old lady. "Now we're all nice and cozy. No drafts from the door. I catch cold so easily, you know. Cindy, be a dear and get me my shawl from the top of the shelf."

It was an old pine chest with the top doors off. It had been painted over many times and then scraped, but the paint still showed at the indentations for the hinges. The top shelf could only be reached by a stool. One happened to be there.

Cindy climbed up. The shawl was hanging out over the edge of a pile of blankets. She pulled on the shawl.

"There's something on top of it," she said.

"Land sakes, child, just pull it down."

"What's on top of it?"

"Don't make a fuss. Pull it hard."

Cindy climbed up on the middle shelf.

"What *are* you doing, child?"

Cindy's head was now level with the shawl. There was an open can resting on the shawl. Sniffing it, she put it on the next shelf.

"Turpentine," she said.

"Up there? Who would have believed it?" The old lady felt affronted. She huffed and snorted.

Cindy climbed down with the shawl.

"Tony must have left it there," the old woman continued.

"I wouldn't want to spill it all over your rug," my cousin said. "Why, it might have even spilled on me," she continued.

The old lady didn't hear her. She had opened her eyeglass case and was talking into it. Cindy handed her the shawl, which she snatched with ferocity.

"I might have even spilled it on you," Cindy said. "Imagine that."

The old lady still didn't hear her. She was putting on her shawl, at the same time shouting at her glasses and spitting on them.

Then she looked up, hesitated, her face suspended between emotions, and smiled at my cousin.

"Well, I'm sure that's all right," she said.

"What is?"

"Tony, of course," she snapped. "What else?"

There was a flash, a momentary crack, when all the lines in her forehead snapped and confusion reigned in her face, and then her features drifted, rotating slowly around her nose.

"Tony's fine," she said, "and we don't have to talk about him anymore. We're quite done with him."

"Of course not, Grandmother," my cousin said.

"Would you like some cake?"

"I would," I said.

"It's strawberry meringue," she said. "I don't think you would like it."

"What's that?" I asked.

"It's special. Cindy's favorite."

"Sometimes."

"Sometimes? Well, now is a sometimes."

"I change."

"You're at a difficult age," the old lady said. "What are you doing for your skin?"

"Pee."

"What?"

"P-H soap."

"I thought you said something else."

"Piss urine."

"What?"

"The name of the soap. Can't you hear?"

"I thought you said something else."

"Well, I didn't, sonofabitch."

"What?"

"I said I didn't shit. Turn up your hearing aid."

The old lady walked to her kitchen. She had wide, flat hips and legs that bent out like G clefs. She rocked from side to side when she walked, which made her appear to be steadier than if she had walked straight forward. Black pumps with heavy inch-high heels were worn in such a way that she walked half on the sides of her shoes. She had thin arms, with huge veins that looked like strings lying on the outside of her skin. Whenever she moved, we could hear her fart.

She came back with a slimy cake. I couldn't tell if it was mold or green frosting tinged with red. There were three layers, each one in a slightly different position. I counted thirteen candles, some stuck in the sides.

"It's for your birthday, dear," she said.

"It's not my birthday," Cindy said.

The old lady sucked on the end of her shawl.

"And I'm not thirteen."

"I'm sure all that doesn't make any difference."

"I don't want to eat it."

"You know the rules. You come here, you eat what I bring out."

"I won't eat it."

"Well, we can all sit here and look at it."

She sat in a lap-size folding chair. Then she got up and went to her own chair, one with a high, fan-shaped back and purple stains on the arms.

"Isn't it pretty?"

Spiders crawled from her eyes when she talked. Her hair was held in place with cobwebs, and a huge brooch covering her chest looked like it had been nailed in place.

"No."

"Well . . . anyway."

We waited for her next sentence. We could have waited until next year. The room seemed to be suspended, as if it were floating in the kind of airless wind found in glass-ball paperweights. Old honeymoons and photo albums drifted about in the corners. The old lady opened her mouth, sucking all the air from the room. We were part of a painting. Then it cracked, and I exhaled.

"That was nice," she said.

I could barely follow her words. My head felt groggy. I stood up, swaying slightly.

"I have to go," I said.

"Of course, child."

I opened the door and ran into the street. I had to see if the house was still there. I wanted to make sure I was not somewhere else. She had put us in a spell, taken us to a different place.

Sunday night I talked with Cindy.

"She tried to cut my finger off," she said. "Look."

There was an inch-long slit at the end of her index finger.

"We were cutting vegetables. She was showing me how to cut cucumbers. The knife slipped, she said."

"Weren't you afraid?"

"A bookcase fell on me. I ripped her dress. The cat ate the cake and got sick on the bed."

"How did you get out?"

"She bit my arm. I broke her glasses."

The following night my uncle invited the old lady to dinner.

Table leaves were retrieved from the closet and the table was extended beyond what was needed, making it look like a small white whale. The tablecloth my aunt used was so thick you could bounce a plate off it or hide a finger in its folds. Crystal glasses glimmered like waterlogged candelabras.

The old lady swayed into the room on my uncle's arm. She sat at the middle of the table, next to my father. My uncle sat at one end, my aunt at the end near the kitchen.

The first course was fruit salad.

"What time is it?" she asked my father.

"I don't know," he said.

"Tony always knows the time."

She gummed the fruit salad.

Next came creamed corn, creamed spinach, a cucumber salad, chowchow, a plate of dark turkey and a plate of light turkey, two great tureens of mashed potatoes, each with its own gravy swimming pool, pitchers of milk, water, iced tea, and a tossed salad.

"Have some spinach, Mother," my aunt said.

The old lady helped herself, carefully, gingerly, dishing it on her plate.

"Everything looks so nice," she said. "I bet you don't get a chance to do this often."

"Not often," my aunt said.

"What's for dessert?"

"Pie."

"What kind?"

"Rhubarb."

"Ice cream?"

"If you want some."

We ate in silence. My brother burped, and then tried to pick his nose. He had mashed potatoes on his finger, which got pushed up his nose. My mother sent him to the kitchen.

"That's a charming boy you have there," the old lady said to my mother.

1 7 5   "Thank you."

"What's his name?"

"Johnny."

"He puts mashed potatoes up his nose."

The old lady worked on a piece of dark meat, and then, unable to make much of it, took it out of her mouth and placed it neatly beside the creamed spinach, evening out the edges with a fork. She speared a piece of white meat and started to work on that.

My brother, back from the kitchen, started mixing all his vegetables together until they were one lumpy mess. Then he poured milk in the middle of them.

"Pass the gravy," the old lady said.

She was sucking on corn, as if she didn't trust it to go down her throat unsucked. I could hear each kernel as it popped down her throat, and could almost see the kernels outlined in her neck. What she couldn't eat she retched up, cut with a knife, and reswallowed.

CONVERSATIONS: ACT I

ACT II

9
6
7
2 7

ACT I, SCENE I. THE BOY AND HIS FATHER ARE IN THE BOY'S bedroom. The boy is seated on the edge of the bed. His feet refuse to touch the floor, and he kicks them back and forth, his calves bouncing against the mattress. He holds a ball in his hand, which he keeps squeezing, sometimes throwing it up and catching it. The father is seated in a maple captain's chair. He is dressed in a business suit. During the conversation he gets up from the chair and walks around the room, looking out the window and then back at the boy. The boy remains seated on the bed. The father speaks first.

"There is something you wanted to tell me."

"No."

"Perhaps something you've forgotten."

"No. I told you before, I don't like to talk to you."

"You're afraid of me."

"Yes."

"And that's why you won't talk to me."

"Yes, that too."

"That too what?"

"That's part of it."

"The other part?"

"I'm afraid to tell you."

"Why are you afraid? Do you think I'll hit you?"

"No."

"If I hit you would that make you feel better?"

"No."

"You must have something to tell me. You've been through my closet. You've seen my papers."

"I was afraid to tell you that."

"Why did you do that?"

"I don't know. I can't tell you."

"Because . . ."

"I don't know what I'm afraid of."

"Maybe if you told me . . ."

"I can't."

"Get it off your chest."

"I can't."

"You saw those books."

"Maybe."

"You've got that look on your face."

"Why?"

"You've got to understand."

"I don't want to talk anymore."

"You read the letters. Anyone with normal curiosity would."

"You wrote them."

"Let's say you did. Don't apologize for reading them. Let's assume you read them."

"Why?"

Ignoring him, speaking to one side. "I needed companionship. I had to have it. It was not a choice."

"That's a funny way to get it."

"They were lonely. I was lonely."

"Those are strange things to say to people."

"You don't understand."

"I read."

"All you know are the words. You don't know what's behind them."

"The pictures in that book."

"It's borrowed."

"Fat people. Ugly people."

"How can you say that?"

"Why do they do those things?"

"Look, you don't understand. Believe me."

"They look angry, those people."

"They're not. They're sad."

"Sad and angry. They look like they don't want to be doing that."

"Who knows what they want to be doing."

"They look uncomfortable."

"How can anyone know what people want to be doing?"

"They look very unhappy."

"They're not."

"I didn't know people did that."

"They're paid. Most of them."

"What can they do with the money?"

"Whatever one does with it."

"Did they do what you asked them to do?"

"Who?"

"The people in the letters."

"I don't think that's any of your business."

"Do people mind when you say those things to them?"

"You don't seem afraid to talk to me now."

"Does it hurt?"

"What?"

"In those letters."

"Everything hurts."

"Then why did you say that?"

"It doesn't make any difference what one says. Don't you understand? Everything hurts."

"Those words seem different when you say them."

"They're no different."

Act I, Scene 2. The boy and his father are in the living room. His father wears a dark suit, a stiff white shirt, and a dark tie. He looks very somber. Someone has just died. There are other people in the room, but they are in the background. They barely move, and when they talk they talk in whispers. Through the curtains, lace curtains with velvet drapes, one can look out into the street and see a big Packard, black, with running boards. It was made just before the war, though it is after the war now. The boy speaks first.

"How old was he?"

"He was old."

"In years?"

"Seventy-five."

"Is that old?"

"Yes."

"Will you be seventy-five?"

"Someday."

"Will you die then?"

"Maybe."

"What about me?"

"You?"

"Will I die then?"

"You?"

"When I'm seventy-five."

"No."

"How soon is it until you're seventy-five?"

"Years. Many years."

"Does everyone die at seventy-five?"

"Many do."

"I don't want to."

"OK."

"Why was he smaller than you?"

"They didn't eat as well then."

"Do I eat well?"

"Pretty well."

"Will I be bigger than you?"

"Maybe."

"Was his hair white because he drank milk?"

"He didn't drink milk."

"I do."

"He hated milk."

"I don't. I don't hate it."

"He drank coffee."

"What else?"

"Water. He drank water."

"What's it like?"

"Water?"

"Dying. Lying down and having all your blood taken out."

"I don't know."

"Does it hurt?"

"I don't know."

"He can't move anymore. Do you think he wants to move?"

"No."

"What does he want?"

"Now?"

"Does he want to get up?"

"No."

"Does he miss things?"

"Sure. He misses them a lot."

"He wasn't that big. He wasn't as big as Nann."

"He didn't need to be. He was big enough."

"I could be as big as he was."

"You have a way to go."

"Just some inches, feet."

"You have a long way to go."

"Did he hit you?"

"Yes."

"Did you need it?"

"Oh God . . . Ah . . ."

"You don't hit me. Not much, anyway."

"Ah . . . yes . . ."

"Did he hit hard?"

"Not as hard as he could. Not nearly."

"Can he hear us?"

"Yes. He can hear everything we say."

"Even if we whisper?"

"Even then."

"Was he born here?"

"No."

"Why did he come here?"

"They wouldn't let him work there."

"Why not?"

"The bastards wouldn't let him work there."

"Did they let him work here?"

"Yes."

"The bastards let him?"

"Yes."

"Can we talk to him?"

"Sure."

"Will he talk to us?"

"No. But he'll listen."

"That's half of talking."

"We can do the other half."

"I don't know if I like being dead."

"Would like. You're alive."

"I don't think I would like it."

"He was small but he was strong. Very strong. He liked to work with his hands. He had good hands."

"Do I have good hands?"

"He never learned how to drive. Sis drove him everywhere. He could do anything but drive. That and swim. He never learned how to swim. Never wanted to."

"I don't know how to swim."

"I tried to teach him, but he wouldn't learn."

"They tried to teach me how to swim."

"He would rather drown than swim. The damn fool would rather drown."

Act I, Scene 3. A rowboat in the middle of the pond. The boy and his father are fishing. The sun is overhead; the day is suspended, still, motionless. There is not a ripple on the water. The boy moves around in the boat, checking his line, watching the bobber, trailing his hand in the water, looking at the lures in the fishing box. The father does not move, except to wipe off the sweat that accumulates on his upper lip. The father speaks first.

"The object of fishing is not to catch fish."

"Why do they bite?"

"It spoils everything when they bite. If I want fish I go to a fish store."

"How can they breathe down there?"

"I get upset when they bite. I've been fishing for thirty years and they haven't bitten yet."

"What do they eat down there?"

"They know me. They wouldn't dare bite. We have an understanding, the fish and I."

"Why do they live down there?"

"Who knows why fish do anything? No one has bothered to ask them."

"How do they dry off?"

"No one knows me out here. It's very peaceful when no one knows you. It's calming. It's better than whiskey. You're not angry, are you?"

"I'm not angry, no."

"I was coming in. I slipped. I thought you were in bed."

"They let me stay up late."

"It's that damn canasta. They've got you playing that old woman's game."

"They taught me the game."

"You're not angry, are you? With what I said, with the way I came in?"

"Then they let me stay up and play it."

"It was late. I get tired of speaking when it gets late. I don't want to say all the words."

"No."

"They want you to explain everything and then they get angry when you don't. You're not like that, are you?"

"I'm not like that."

"I think you've got a bite. Take it off the hook and throw it back."

"I don't like to touch fish."

"I'll do it for you. . . . I think you lost him."

"I wasn't angry."

"I didn't think you were, but I wanted to ask to make sure."

"Not me."

"That's what I thought. But they've got so many busybodies running around you don't know anymore. That's why I had to ask."

"I was tired. I was falling asleep."

"You were asleep. Even when I shouted, you didn't wake up."

"I never heard you."

"I was shouting because of where they parked the car. That car should never have been there. I never expected a car there. No one would."

"I wasn't angry."

"People don't know how to drive anymore. And they get upset at a little scratch on the fender, a little dent in the bumper."

"Who fell?"

"That was me. I fell coming in. I tripped over something; they had no right putting it there."

"The castle."

"A man's home."

"I built a castle. It broke."

"I fell against the china cabinet. It made more noise than it should have. Ever notice how things make too much noise these days?"

"It's quiet."

"No? I'll get you a new castle. I had to hit you. You understand that, don't you?"

"I was bad."

"Not bad so much, but . . . well, OK, bad. It doesn't mean that I don't care for you."

"It hurt."

"It hurt me."

"How do they breathe?"

"They breathe water. It goes through their body. The other day you looked upset at what I said."

"Up set at what you said?"

"Angry, upset. I didn't mean it. I don't think you understood. I don't think you understand now. That's why I'm talking to you. It's as if, well, as if you're the only one who does understand."

"My bobber went down."

"Leave it alone. It will go away. Do you understand what I'm saying?"

"No."

"Good. That's a relief. You will. I hope you're not angry."

"The bobber is still down."

"I'll throw it away for you. You don't want to eat these fish."

"Eat them?"

"Do you remember the time the damn goldfish jumped out of the bowl? You and your brother wouldn't touch it. Your mother ran up to get me. She was afraid of the damn thing. I was on the toilet. I had to come running down and put it back in the bowl."

"It's hot."

"Damn right it's hot. Hot as hell."

"What is hell?"

"Hell is heaven backward. Heaven upside down. It's what people do. It's what I find in a bottle."

"I collected bottles."

"I know. It drove your mother crazy."

"Why did I have to kiss the stones?"

"Don't worry about that. He's just another lush priest."

"What's a lush?"

"Do you remember Canada? Where you were born? The tiny apartment on the fifth floor? I caught you crawling out on the balcony once. Do you remember the Frenchy who used to play with you? God, it was simple then."

"The bobber."

"Those beautiful wood floors. We used to eat fish on Fridays. I still went to church then. The sky is different in Canada."

"Now it's up."

"You don't get those magentas here, those purples and oranges. You mustn't worry about what I said to your mother."

"I'm not worried."

"Of course you're not. You don't know what it means. Did she say that I hit her?"

"You wouldn't hit her."

"I've been under a lot of pressure. Pressure makes your head grow bigger. My head is huge. I can feel it huge."

"Sometimes I forget to breathe."

"I can feel it. There are times it makes my head heavy. You can barely hold your head up. It makes me sleepy, pressure does. You don't know about heads growing bigger. Your nose and ears get bigger too."

"Do I have a big nose?"

"Huge. We all do. What do you smell with it?"

"Worms."

"Worms don't smell. You smell what you think are worms. Worms thrive in shit, in putrefied meat, but they're the cleanest creatures on the earth. That's one of God's little jokes. He likes to play jokes."

"What's a joke?"

"Something funny. When you laugh. When I fall down, or swear at someone."

"I'm thirsty."

"Have a soda. Throw it overboard when you're finished."

"I haven't started it yet."

"Just drink it. I thought you said you were thirsty. We're going to be without a car for a while."

"I like cars."

"Let's go back. I borrowed your uncle's car. He won't mind."

Act II, Scene 1. An old kitchen that has suffered an attempt at updating. The floor is covered with "modern" linoleum. The refrigerator sits on tall legs, with the coil, condenser, and electric motor on top. Hanging on the wall next to the phone with the emergency phone numbers is a Catholic calendar with the days of the saints. There is a chrome-tubed Formica-topped table with chrome-tubed chairs covered in heavy plastic. Something hard and bouncy is hidden underneath the plastic. An electric coffeemaker on the table is plugged into a light socket that hangs from a long frayed cord attached to the ceiling.

The boy, now a young man, and his father sit at the table,

drinking coffee from cheap milk-glass cups. Someone else is sitting at the table with them, but the light is dim where this person sits and it is impossible to make out who, or what, this person is. The boy, the young man, speaks.

"When did you first see them?"

The older man, his father, is slow in forming his words.

"About six months ago, maybe a year ago."

"You don't remember when?"

"They were there; I just didn't notice them."

"Why did you begin to notice them?"

He looks at him as if the young man is stupid.

"Because of what they were."

"What was that?"

"What I told you."

"I thought you said they were members of your family."

"They were."

"But you called them monsters."

"I'd be shaving. They'd be in the mirror. I thought they would go away."

"And they didn't?"

"No, they did. But they knew when to come back."

"In the mirror."

"There too. Sometimes I'd find them in the car. Or sitting at the table with me."

"How long did they stay?"

"At first only a minute or two. They didn't bother me at first."

"Did they say anything, or do anything?"

"No. They never did. They still don't."

"Did anyone else see them?"

"Of course not."

"Why do you say, 'Of course not'?"

"That's their plan. That's the idea behind the whole thing."

"How long do they stay?"

"Five minutes, ten minutes, rarely longer, sometimes shorter."

"Why are they monsters?"

"They're dead."

"Does that bother you?"

"Don't be stupid. Don't play that game with me."

"Why are they monsters?"

"Don't be so stupid."

"Do they want you to do something?"

"No. They're just there."

"Are they trying to frighten you?"

"They don't make any noise."

"Do they want something?"

"They don't say."

"Maybe they're here to watch you."

"That's not enough. They've been watching me all their lives."

"Maybe it's hard for them to stop."

"I don't give a goddamn how hard it is."

He stopped for a minute, as if he remembered something.

"I've got some stories and a novel out with an agent. If I go on television I don't want them tagging along."

"Why do you think they would?"

"That's the kind of thing they do."

"Do you see them after you've been drinking?"

"Before and after, to that stupid question."

"Why don't you stop?"

"At my age? Why?"

"For me."

"I never did anything for you. I never asked you to do anything for me."

"You're a liar."

"I did a few things for you. But no more. You're old enough now."

"It seems that way."

The old man was silent. The young man continued.

"You could have ten, twenty years left."

"For what?"

"What do you want me to do?"

"Get rid of them."

"How?"

"Ask them. Maybe they'll listen to you."

"Why should they?"

"Because they like you. They never liked me."

UNCLES

ALONG WITH MY CHEESE UNCLE I HAD A HARDWARE UNCLE

and an eyeshade uncle. They all smoked cigars. They're all dead.

My uncles came from Michigan. They smoked White Owls and Dutch Masters, came with and without hair, drove bottom-of-the-line cars from Ford and General Motors with neckers' knobs, and died from strokes. I had another uncle who was an elf. He came over from Russia and sold used cars as soon as he got here, as if he had been waiting all his life to sell second- and third-hand automobiles. I don't know what brand of cigar he smoked, but he sold every brand of used car. He may not have died from a stroke.

My cheese uncle liked practical jokes. There was rarely anything practical about his jokes.

He enjoyed making things disappear. He made his friend's house disappear, and also made sure that other things, objects, vanished.

"Anyone," he told me, "can make things appear. Businessmen do it all the time. They make something out of nothing. But to make nothing out of something . . ."

He said cheese was merely a hobby with him. He called it flavored air, somewhat more condensed than most air. He mentioned other things that he had made into nothing. I had this vision of a reverse factory, where the raw material was fully assembled products, and little by little, as they proceeded down the assembly line, parts of the product were "disappeared," until the end result was nothing. No matter how hard I tried, I couldn't stop believing him.

"What if I should make your father disappear?"

"How?"

"The way I do everything else."

"You wouldn't."

"Don't bet."

I didn't.

I was fascinated and horrified by the prospect of my father's disappearing. I begged my uncle to tell me how he would do it, but he refused, and having given up asking, I imagined various ways he might accomplish this, and then finally stopped my ruminations when they became all too real and the possibility existed as a fact. I had dreams at night before I went to sleep. My father's face appeared in a variety of guises. He was held forcibly by Brazilian Indians, buried up to his neck in sand. They heated him until he shrank to the size of a baby. But they could never get him to disappear, despite all their poisons and witchcraft. Finally they threw up their hands in despair and left him alone in the jungle, a tiny man the size of a tree squirrel.

(My father conducted many wars. He fought my mother, his friends, and anyone who employed him. But the Michigan uncles remained ignorant of the war he conducted against them, probably for the reason that they mystified him, and the war he conducted against them was not so much a war as a series of minor skirmishes:

petty accusations, bruised feelings over imagined wrongs, slights over subtle tones of a voice, annoyances over their lack of order—all small potatoes compared to what he was capable of. The Michigan uncles were agreeable to a fault, always ready to give in, to admit a wrong, to admit an unwrong, and this willingness on their part to bend, to step aside, annoyed him and later mystified him. To him, the algebra of war was simple; it was the choice of weapons, the conduct of the war, and the reasons for it, that remained complicated. To battle was noble. To battle for simple reasons was stupid. To avoid plots, to escape the mesh of paranoia, was the sign of an undernourished mind. It was a violation of the natural order. God had willed that man was meant to be miffed, and my father was only carrying out His commandment.)

I never saw my uncles drink wine. Catholics, Italians, and old ladies drank wine. They, my uncles, drank beer, and that's what all Protestants drank. My hardware uncle kept a case of it in his store. He had a Western Tire & Auto Store in northern Michigan and the biggest belly I have ever seen on a man his size. His belly was really below his belly; he had saved his immenseness for the area under his belt. I always felt comforted by it. It protruded from underneath his belt like the trunk of a car. He used it to collect the ash from his cigar. He had a long face with heavy jowls and a thick beard that he had to shave twice a day. He was the one uncle who drove a Mercury. He felt hardware store owners should drive Mercurys, being a step above gift shop owners. His was a coupe, maroon, that looked like a series of bumps getting smaller and smaller, ending rather abruptly at the rear bumper.

My hardware uncle had a talent for appearing in pictures. Whenever anyone took a picture, he was in it, whether they took a picture of him or not. Everyone asked him how he managed to do it, but he refused to say, modestly shrugging his shoulders. I don't think he knew himself. I think his image was refracted all over the state and called forth to appear at the click of a shutter. Since he kept appearing in pictures, no one took any pictures of him. His was a strange, nonnegotiable talent, and one that he, a firm believer in free enterprise and hard work, never took seriously. He was, in fact, embarrassed by it, saw it as an aberration, a kind of discomforting out of the normal fact he had to live with. We soon got used to it. My father claimed he showed up in all the pictures taken in northern Michigan, that his light rays were charged with a desire for exposure.

I was extremely fond of my uncles. I never told them, never would, too embarrassed, told myself to keep it a secret. In trying to be around them I learned they had their own secret, which they kept so well their secret has gone with them.

My elf uncle came here from a German-speaking part of Russia, which made him either a Russian German or the other way. Even though he spoke both languages, I always had the feeling he came from somewhere else because of his religion. He prayed to machines, or, more specifically, cars. He got down on his hands and knees before every car made in this country. I saw him praying to Crosley Hotshots and Hudson Hornets with equal fervor. But I never knew what he wanted from them. Perhaps the secret of machines, what made gears work and pistons turn a crankshaft, why camshafts could lift and lower valves at precisely the most opportune moment. I couldn't understand the words he used in his prayers. I don't think anyone could. They weren't Russian or German.

He was short and round, like a dirty snowman. He kept getting knocked over and rolling up again, sold used Fords, used Chevrolets, used De Sotos. He drove backward, everywhere, to reverse the mileage on the odometer. He bit through the ends of cigars and smoked them down to, but not over, the band.

My uncles sang a soft song of cigars and cars, wooden garages with overhead racks that held never-to-be-used pieces of wood. They kept empty Valvoline cans, wore butter-smooth black shoes, and had swollen ankles underneath tissue-thin black socks.

My father was looking for immortality. They were looking for a good brand of antifreeze. I stood between, trying to connect.

Now they are gone, and I can't even find the lake where they went fishing, though I did restore the old '48 Buick Roadmaster they used and even filled the ashtrays with fresh-smoked dead cigars. I found a woven straw steering wheel cover and a neckers' knob and also a straw-mesh seat cushion with little steel springs that keeps your butt off the seat on hot summer days.

The steel springs still poke their way through the straw, just as they did to my uncles. I can't find the kind of suits they used to wear, or the gray sweaters they wore underneath their suits.

I keep looking.

I follow the air, sniff for their scent. Fire up the straight-eight Buick, Dynaflow transmission, Roadmaster ride, and drive around at night. I can't get their air out of my head. I pass the house where my eyeshade uncle lived. It looks like a derby hat on stilts. There's the driveway with the two bumps—the second one scrapes the oil pan—and the huge elm in front. That's dead too. My eyeshade uncle came home one night and drove his car into the tree, not against the trunk but right up into the branches. No one could figure out how he did it. They needed a derrick to get the car out. He never told anyone how he put the car up there, but he got a new car soon afterward and drove it up on someone's roof. He drove the same car into a fish tank, into his wife's kitchen, and eventually had it flown to Duluth, where it was squeezed into a giant paperweight and then melted into ball bearings, which he mailed to his clients as Christmas presents.

He loved magic. One trick he did involved burning my shoes, which, mysteriously, from his point of view, stayed burnt. He collected energy in an adding machine he kept by his bed. By adding the proper series of numbers, he could make things move. All this took place in Lansing, Michigan.

He liked to dance. He and my aunt would dress up at night when everyone was asleep and fox-trot across the fake Persian rug, then rumba over the linoleum. He had an old Victrola that worked with a crank. My aunt turned the handle, he picked the record and placed it carefully on the machine, she tipped the needle into the wax groove. Sometimes late at night I can see them dancing through the window, even though they don't live there anymore. That section of town is all black now. Sometimes I see him sitting up in the tree, grinning at me. He's gone now; they're all gone, even my aunt.

That secret, what they took with them: they were all part of the same uncle.

FORGETTING

TO BREATHE

13 ½ - 14

LOOKED AT THIS WAY, HIS MOTHER IS MUCH FATTER THAN SHE really is. She is squat, hips like clam-shells, breasts that hang down to her belly. She is naked. She invites other friends, women friends, to come over to the house and be naked with her. The women are naked in a circle. Their hair is rinsed blue. They stand as straight as their bodies allow. They are not confused. They know what they have to do. They have to walk in a circle. They are telling the boy something. He doesn't want to know what it is. This makes little difference to them. He has no choice. There are things we can't stop learning. They know he will know. It is the dumb wisdom of old bodies they have in their favor: flabby thighs, buttocks that roll and crest like slow waves. These will prevail. They wave him in,

knowing that he does not want to go in. He is embarrassed at seeing old women naked; this does not bother them. They have lived in their bodies a long time. They've had time to practice in their bodies. It is the only thing they own, and part of their explanation is about that. He stands watching them, ashamed, vaguely full of lust (can a woman ever be old, can she ever be too old?), thinking they will acknowledge his presence by refusing to notice him. But they do notice him. They wave at him, wink, and walk, he thinks, as if they were wearing clothes. They take him by the hand, pass him from body to body, and he can smell their flesh, smell the skin on their flesh, the perfume, sweat, oils on the skin. He can read the map of their skin, the hills and valleys, crags and creases, texture, all the depressions and elevations. He can see the pimples that blossom (fed by fat), the dark leaf-colored patches, the tiny forests of hair, the veins that run like underground utilities. He is passed from woman to woman, from smile to smile, from hip to hip. I don't understand this, he says. He looks around for his mother, but she is gone. They make sounds when they walk. Not with their mouths, but with their thighs, wetly, damply brushing against each other. Their ankles creak and crack, as does the floor under their feet. Their breasts get in the way of their walking, loose bowling balls that swing and then bang against their arms. Their faces seem to rise in the air, loose and tight, eyes that no longer have the capacity to be amazed (they are perpetually amazed), as if the wonder of their bodies and those who have prayed at this shrine (men, lovers, children) no longer concern them. You have made of us what you want, they say, and we listened to what you wanted and became that, but now it is time to take leave of that, to become what we always were, which is what you wanted us to be and something else. The boy is confused. Would you be more comfortable if you were naked? one of the women asks. No, the boy answers. Come here, she says, and she is so insistent, as are the rest of them, that his clothes leave his body as if by special pleading, by prayer, by the comfort and service of their hands. Now what will you do? they ask. He does not know. He is embarrassed by his hard-on. Don't worry about that, they say. We've seen that many times before. But their saying this does not comfort him. He wears his embarrassment on his groin; he cannot hide his excitement. They, on the other hand, are designed differently. Their excitement, their mystery, is hidden. Come dance with us, they say. No, he says. Are we too old for you? they ask. Are you ashamed because we sag, we bulge, we are loose where you are tight? Before he can answer, they pull him along, whirling him in the room, and he is afraid that if they whirl too fast they all may turn into butter, like the tigers in "Little Black Sambo." They bounce and skip, and their flesh bounces and skips with them, half a beat behind. They are their own sea. Their bodies crest and surface, waves flowing along thighs and bellies. Now their elaborately coiffured hair begins to fall, scattering itself about their heads, and the blue dye runs, streaking their faces, blotting the mascara, dulling the lipstick. Their faces become parodies, their makeup drunken. Sweat blossoms; salty underground springs gush forth. They stumble, they fall, they are tired. They collapse, looking as if bones had been sucked out of them, as if jellyfish had invaded their bodies. They pull him into the heap and stuff his face in the swill of their bodies. He is outraged at these women. What liberties they have taken with him! He is full of lust and anger, shame and desire. Stink fills his nose. His mother stands over him. Now look what you've done, she says.

He had forgotten to breathe. He woke in a panic, thinking it was fortunate he had picked this particular time to wake up and that if he hadn't he would have slept through his not breathing, slept through his death, never knowing that he had died not from some majestic disease but simply from forgetfulness, death by lack of memory, forgetting to breathe. And yet there was something easy about it. Minus the effort to breathe, his body lay absolutely still, mute, and even the sounds that usually bothered him when he was quiet, the sound of blood rushing through his ears, the creak of his lungs, the whispering of his joints, all these sounds were blessedly silent, and he could feel himself without motion, come to a halt, still alive. It was as if he were living between breaths, waiting between lives, suspended between life and death, somewhere in a region that was more than life, that was a kind of exalted life, the sort of thing that would not last long, and because of this was infinitely precious. So when he woke up and realized that he was not breathing, he did, indeed, panic but then quickly withdrew from his panic, realizing he was in a place he had never been, and a great peace settled over him, a stillness that seemed to incorporate the objects around him: the bed, the room, the house, the night. It was what he had heard about drowning, about freezing, just before death occurred, that a peace of such exquisite beauty came that one longed to remain there forever. Death did not beckon, but this beauty that accompanied death, this cavern of infinite peace, this country of joy, held out its arms and beckoned, and he was moved, wanted to act by not acting, thinking that whatever this was, he would never experience it again; it was a gift, exquisite, not to be ignored. He thought his lungs would be gasping for air, but they were not; they remained at the service of his will. He could slow his heartbeat if he wanted, he could stop it and not die, heart and lungs would obey. The entire machinery was at the service of his will. He lay motionless in this place, in this space, barely thinking, thinking about stopping thinking but not stopping consciousness, letting his body simply be. Existence equals essence. Then he rose up, filling his lungs with air.

There was a party, a gathering for some reason. Many people milling about. His father had invited a guest, but when he tried to introduce this guest, people turned their backs on him. He tried others, but they ignored him, remaining deep in conversation with a partner, and refused to turn toward his father, refused to acknowledge his presence. His father's guest stared blankly ahead while he kept trying to introduce him.

Someone tapped on a glass with a spoon and stood on a chair

to make a speech. We have an honored guest today, he said, someone I'm afraid we've been ignoring for too long, but now the time has come to make amends and introduce him. The speaker's eyes swept the room. His father smiled, holding his guest in front of him, a rather famous man, as if the man were a banner his father was carrying into battle. The speaker looked right at his father's guest, halted momentarily, and his father started to say something, the words forming in his mouth, his lungs shutting down to expel the words into the air. Perhaps he would introduce the speaker, perhaps he would be called on to list the accomplishments of his guest, a formidable man in his field. But the eyes of the spoon tapper moved on, continued to sweep the crowd, and after several moments he said that the honored guest had not yet arrived, but that when he did he would scarcely need an introduction, he was quite well known by everyone. But that, his father thought, was an ample description of his *own* guest, a man well known, honored not only in his field but outside it, recognized for his many contributions. Trying to capture the end of the spoon tapper's speech, to interject himself into the brief silence that followed, his father started to say something, but the spoon tapper stepped down from his chair and everyone started talking, drowning out his father's words. His guest was unfazed, too sure of himself to be bothered by the slight, but the boy's father rushed around with his guest in tow. It's all right, his guest said, I can understand in the rush of business how people can forget. No, no, his father insisted, I must introduce you; after all, you deserve to be introduced. I know that, the man said, but people here don't seem to be terribly concerned about me. Please, his father said, let me try. If you wish, said his guest, but I'm quite content to be here this evening and talk to you. I know, his father said, but there must be some mistake, some misunderstanding. Let me iron it out. As you see fit, said his guest, but it makes no difference to me one way or the other. Near the punch bowl, a three-tiered affair sporting ever-decreasing bowls that spilled over into the one below, his father spotted an old friend. It was a man he had gone to medical school with, graduated with (in the days when the graduating classes were one quarter the size of the entering classes), and at one time shared an office with. His father walked over, dragging his guest, and tapped his friend on the shoulder. When the other man turned around it was someone he had never seen before. They stared blankly at each other for a moment, and then the other man walked away. Look, his guest said, it's quite all right. You don't have to go to all this trouble. No, his father protested, it must be done. Don't make an issue out of it, his guest said. I can't stand someone making an issue out of something as trivial as this. No, his father said, it's just some simple misunderstanding. I'm sure, said his guest. Look, there's someone I know, his father said, pointing across the hall to a tall, thin man who wore a striped shirt and a bow tie. We worked on ACTH together. Guest in tow once more, he quickly strode across the hall to his friend. But the tall man seemed in a panic, looked quickly for the exit, and reached it before the boy's father could reach him. Now, really, his guest said, this is quite silly. Let's not be wasting our breath running after people who don't want to meet us. I include you in that category, though for the life of me I don't think you fit in, since these are *your* friends, and so I must suppose that for whatever reason, they simply don't want to meet me. No, his father said, it can't be that, there must be some reason. Well, look at it this way, his guest said. Suppose we stay here, in one place, and see if anyone wants to come to us. Perhaps they are just put off by our running after them. Perhaps, his father said. They stood around, drinks in hand, the center of an empty, widening circle. Someone kept throwing confetti on them, but his father couldn't see who it was. A band played martial music, an odd choice for a pathologists' convention. Is this your first time in Chicago? his father asked the guest. No, said the guest, somewhat annoyed. I've been here many times, never, fortunately, for very long. I see, his father said. These drinks are quite warm, the guest said. Are there any ice cubes? I'll look for some. His father strode off, leaving the guest in the middle of the floor, isolated, like some plague-infested mouse. There was much liquor left, but when he leaned over to look in the ice bowls, he discovered that most of the ice had melted, leaving blobs of congealed cubes unable to fit in any glass. I'm afraid there's nothing left, his father said. The guest squinted, as if he had just tasted something unpleasant. No ice? I know it sounds absurd, his father said, but I can't find any, at least nothing that will fit into a glass. The guest snorted. It was the first truly upsetting thing that had happened to him this evening. Can't you chop something for me, make something work? I'll try, his father said. He went looking for a knife, but could only find plastic ones. Finally he found a metal serving spoon. Hey, where are you going with that? shouted a waiter. His father ignored him, taking the spoon over to the ice bowl. He started to chop at the ice, but the only thing he could produce were small chips that landed in the icy water and quickly melted. Then he realized that he didn't have his guest's glass. He walked back to where he had left him and found no one. He looked around the room, unable to spot him. Perhaps, his father thought, he left in disgust, miffed at the unpleasant reception. His father had another highball, swallowing the liquor neat. He hated the taste, but loved the glow in his stomach and the drumming in his head. His head buzzed, his nose turned red, he could feel the veins stand out on his face. He noticed the spoon tapper climb up on a chair. Ladies and gentlemen, he said, oblivious to the fact that no ladies were present. Directly in front of him, the spoon tapper's hand on his shoulder, fresh ice in his glass, was his father's guest.

SOBERING UP

THERE WERE TIMES HE GOT SO BOOZED UP, LITTLE TURNIP-colored explosions appeared on his face: It was the revolt of liquor-soaked blood, the revenge of drunken cells, a stomach pickled and pushed beyond reason. These purple patches pushed up with alarming force from underneath his skin. Terrified, warned of mortality, he stopped drinking. The vegetable eruption was a signal to dry out. Booze had taken some of the hair from his face and replaced it with capillaries, until the only beard he had left was a patch on his upper lip and chin. Nevertheless, he would shave his entire face, from upper earlobe to upper earlobe. He liked to shave. It was one of the few things that gave him enjoyment.

We drove him to the outskirts of the city, to one of several expensive drunk

tanks. He sat in the back seat of the car, sobbing, and I felt uneasy witnessing this. My mother cried too, and that also embarrassed me. I was used to seeing them argue; I was upset by it but familiar with it. I didn't know what to do when they cried. I was afraid to show any feelings, afraid to know if I had any. Feelings, like moles, best lived in tunnels, away from the light. The only thing I showed was my fear of showing feelings. And I was even afraid of that, afraid that it may have been the only feeling I had.

Except for a few details, I don't remember what these places looked like, but I do remember what he looked like when he came back. He looked as if he had just returned from the laundry: clean, white, stiff. What made these places memorable wasn't the buildings or the quality of the care but the grounds. They always looked as if they were freshly rolled out for the occasion, a sort of gardeners' salute to drunks. The entrance to these buildings was never on the street but at the end of a coiling, serpentine gravel driveway that sliced its way through a putting-green lawn. There were two he stayed at that I remember fairly well.

One, on the North Side, had a doorman with a rear admiral's uniform, who welcomed guests with a nickel-plated whistle and a snappy salute. This place looked like a resort for rich, heavy, arthritic travelers. The other, just outside the city limits on the South Side, on the top of a hill, had a director who got himself drunk once every six months and fired a cannon into the heart of a residential district. No one ever complained.

My father was good at sobering up. He had lots of practice, had done it thousands of times. Part of getting drunk was sobering up. It was an occupational hazard of drinking, the most traumatic part. It had to be done, but it cost. A piece of him was expunged, along with the booze. Bit by bit, he was tossing himself away.

Sober, my father was no bargain, and I think he probably irritated the staff enough for them to send him home before his time was up. We came to get him in a postwar Studebaker, which was later sold to pay off debts. Six months after we sold it, I saw the car filled with strangers. A tremendous feeling of regret hit me.

He came home smiling, full of ideas, ready to appear on local television. His shoes were shined. His trousers looked as if they would cut glass. His shirts were starched in sections. Some mornings the joy of shaving would strike him and he would shave twice, though he barely needed to shave once a day.

We didn't know what to do with him.

My mother was mad when he was sober. She couldn't help complaining, feeling she had a captive audience. (He was sober, he had to listen: that was one of the detriments of being sober.)

Once in Michigan during a bad drunk she had him committed to an asylum. They came and got him in his office, driving out his patients. Tables and chairs were overturned in the melee and he punched someone in the mouth, a sheriff, and was punched in return and then went berserk and had to be chained and dragged down the stairs and through the lobby of his office building. At this stage of his career he had lost much of his skill and knowledge, a lack which still allowed him to perform as a slightly above average doctor. Now they were dragging him away, and I saw him crying on the sidewalk as I was walking toward his office and was afraid to help him, couldn't stop them and was ashamed, for him first and then for myself. In the asylum they took away his watch crystal and his shoelaces and wouldn't let him shave himself. There was no belt for his white pants, which were several sizes too big for him. Patients with belts, they believed, hang themselves. He walked around the asylum holding his pants up, still holding them up when he talked to someone, still holding them up when he talked to the doctors to try and convince them to let him out. When I visit him, he hides holding up his pants by putting his hands in his pockets. I can still see him, talking while he holds up his pants. It is the worst kind of thing to make him do. I turn my head away.

They put him to work washing dishes. He cleans test tubes. He scrapes the carbon off Bunsen burners. He scours, scrubs the residue off pots and pans in the staff kitchen.

My mother and I talked with the director about letting him out. There were reasons for and against, and I remember none of them. The asylum was not in Battle Creek, but they had chained him up and dragged him out of his office in Battle Creek. He had gone there and interned for a year when he was in his fifties and set up an office (internal medicine) and lived in a hotel room in a gray building that looked like a cereal box and we came up on the train from Chicago one Christmas Eve to be with him. The train ride was the best part of the trip. It was a dirty day; the snow was gray, and more sooty snow was falling, and we had a compartment on the train—I don't think they have those anymore—and had a meal served in it, and we could do whatever we wanted to in the compartment. When the train pulled into Battle Creek he stood on the platform, drunk, though I knew he'd be sober by the next morning, and I thought: *The hell with this. Fuck you.*

We got off the train and lied and pretended everything was fine and he lied too and pretended he was sober and tried to walk a straight line to a restaurant. Everyone at the restaurant lied and pretended he was just fine, and everyone pretended he could pull out the chair by himself and sit in the chair by himself and that he didn't look sleepy and his mouth wasn't hanging open and that his chin didn't rest on his chest. We pretended he was sober and he pretended he could pronounce all the things on the menu and that he could light his cigarette without burning his fingers or that he could make conversation, that words would come to his lips fully formed, and I had the feeling that someone had written out the conversation for us on bubble-gum cards and we read the cards but forgot most of the lines or said them in the wrong places and that there was no point to the cards anyway, even if we had gotten all the lines straight. My mother looked green and my father looked white and my brother and I looked red and there were little Christmas trees on every table, with tiny dribbles of tinsel. I put a piece of tinsel behind my ear. For some reason I was wearing a badge that had my name on it. I had forgotten all about it. My father leaned over the table and stared at it, trying to make out the letters. He needed glasses to read, but he refused to wear them, so he guessed what he read and when no one was looking would pull out his glasses and read what he'd guessed. "What are you selling?" he asked. I didn't know. What was I selling? All of a sudden I heard "God Save the Queen" come out over the Muzak.

"It's the fucking British," my father roared.

It was during a momentary lull, and he was heard all over the restaurant. Everybody turned toward our table.

"What the hell are they doing here?" he continued.

"What am I doing here?"

He asked me that question in the asylum.

We were sitting next to a heat register. Everywhere I looked, there was marble. Floors, walls, ceilings, tables, even the chairs, were made of it. It was a green marble they had imported from Italy. There were little strings of soot that blew upside down from the hot-air register, and I thought of the register back in Chicago in the house my father was born in and had lived in as a child and would soon go back to live in as an old man.

"You were committed," I said.

"I know that," he said. "You don't have to tell me that."

"You'll get out."

"When?"

"Soon."

"I can't stand this damn marble. It gives me a cold. My nose runs all the time. Do you have any Kleenex?"

I gave him my handkerchief. He blew his nose in it, honking loudly the way he always did. His nose was in two parts; the lower part moved back and forth when he wiped his nose, fluttered when he blew it. I was uneasy talking to him.

I made conversation, skirted the main issue. I knew what to say and didn't want to say it.

"They hose everything down," he said, "even us."

There was a drain in the center of the room. I could see small beads of water clinging to the top of the chrome grille that covered it.

"They don't tell you that," he said.

"There's a lot they don't tell us," I said.

"Then get me the hell out."

"I think maybe you should stay in."

"Maybe you should."

"I'm sober."

"So am I."

"But you won't be when you get out."

"What's the big fucking virtue about that?"

"I don't want to know you then."

"Who said you have to? Who wants you to?"

He looked up, noticed a doctor standing nearby.

"They're all cocksuckers in here," he said.

I flinched.

"They're all queers and they resent that I know more than they do. It galls them. They can't stand it. I can treat half the patients here better than they do and the other half no worse, and furthermore I have the advantage of knowing which half is which and they know that and they even know that I know they know. They are bitter, full of revenge, and do not take my suggestions."

My father decided that the problem about being in an asylum was not so much being in one as not being able to get out.

"They won't even let me work in the lab," he said, "afraid I'll break glass and slash my wrists. I wouldn't give them the honor of bleeding to death in their fucking laboratory."

Michigan seemed like a good place for asylums. They all had high ceilings, so high you could hardly see them. To heighten that effect, they painted clouds on the ceiling, right over the marble.

"The ceilings are too high for the sprinkler system to work," my father said. "By the time the water reaches us, it's all mist. We'd fry like bacon if there was a fire. Of course they don't care; they'd get their asses out in time."

He loved things that didn't work. His favorite pastime was watching a machine malfunction or observing a bureaucracy systematically destroy what it set out to preserve. Ostensibly he liked to point out the irony of such situations, but secretly it thrilled him that things worked as badly as they did, and he was always afraid his complaints would cause corrections.

The next time I went to see him he was wearing a key around his neck. I asked him what the key was for, since I knew none of the rooms were locked.

"It's for my room," he said.

"There's no lock on your room."

"I know."

My stepgrandmother died, and we had to go to Saginaw. The body had lain in the rocking chair for a week. A cat was sitting on her head, eating her nose. Her son Tony was off hunting deer in northern Michigan. He came back with a buck's head in time for his mother's funeral.

Her apartment was full of tiny things: little bits of glass and wooden chests with small locks, miniature porcelains, scraps of velvet, and old razor blades, some of which had dried blood on them.

"Aren't you happy?" I asked Cindy.

"About her?"

"Of course."

"I knew she was going to die. The last week she cut me three times with razor blades."

"And now you're happy she's gone."

"Why do you say that?"

The cemetery was on the edge of a cornfield that was being plowed. One of my elf uncle's daughters was there, pregnant. Another had just given birth. A third was desperately hoping to. His daughters were born breeders. As soon as they looked at a pair of pants they got pregnant. A fifth daughter, slightly plump around the vagina, with a face that looked like a partially slept on mattress, was at the funeral looking for a husband. Years later, after they had given birth to all the eggs they could, their bodies deflated, becoming lumpy pieces of airless rubber. They slouched around their homes, envious of their children.

There was a canopy over the grave. While the minister gave the eulogy, the slow chug of a tractor came from across the field.

There is something wrong with the mechanism that will lower her into the grave. It will not release the webs the casket rests on. Two men are prying at the roller mechanism with screwdrivers. They are dressed in green khaki work clothes and wear caps with long sun visors. They do not like being surrounded by people when they work, especially people who wear suits. How my father would have wanted to be here, to see that wonderful jammed mechanism. He would insist on giving advice. He would hope that the advice would be faulty. He would blame the men for not following the advice, which if followed would not free up the mechanism. The men work furiously. The minister has finished his sermon. People shift uneasily. Perhaps she could not be buried. Perhaps she would be suspended, for eternity, over the open grave. But everybody wanted her buried, out of sight, even Tony. He wanted to bury her with a pair of antlers. Some shotgun shells. Map and compass.

Finally the mechanism is freed up. People want to cheer, but hesitate. The tractor across the field, having been silenced, starts up again. Crows settle in the upturned dirt to eat the worms, and the old lady, bent legs and all, is lowered into the grave along with her poisonous intentions. (The grave is her asylum. She cannot leave. She is locked in.) I look into the faces of all those pregnant or soon to be pregnant women, marveling at how wonderfully soft they are. They are like mud, like slowly boiling corned beef. I envy them their comfort.

"What are you going to do?" I asked Cindy.

"I'm going to live," she said, turning toward me.

"Will you miss her?"

She said nothing. We drove back to their house and had a light supper. It was very hot and dry; the cicadas were noisy. Daylight was disappearing behind the wooden gothic houses that surrounded my uncle's house. I kept imagining I heard owls hooting from the gables.

Later that evening we unbolted the door to her apartment. We looked for arsenic and thumbtacks and found cyanide and razor blades. There were bundles of old seed packets and letters to non-existent post offices. An entire chest of drawers held sweaters, except for the bottom drawer, which was filled with boxes of poisoned pigeon food. A yellowing strip of lace was imprisoned under a sheet of glass on top of the dresser. On top of that were framed photographs of Tony and his family, bright-colored fat people who lived in trailers. Tony was holding a shotgun to the head of his wife. They were both smiling. Everybody was smiling, even the photographer.

Outside, Saginaw felt numb, a burr under the saddle of Michigan. The city settled wistfully into night, drew darkness about it like codeine.

Cindy and I sat listening for sounds. I remembered the old lady's whispers and the way she fingered objects in her room as if she had to coat them with glue to keep them from flying out the front door. We sucked on the hard candy she kept in little bags for the neighborhood children. The cicadas had quieted, their places taken by crickets. I wanted to kiss Cindy, wanted to feel her lips on mine.

"Once she tried to slit my throat," she said.

She got up from her chair, walked over to me, bent down, and kissed me on the forehead. It reminded me of a kiss I had gotten, several years before, when I was twelve. I was in love with a girl who was the toughest kid on the block. She was the only kid on our block who could beat me up. Her father was a steelworker and had a vacation trailer in a mosquito-infested swamp near Chicago. We went there one summer, and ten of us slept in our underwear on the floor in one room. Around midnight she got up, tiptoed over, and kissed me on the lips. It was a full, slow kiss, and when she finished I lay on the floor rigid with fright.

"Let me kiss you," I blurted out.

"We'd both get VD," Cindy said. "Cousins can give each other VD. If we got married we wouldn't have babies, we'd have toads. It's bad for cousins to think of one another. A doctor told me that."

The light from the streetlamp poured in through the windows.

I thought I could hear dogs, or pigs, sniffing outside the door and digging in the flowerbeds.

"If she were alive now I'd probably kill her," Cindy said.

She walked through the door and I fell asleep in the chair. Hours later I woke and heard someone crying in the next room. Then it stopped, and someone grunted. I walked through the living room to go to bed. Cindy was on the couch, twisting and moaning. Someone was with her. I rushed upstairs.

The next day my father escaped from the asylum. He had stolen some clothes from a termite inspector and walked off the grounds with a spray gun and a gallon jug of DDT under his arm.

"The whole place is made out of stone, and I walk out as a termite inspector," he said. "Can you imagine?" he continued. "If I had walked out as a marble restorer, they would have been suspicious."

They issued a warrant for his arrest. He returned to Battle Creek, bought a green house, and was never bothered again.

SMOKING

7
14

HE SMOKED PHILIP MORRIS. PHILIP MORRIS WAS ADVERTISED over the radio by a midget whose face looked like a piece of wood left out in the sun and rain until the grain had run to sharp ridges. The midget had a cutting, high-pitched, ball-less voice. The midget used to say: *Call for Philip Morris*. That is, he tried to say it, or was supposed to say it, but what he said was something else: *Kawl fo-re* (or *ka-well fo-were*, turning two or three syllables into four, stretching them into an invocation, like a Muslim's call to prayers) *Fil-leep*, or *Phil Leap* (sometimes spending two seconds on the first vowel and running quickly through the next vowel so he could get to his favorite part in the pronunciation, the final *p*, which he loved to explode over the radio, as if making the first part of the

sound effects for a bomb going off, or sometimes deciding to reduce
the first vowel to but a second's duration and then really jumping
into the next, letting it rise and fall as if on a roller coaster, and
then in a switch he would ignore the last consonant, slurring over
the *p* that he had exploded just the previous night), and then the
midget's crescendo, the witch's whine that he turned into a Wag-
nerian solo, *Morris*, which was not really Morris but *Mo-reeeiiss*, or
More Reeece, or, when he was drunk, *Mo-reeze*. (He seemed to prefer
leaving off the *r*, that being a letter unsuitable for utterance by the
tiny vocal cords of midgets, and get right to the meat of the matter,
everything that came after the *r*, so that *Mo* was more an introduction
to what would follow, a prologue, a guide to the song ahead. But
attention paid to the midget's moment of glory revealed that the *r*
never disappeared, it just transferred itself to the second syllable,
where it served as a convenient bookend, a beginning, a justification
to the spiel, the *Reeece*, the triple *eee* hitting the high end of the
midget's register, held for what seemed an interminable length of
time, and then suddenly dropped, dismissing the *c*, as if one had
run up a mountain screaming and reaching the highest pitch on top
of the mountain, held it, and then jumped off.) The midget was a
drunk who had to be watched by a normal-sized man and kept sober
enough to shout these four words over the radio. The midget was
despondent over his size, his tiny prick, and the ravines of flesh in
his face, and he loved to go to bars and complain. He would shout
his famous four words before he passed out, his head bouncing off
the bar or the barstool if he was lucky or in attendance with his
male nurse, sometimes bouncing off the floor, if he was unlucky or
his attendant slow. The midget had many women, large and small.
They were fascinated with his tiny prick, fascinated by how it turned
into a small prick; performance rather than size was what they
counted on, but the midget could not persuade himself to believe
that.

    The boy's father was a drunk, and he shared that with the
midget, along with the Philip Morris cigarettes, but beyond that
little else. Smoking had a hypnotic effect on him. It calmed him

beyond words. He liked to sit and smoke. He liked to smoke and sleep, sometimes waking to a small fire on his lap, which he would put out with an angry flap of his hand. His arm would rest on the edge of the chair, wrist falling over the edge, the cigarette between his fingers. He had smoked for so long the tar had etched a dull yellow (later re-etched brown) on the facing sides of his index and ring finger. These fingers were constantly groping for something, never comfortable until a cigarette rested between them, lit, burning slowly to reveal the white ash, which he let fall anywhere.

Immobile in the chair, a figure of resolute calm, he was able to lift his arm without moving any other part of his body and place the cigarette at his lips. This was the magic moment. The tip of the cigarette, pale ash before, turned red, became erotic. A great rush of air and smoke swept the length of the cigarette, sucked into the mouth. The boy watched as his father, eyes now widened, directed the fumes into himself. He commanded the smoke: Inside, inside! The boy marveled at how long the smoke would stay inside him, as if he had swallowed it, let it churn inside until he burped it up. How could he keep it down there so long?

Smoking seemed to calm the drinking, ease the entrance of alcohol into his system. It removed the impurities from bourbon. He could drink with a mouthful of smoke. What an elixir in the stomach! What dreams were trapped there!

He enjoyed the first puff, relaxing immediately. The first puff is a tonic: stimulant, relaxant. It takes the freshest part of the oxygen from the lungs. It is heady, reassuring. It reminds one of vast order, a complacent social structure.

Every puff after that seemed to tighten him up, undo all the work of the first. Order crumbled. The smoke changed to a deeper hue, oxygenless. It no longer mixed with air but crawled along the skin, taunting the eyes, crawling in pockets. It is obsessive, demanding, the smoker is no longer capable of choice.

"I should stub it out after the first puff," he said. He never did.

"I smoke for nostalgia," he said, "a dream of what was." It is enhancement of the ideal, a recognition of the transitory. Smoking is an invitation to his mouth.

He could go for hours without cigarettes, sometimes days. But the minutes were different. He could barely stand the minutes without a smoke.

Watching the smoke rise, he never looked up to see where it went. He assumed it went to the clouds.

He could smoke in his sleep. He set things on fire in his sleep.

"What the hell is going on?" he asked.

The armchair was burning.

The boy's mother battled the flames, beating them with a broom, somehow thinking that she could sweep them away, that fire, like dust, like dirt, could be disposed of with a dustpan.

A glowing ash had dropped into some acrylic. It made a tiny fire.

"What is it?" he asked again, exasperated at the commotion around the flame, standing up, watching the arm of the chair glow and curl toward itself. The boy's mother kept beating the fire as she would an errant child, perceiving the flames as a sort of moral outrage.

"What the hell are you doing?" he asked again, raising his arms, the cigarette still between his fingers, still dripping bits of glowing ash.

Now the boy's mother beat the flames in earnest, giving them a proper whipping.

"Goddamn, you're just making it worse."

The boy's mother would not listen. She was truly angry with the fire, and felt that if she could just give it the right beating, really lay into it, the fire would learn its lesson, relent, stop eating the chair.

"Goddammit, look what you're doing!"

The boy's mother stopped, and looked up at his father. She seemed to be pleading with her husband, asking him for a favor. The fire, sputtering in the chair, took to the straw broom. She looked down at the broom, at the torch at the end of the broom, now threatening to engulf the broom, and started to scream. She lifted the broom up and began swinging it around, the air fertilizer to the flames, which now roared like a small desk fan. She kept twirling the broom around, prompting the flames, screaming at them.

"Give me the goddamn broom."

He tried to wrestle it from her, but she stepped back, thinking that he did not want to put the flames out but to torch the draperies, the rug, the furniture. She thought: The fire is spoiling my house-keeping.

She looked up at the flames. If she stuck the broom in the goldfish bowl, would it boil them to death?

Smoking is a pause between significant events. It is a recognition of that pause. Smoking is dead space, chinks between time.

Smoke the verb; *smoke* the noun.

The boy's father smoked from a pack of Philip Morris he kept in the breast pocket of his shirt. It had a cellophane wrapper around it, with a red cellophane strip that broke the seal. Small, neatly-folded-over ends of tinfoil were pulled back and carefully ripped so that a cigarette could be extracted.

Sometimes he used a dented Zippo lighter. The *zip* in the name meant it could be done quickly, without a worry, and the *o* at the end meant it could be done over and over again, that it was re-peatable, reliable.

The boy had never seen his father open a cigarette pack. He saw many unopened packs around the house. Later they would appear in his father's breast pocket, a small square torn from one end. The boy thought his father did the tearing in the bathroom, that there was something about it he was ashamed of.

It wasn't the smoking he enjoyed so much, the boy thought, but the smoke. He preferred the noun over the verb. He preferred to have the cigarette lit between his fingers, preferred to see the smoke, the noun, rise up between his fingers. He preferred that to putting the cigarette between his lips and smoking, the verb. The function of the cigarette was to remain between his fingers. The job of the cigarette was to smoke itself, the noun to smoke the verb.

He never promised to give it up. He never tried to give it up, never attempted.

"My fingers were born to hold a cigarette," he told the boy.

The boy thought he said, "My fingers were bored to hold a cigarette," meaning that small holes, niches really, were drilled into his fingers so he could hold a cigarette more easily. His fingers were cut like the grooves in ashtrays.

When he smoked it meant he had stopped doing something.

He never did anything while he smoked, except set fires, and once try to shoot someone. Smoking was total immersion. He could not keep his hands busy while a cigarette was burning. One hand had to remain free for the cigarette. One hand was an extension of the cigarette. When he put the cigarette to his lips he was completing a cycle, his body was recirculating itself.

At first the boy thought that smoke lived in his body and that he used the cigarette to "tap" it out, that the cigarette was a special tool for releasing the pressure of smoke. Then he thought the smoke was in his fingers, and that cigarettes helped him suck it out. The day he realized the smoke came from the cigarettes was a day of revelation. Another one: the day he finally realized that the smoke came from neither his body nor the cigarette, but from the very air itself.

That is where I will be someday, the boy thought, in the air, and he'll be there too. Smoke was air defined. Smoke shows us the place where we live.

When his father was younger he smoked at an oblique angle, feet up, hand in front of his face. Later his feet came down, no longer stool-propped, his head began to sink, his hand drooped, and he seemed to sit higher and higher in his chair, until at one point, though he was sitting, it seemed that the chair was so high he was standing. His body seemed to stiffen and hold itself closer together, become boardlike. It was only when his father stood while he smoked that he seemed relaxed, as if the effort of standing on his legs loosened something in his body.

The boy's mother is still beating the burning chair his father sits on. She raises the burning broom.

"See what your smoking has done," she said, accusing him, forgetting that until several months ago she too smoked (but never the way he did, never with the same passion, the same obsessiveness, the same need to command the smoke, to possess it).

"You almost burned the house down," she added (secretly hoping that he would have?).

"We could have all been burned to death, even the boy," she said (and the boy was puzzled by the remark *even the boy*, thinking, Did that mean he would burn all over, very evenly?).

She looked up at the broom, the fire, as if it were an embarrassment, a fresh shit in the middle of a just-vacuumed rug.

"Did I ever tell you about the time we taught the bear to smoke in Banff?" the boy's father asked.

She did not answer.

"It was a hot day, too hot for Canada. The damn bear was tame. You could get him to do anything. He was quick, smart. The hardest part was getting him to not eat the cigarettes after they were lit. That was the hardest part. He didn't seem to mind the fire in his mouth. They must have fireproof mouths, these Canadian bears. We taught him to fart too. You had to feed him something special to get him to fart."

The boy's father looked down at the chair, no longer on fire, merely smoldering. He seemed disappointed.

She lowered the broom. The flame had gone out, leaving a charred stubble of straw on the end of a stick. The fire spirit had left the room. A thick layer of acrid smoke filled the room.

"Open the windows," she said. "We have to get this stink out."

She went to the kitchen and put the broom in the sink (why hadn't she done that before, stick it under the faucet, turn on the water?) and filled some buckets with water and cleanser and brushes and carried them back to the living room, throwing more windows open, bustling about, feeling that the energy of her movement, her goodwill, her Lutheran intentions, would drive the smoke smell from the room.

"We have to clean," she said, "we have to clean for hours. I know these smells. They can last for years. We have to spend hours cleaning. We have to scrub everything, and then we have to go back and rescrub it, and then we can't wait for it to dry but we have to scrub it again, really soak it, a bit of vinegar, ammonia in the water, and scrub again. All the furniture, the walls, the woodwork, the ceiling, the rugs. Especially the rugs. The stink of smoke will live in the rugs for years."

"Let someone else do it," the boy's father said. "We'll pay someone to do it. We'll roll up the rugs and send them out."

The boy's mother looked as if someone had poured a pitcher of ice water down the front of her dress.

"We can't send it out," she said, shocked. "That would be shameful."

The boy's father lit another cigarette.

The smoke from the first puff curled slowly, wound its way thoughtfully around his father's head, and then continued on a spiral, a slightly discolored bit of air, a nicely shaped cloud, settling in along the edges of the ceiling.

"We can send anything out. That's what you pay people for."

GOLF

I COULD SAY IT WAS BECAUSE HE WAS ANGRY, BUT THIS EXPLAINS little since he is always angry, his mood simply degrees of anger, so that if I search for an explanation as to why he was beating the man with the knickers and the clam-colored hair with a golf club (a mashie, or a niblick, a half mashie, a baffy, spoon, brassie, mashie iron, spade mashie), using the business end of this hitting machine to deliver considerable force to a small, precise area, and claim anger for this reason, it tells nothing.

They stood on a small hill, and I marveled at how calm the light-complexioned man he was hitting behaved, as if this were just a small variation of the game, my father his teacher, that golf in fact was a contact sport, a game of blood violence, the ultimate entrance into death. My father squatted when he hit, as if to chop wood, the golf club over his head, considerably behind him. His legs and torso are positioned to extract the maximum force from his swing, the object of that swing not the white balls that are scattered about the warring men but rather the skull that held the hair, clam-colored, of the man opposite him. Question: I have always wondered why a man who wears knickers would fight. It seems an anomaly to me. There is something about knickers that precludes fighting, the ridiculous sight of these—what to call them?—surely not pants, gathered skirts perhaps, elasticized below the knees. Perhaps my father was fighting the man because of the knickers, but I doubt it, since he was hardly an authority on sartorial wear, couldn't care less, in fact (he had once played nine holes in his pajamas). No, there was something more elemental here.

The man in the knickers assumed a more upright position when he swung, feeling perhaps that the decorum of wearing knickers demanded that he bash my father's head in a certain style, one befitting his choice of clothes. My father cared little about style. He was wearing white pants, bloody by now, and a tan polo shirt, also bloody, and my first thought on seeing him was not the marks on his face but how to get the blood out of his clothes. He would simply want to throw them away, assuming he lived, after the fight. I on the other hand would want to save the clothes, reuse them. I hate to throw anything out. My father throws everything out. He was then in the process of throwing himself out.

The man landed a blow on my father's leg, cutting his pants, gashing the calf. I saw a slow blot of blood form on his pants, and the way my father dipped to the side, a heavy ship listing to the lee side in a storm. Down came my father's club—mashie, niblick, baffy, spoon, what have you—and though the other gentleman was able to stop most of its entrance into his head, the tip did lodge there, and the man's lower jaw did not drop so much as the upper part of his head rose, as if he had just seen something astounding and wished to communicate that fact to my father, wished to point out some marvelous sight, a great surprised eagerness on his face. It seems to me too that this man has a British face, though I have no reason for assuming this, except for the extreme politeness he shows in fighting. My father raises his club in preparation for another blow, and I notice the shaft is bent. The two men do not circle each other, do not feint, dodge, or seem overly excited. In fighting, most men are highly agitated, nervous in a way they cannot contain. But here the intent is calm, almost sullen, as if this fight were simply an unpleasant task both men had to complete, the bludgeoning of each other's brains a nasty but necessary business, no need to get upset about the prospect.

Now it was the other's turn to strike, and this he did, the blow landing on my father's shoulder. It was the same shoulder he used to hoist me up to when I was younger, lighter. It was a glancing blow, but it landed. I heard a sharp noise, like two pieces of slate clacking together. I saw no blood, but my father paused, moving that shoulder slightly, and then rubbed it with his other hand. He whipped his club around and caught the other man in the side. It made a sound like a stick hitting a pillow. Small puffs of something cottony exploded from where the blow landed, and the gentleman in the knickers suddenly looked extremely sad, as if someone had told him some unimaginably depressing news, something of such magnitude as to cause him to draw his breath in quite forcefully and cry. I have never seen a man's face look as sad as his looked. He looked as if he were responsible for dooming an entire family line. The sadness seemed to be catching, because my father, rather than looking triumphant, also saddened, and the blow the knickered man then landed on my father, short of his head but fully on his ear, neck, and shoulder, taking a long slice out of that area as neatly as someone working a roast beef with a skilled hand and a sharp knife honed for the occasion, put a look of immense resignation on my father's face, like a historian who can see the shape of human civilization for centuries to come.

I wondered how long this carnage would last, and why no one came out to stop it. I would not. If my father had wanted me to stop it he would have said something. It seemed to me that more than just blood was escaping from these two. In addition to the clubs and balls that were scattered about, testimony perhaps to the argument that preceded the fight, I imagined I saw parts of both of them lying on the ground: small, precise strips of skin, tips of ears, nubs of fingers, lumpy balls of flesh, fat, and blood, the stringy residue of bloody sinews lying forlornly against the bright green of the golf course. I heard no one yell. Why were they not yelling at each other? Why were they not shouting?

If there is such a category as golf samurai, my father and the other man epitomized it. There was such gentlemanliness in the way they attacked each other, as if death were the ultimate prelude to politeness, a bloody bit of decorum that would stand as a model for generations to come. My father refused to bend his back when he hit. His spine remained straight when he struck his vicious blows. And the other gentleman, a man who reminded me of nothing less than a harried butler, fought on his toes, hardly bending his knees when he carved pieces of flesh from my father's body, or pulverized his muscle, or shattered some small, fragile bonework, something intricate and finely connected.

Honor perhaps had something to do with it, though frankly my father never made a point of honor. Principle, yes, rightness, yes, but honor? Still, the extreme way they hacked into each other, without vindictiveness, made me think that honor was involved, and that this was a facet of my father's personality that had escaped me. But then, if I examine the matter, his entire personality escaped me, as it surely did everyone else, and the behavior of this fight may have simply been one of his many whims, a thing that existed for itself, a gamble he and the other gentleman were willing to undertake and see to its conclusion. Who knows?

With each swing my father attacks himself, attacks the very possibility of himself. This is a prelude to one of his great "thrashes," a time when all he can do is thrash about, wildly striking at himself.

Finally the two gentlemen sit down, their legs giving out before the other parts of their mangled bodies. Facing each other, seated, legs stretched out before them so that the soles of their feet are opposite, they keep feebly striking one another. And then they whisper something at the same time, and stop. My father never told me what the fight was about, though years later he did tell me that the gentleman in knickers lay at the bottom of a water trap on the fourteenth hole at a golf course in Scotland. "He is fully clothed and his golf bag is slung around his shoulder," my father said. "His clothes are remarkably well preserved, and though you can't see much in daylight, on a moonlit night he presents an awesome figure, spread-eagled on the bottom in all that muck. No one knows what happened to his caddy."

Golf was a contact sport for my father. I caddied for him. He believed that golf was the power of white against green. He also said that each golf ball had a soul, a tiny soul rising in the air, trying to stay in the air, that it represented the overcoming of weight, the triumph of air, and the transformation of the soul into air.

He played by himself, rarely counted strokes. The area around his ball always looked mangled, fire-swept. He attacked the ball: clubbed it, sliced it, hacked it, chopped it, tried to pound it into the ground. On several occasions he destroyed the ball and drove the windings deep into the earth, burying them along with a corkscrew-shaped putter. He liked to tear up greens, send huge divots sailing through the air. He speared the ground with cup flags. When he got mad, clubs, golf bags, golf shoes, flew through the air. It was the nearest I ever saw him get to joy.

This took place on Saturday afternoons, quite regularly, until something happened that caused him to give up golf.

He hit a ball into the air that refused to fall to earth.

I was there. I saw it. The ball took off slowly, thoughtfully, almost casually, holding a parallel to the ground before it began to rise and pick up speed. It flew straight off the tee, and then, about one hundred yards out, jumped up, reaching the top of the trees. The ball soon became a dot, a pinprick, nothing, swallowed in an immensity of blue and green.

My father stood still, watching it disappear.

There was a look of nostalgia on his face, as if he had killed something he loved. He wore a white handkerchief soaked with sweat around his neck. His neck and arms were pink, getting pinker. Small water blisters appeared underneath the handkerchief.

He is calmer than he has a right to be. He realizes the absurdity of his calmness, clasps his fingers together and leans over, holding an imaginary club. He swings. The imaginary golf ball rises in the air, following the real. At some point they join. For a moment, what is real coincides with what is desired. Then they separate, the imaginary beyond the real, a golf ball of stupendous proportions.

The sun had been up for a while, and the bunkers and traps seemed to shiver in the heat. Off in the distance, the greens lay like postage stamps slowly curling off vegetable-colored envelopes. And then for a moment it seemed to me that the entire golf course had been lifted and suspended in air. I could feel the ground shudder, as if something was wrenching itself from the earth.

He is sweating heavily. Years of booze are pouring through his skin. Everything he does—smoking, drinking, golf—rises up in the air, evaporates, disappears.

I can sniff a room and tell you if there are golf clubs, golf balls, or golf shoes there. I can tell you how old grass stains are, how old golf shoes are, how long a golf bag has been lying around. It is not a negotiable talent. I mention it to no one.

THE ROCKING

HORSE

3
4
6
8
1 8

THE ROCKING HORSE WAS ONE OF HIS FIRST TOYS. IT CAME ONE evening unannounced, tucked under his father's arm. It was a crude affair: maple dowels for legs and neck, curved slats for the rocking part, a head hacked into a wedge with an ax, thumbtack eyes, rag-mop mane, a trunk rounded on top, with flat sides and bottom, and a square of blue felt for the saddle which was nailed over the trunk. The wood was dark maple, glued and doweled. When the boy got on it he noticed it rocked unevenly. The slats were mismatched, the curves not congruent. He rode it with the bump. Later the bump would remind him of many things, but now the bump only reminded him of a bump. The boy said to himself: This is the way horses gallop, with a beat, a bump. He believed this because the horse looked more like the idea of a horse than a horse.

At night he took the horse into his room. He placed it alongside his bed, and before he shut his eyes gave it a push and watched as the horse rocked back and forth with its built-in bump. That happened in Canada, Montreal, before Chicago. It was a city of red brick, dark woods, and bright sun. At first the boy thought the sun was white, that the sky was the sun. He would look up and see the white sky and become frightened. The sky was too big, it covered everything, and it was so white that nothing could hide in it. He didn't like being in the open. He could feel the hugeness of the sky and wanted to run, but the sky was everywhere. Later he would deliberately run into open fields to frighten himself. He did not know what he was frightened of, and that magnified the terror. He liked to frighten himself. He forgot about himself when he was frightened, and he could feel himself more completely: his skin, his toenails, his hair. But he did this too often and soon was no longer afraid of the sky. He noticed that the sky was not white, or not white all the time. The white was clouds. Behind that was blue, and the sun was a color so bright he couldn't look at it.

His mother was slim and pretty. His father was tall and handsome and wore dark suits and dark shoes with tiny put-there-on-purpose holes. He lived in an apartment, which was dark, except near the windows, where it was light. The floors were polished maple, and the boy could ride his rocking horse over the glossy waxed floors, skidding, bumping into furniture. He rode from the light part of the apartment to the dark part, and back again. The apartment was divided into two worlds, and he was riding from one to the other. The best part of the ride was the boundary between the two, the area that was neither. He liked this best of all because it confused him. No longer terrified of the sky, he liked being confused, especially by things that were neither this nor that.

There was little furniture in the apartment. His mother and father had been married only a few years, and his father taught bacteriology. His father told him that bacteria were everywhere, that you couldn't see them, that where everything else wasn't they were. They are ghosts, the boy thought. He had learned about ghosts from the woman who came to take care of him on Wednesday afternoon when his mother went out. His mother said she was not all there, but enough of her was so she could watch after him and tell him stories whose beginning and end she could never remember, any more than she could remember if the story she told was just one story, or half of one, or two or three mixed into one. It made no difference to the boy. He was no critic, and as she told the stories he assumed that was the way stories were: that names of characters changed in stories, that characters themselves changed, that rivers turned into deserts for no reason, that evil became good, right wrong, that what happened didn't happen, never would, and that what didn't did. Old people turned into babies, and the babies into their own grandparents. It was the change that he liked. It made little difference to him who was changed into what. He liked the change part because that was where the boundary was. He never knew how these changes took place. They just seemed to happen, mysteriously, and as the boy rode around the room he had the feeling that nothing was. Things just happen, he thought, with no order.

One Wednesday afternoon she came and took off all her clothes. He was on his rocking horse, bumping across the floor. She stood before him, a short, squat woman, not particularly pretty. She removed her clothes in front of him, tossing them as if she never wanted to see them again. The boy stopped rocking and stared at her. The only unclothed person he had ever seen was himself. She stood before him naked: thick legs, hips that bubbled over themselves, hanging breasts with nipples that pointed toward the floor, sloping shoulders, and a hill of hair below her stomach. She held up one of her great breasts and pointed it toward him as if it were a gun, the nipple the barrel of the gun and the dark area around the nipple and the heavy veined breast the business end of the gun, and asked him if he had ever seen one of these before, one like this, one as big as this. The boy said nothing. He felt the rocking horse between his legs, and gave it a little nudge. He lifted up his arm and pointed toward her middle. "What do you have all that hair for?" he asked. She said nothing. "What's it doing there, anyway?" he said. She walked over to his toy box and got out a ball and tossed it to him. He caught it and tossed it back to her. She went to the kitchen and opened up a box of marshmallows and began to eat them. She asked him if he wanted any and he said no. She stuffed the last two marshmallows in her ears. Then she jumped up in the air and touched her hands over her head. The boy could feel the floor shake each time she came back out of the air. As she jumped, her breasts followed after her, lagging, as if they were independent. Sometimes they followed her hands, rising up to touch each other. When she stopped, the boy noticed sweat rolling down between them. She took her thumb and forefinger and opened her mouth as wide as she could. With her other hand she pointed toward the inside of her mouth. She made gagging sounds. The boy could not understand them. The sounds she made seemed to be part of her nakedness, her hair, her breasts. Then she took her upper lip between the thumb and forefinger of both hands and lifted it up, showing her upper gums. She grunted as she did this. The boy realized she was making the same noise she had made before. She started to rock her head back and forth, grunting in time to the rocking, shutting her eyes. She took her two index fingers, keeping her thumbs on her lips, and spread her nostrils as wide apart as she could. She continued rocking, grunting. Then, as if hit over the head, forced to stop, she came to a halt. The rocking was slow to leave her, and when it did, even though she stood still she seemed to rock, the waves in the air vibrating around her. She walked over to him and picked him up. He hooked his legs together, lifting the rocking horse with him so that while she held him in her arms, between her huge breasts, one runner of the rocking horse was hooked into her, the other pushing into her fat thigh. "I'm hungry," the boy said. She told him they were going out for air. She walked with him to the window that had a fire escape, the rocking horse clanking against her legs. The apartment was six floors above the ground, and the fire escape overlooked a courtyard with a fountain and a pool. With one hand she removed the offending rocking horse from the boy's legs. Then she opened the window with the same hand and, still holding the boy, put her enormous rump on the window ledge and swung her legs around so that she and the boy were facing the courtyard and her bare feet were on the fire escape. Holding on to the boy, she lay down, the black iron strips of the fire escape pressing against her white flesh, which engulfed the strips like rising bread dough.

She asked the boy if he would like to swing in the air, and he said yes. There was something he liked about the air outside. It seemed fuller than inside the apartment, crammed with more air, air stuffed into air. The sky was white. She took him by the wrist and swung him out over the ledge, swinging him back and forth like a pendulum. The world rocked in a wide arc, threatening him with its presence. He felt as if he should have all his clothes off to feel the air. He was not frightened of falling, but he did not want to fall. He wanted her to hold him tightly, not to let go. He wanted to tell her this. He opened his mouth to breathe, to take in more of the air. Swinging back and forth, he looked down at the courtyard. His mother and father were sitting there, arguing. His mother rose quickly, and looked up. He wanted to wave, but he was afraid. His mother looked upset. She made a noise and ran toward the lobby door. His father looked up, sighed, as if he were about to spit out an egg.

Then his mother stopped running and looked at him. She hardly moved. His father hardly moved. He was the only one who moved, back and forth, back and forth.

Later his mother told the boy that the naked woman wouldn't be coming to take care of him anymore. She had a new home, where she wasn't allowed to take off her clothes. The boy pestered his mother until one afternoon they went to see her. She wouldn't talk to them. She kept standing, rocking back and forth. His mother said it didn't make any difference, because they were going to Chicago, where his father had a new job. The furniture was put in boxes for the trip, but he was allowed to carry his rocking horse with him.

When they arrived in Chicago the furniture inside the boxes changed, just like the stories the squat lady used to tell. He found a house with a rug on the floor and soft, padded furniture that had cushions and pillows, furniture so deep and heavy you could disappear into it. The rug made it harder to use his rocking horse, and he did most of his rocking upstairs in his bedroom. His bedroom was on one end of a landing. At the other end was an empty room; later that would be the bedroom for his brother who hadn't been born yet, and there was another brother who also hadn't been born yet, but there was no bedroom for him, so he died. He rocked out of his room and along the landing and into the empty room and rocked around that room, feeling its emptiness, thinking that another person should be put in this room so the house wouldn't be unbalanced and tip to one side.

He met his grandparents and was frightened by one of them. She was called Nann. Sometimes his father called her "The Madam." He didn't know what to call her. He didn't want to call her anything. His father had a ghost brother they never saw who made calls late at night asking for money. Nann told his father not to give him any. He wouldn't want to disobey Nann. He didn't know if his father disobeyed her. His father was still his father but also her son, which confused him. He wanted to know what he was. Whenever Nann came over he went up to his room and rocked on his rocking horse, bumping over the bare wooden floors. If she wanted to see him he had to come down, because she didn't like to climb stairs. He dragged his rocking horse downstairs and rocked on the rug. Sometimes she made him get off the horse and stand up straight in front of her. She smelled sweet and sour, old and new, and she liked to walk around him, looking down, while he stood there. One time she did that and he peed his pants. He was afraid to tell her. He let the pee run down, soaking his pants and socks, at first hot, then warm, then getting cold. She seemed to be inspecting him for something, but she never told him what it was. She would always ask him how old he was, even if his age hadn't changed since the last time she had been over, and he wondered whether she had forgotten or whether she just wanted to test his memory and see if he still knew. She told him he'd been baptized. He didn't know what that meant, except it had something to do with death, and he didn't know what that meant, either, except that it somehow meant that you weren't anymore, and he didn't see how that could be. Where would he go if he wasn't anymore? Up in heaven with the popes, his grandmother told him. What are they doing up there, he wanted to ask, but didn't, because you didn't ask Nann anything, for some reason.

His father gave his mother a tiny seed, a tiny baby, and she grew his brother until he was born. When his brother was several years old they both went downstairs to see Nann. Now she spent most of her time in a chair and she wouldn't let him bring his rocking horse down. She made them stand in front of her, made them turn around, and he was still frightened by her but he knew he wouldn't pee his pants and he also knew that when she asked their ages it was because she had forgotten.

His father gave his mother another tiny seed, only this one wasn't made right, and before the boy's second brother could stand in front of Nann, he died. The boy had wanted the three of them to stand in front of Nann. It would have made the standing easier. They put him in a hole in the ground and Nann said he was with the popes and he wondered if the popes had come and dug up the box and carried him off, taken him out of the box, played with him.

Then Nann died. That's what they said. He didn't believe it. There was too much of her to die. She was too solid. She had shadows within shadows, bulk within bulk. Her voice was too big. She hadn't died. She just wasn't on the ground anymore, she wouldn't come out of the air. He no longer had to come downstairs and parade for her. He rode his rocking horse in his room. Sometimes he felt she was watching him, and then he would get off his rocking horse and go to his Erector set and work on the drawbridge that cranked up and down.

The air! What was the air like then? It was new, at least it started out new. It filled your lungs many times over. It made you want to jump. It made you want to sing. It was blue. It shook. It sparkled. Then it turned yellow. It was wet, heavy, it curled.

Almost summer, the last week of school. The air began to get light. He brought a school friend home and they pulled weeds out of the vacant lot and threw them in the street to watch the cars roll over them. Several times they were chased by drivers. They ran through alleys, skipped over fences, breathless, arriving in his mother's kitchen, where she poured them each a tall glass of lemonade, the sugar still thick and sticky at the bottom of the glass. They set up a card table in the backyard and made a small pot of glue from powder that came in a package and took out the balsa wood and tissue paper for the model airplanes they were making: P-39 Bell Airacobra, P-38, P-51, Mustang, Hellcat, Corsair. Long, cigar-shaped pods from the catalpa tree littered the ground. The air was warm and heavy. Round white bits of fuzz with tiny seeds in the center floated in the breeze. Hours were spent on the planes for the few brief moments when, propeller twirled taut on its rubber band, they became alive in the air. They were perfect in the air. But they always crashed. They could never be repaired. The unfairness of it angered him, delighted him. He was suddenly aware of time. In the air the plane was outside time. Once it landed, crashed, it was in time. *In* and *out*. Your blood was time. Once it got outside of you, you were outside time. You could go out but you couldn't go in. It was like looking at your self without a mirror.

He went up to his room and brought his rocking horse down and rocked on the grass. He didn't notice that his friend kept looking at him. It was hard to rock the horse on the grass. He had to take his feet off the runners and put them on the grass, give a good push. He looked up, and noticed the way his friend was looking at him. Suddenly, he stopped. He took the rocking horse to his room. His face felt hot.

He rocked in his bedroom. He shut the door before he rocked. Sometimes if he couldn't get to sleep he would rock until he slipped off the horse and fell asleep on the floor. There was a rug on his bedroom floor. Once his father came into his room and stumbled over the rocking horse, becoming so angry he threw it out the window. The boy waited until he had left and the house was quiet before he went into the backyard and retrieved the horse. One of its legs was cracked. He stuffed glue in the crack and wrapped twine around it. Sometimes when he woke in the night, forgetting to breathe, he would get up and ride the horse, thinking that the rocking would help his breath.

He put it on top of his dresser and used it as a hook for his jacket. Friends came over. He told them they could throw darts at it. When the first boy raised his arm, dart in hand, he grabbed hold of the arm. "No," he said.

Sometimes at night he would stretch out naked on the floor and set the rocking horse on top of him. By moving his stomach he could make it rock. Making it rock made his penis stiffen, rise. It throbbed to the beat of the horse on his stomach.

The rocking horse stayed in his room for several years. One night when he couldn't get to sleep he thought about taking it down and rocking himself to sleep. His father had come home, and he could hear him moving downstairs. Sofas bumped against walls, lamps rattled. Soon he would try to come upstairs. The boy was afraid his father would fall down the stairs. He would somersault backward, his arms and legs flapping against the walls like some paralyzed marine creature. The boy got out of bed and took the rocking horse down from the dresser. He was too big to ride it. Why would he ever want to? The broken leg would never support his weight. It would crack. The other legs would crack. He put the rocking horse back on the dresser. The blue felt saddle had been ripped, a few strands of the mane were cut off. One of the eyes was missing. He heard his father start up the stairs. He heard the sound of the railing as his father steadied himself, and the creak of the first stair. There was a pause, as if his father couldn't make up his mind to continue, as if his mind had flown to another part of the world, and then the second stair creaked, and the third, and there was another pause. The boy could imagine his father sweeping the air with one of his feet, wondering where it should go next, or else forgetting that he had a foot, thinking that his foot had evaporated and that he had somehow miraculously managed to climb stairs without feet. Then, the sound of the fourth and the fifth stairs. He could now imagine his father in the middle of the stairs, wondering whether to go forward or back. His mind was no longer in his head; it was dancing in the air; it had evaporated along with his foot. And then it reappeared, like rain. He decided he would continue, that he would climb the stairs, feet or no feet. The boy looked at the horse on the dresser. It seemed to be moving, as if a breeze had pushed it forward or someone had come by and with the slightest touch of a hand brushed it enough to set it rocking.

Soon after, his home exploded. His father flew to Texas. His mother sold their house and moved to Michigan. The boy went to college, where for some inexplicable reason he was struck with a huge joy. It descended out of nowhere, and was the result of no tangible accomplishment, and yet its reality enclosed the boy and shook him with great vividness. It was a terrifying joy. It seemed to demand something of him, and yet he had no idea what that demand was. It propelled him toward inanimate objects that bristled with life. He would spend afternoons watching the water evaporate from rain-coated slate roofs that covered the gothic buildings on campus. In a philosophy class on Kierkegaard he listened to the steam hiss from a huge radiator the size of a small pony. The escaping steam reminded him of snow, of feathers, of stars. The gray floorboards were curled at the ends, as if unsuccessfully trying to hold something down that seethed and surged just beneath. He would stare at objects, wanting to cry, and realize that joy once again had him in its clutches and was bent on extracting some hard-won secret. It was a terrible joy, merciless. He had no power over its coming and going. It held him at odd moments, inconvenient times when he was in public and forced to stare at inappropriate objects. It disregarded shame, propriety, social conventions. He became so engrossed in his focus that the moment became everything, and what remained outside that focus was anesthetized. When the spell of his stare was broken, he felt a balloon of wellness blowing up inside him, and a silent scream, to which he could attach no voice, escaped from his throat. Tears welled up in his eyes, and the joy became so immense it was a burden, an ache, an impediment he could not throw off. The very fact that he could attach no reason to it made it more powerful.

They found him perched on a cornice of the museum, several hundred feet above the ground, sitting on his haunches with his hands placed in front of him like paws, looking as if he expected to leap into the air and glide over the pond and trees and hurtfully bright green grass that surrounded the museum. They made a big commotion over his sitting on the cornice, gargoyle fashion. They thought he was going to jump, and brought in jump pleaders, people whose job is to remind jumpers that air, and the leap into it, is not the solution to any puzzle. The jump pleaders get information about the jumpers, bring friends, family, to the scene. But his father could not be found, his mother was unreachable, and his friends at school were drunk and applauded the act. The ladder from the fire truck did not reach where he was sitting, squatting, and they could not figure how he had gotten onto the cornice. They were puzzled by how satisfied he looked. He would not talk to them but stared ahead. The day was clean and cool, early spring. Buds, flowers, green things, had made an appearance, folding and unfolding themselves like origami. The police hooked up a megaphone and began speaking to him. That was when he noticed the men with rifles. Someone had phoned in and said there was a sniper on the roof of the museum.

He crouched on the ledge, sitting on his haunches. The marble under his feet had a slight tilt away from the building. He could feel the curve of a fluted column at his back. He was up several stories, museum floors, which put him almost one hundred feet above the ground. He got up and walked along the ledge, found a place where he could climb higher. His climbing had no goal. Perhaps the roof was calling him, something above the roof, something in the air. He was calmed by thinking about broken bones, blood. Fresh bone protruding from a leg, surrounded by a gristle of meat and blood, gave him a hard-on. Lying on the ground, the body no longer following the contours of bone but following the shape of the earth, the liquids of the body seeping into the soil, made him feel relaxed, as if anxiety had seeped out of him and into the earth.

He climbed slowly, patiently, with no thought on his mind other than climbing. He knew someone would want to shoot him off the building. He would have wanted to shoot himself off the building.

The air on top of the museum is ancient, distilled from the antiquities in the museum. He is the only one in the world who can smell ancient air. Neither he nor anyone else could figure out how he had climbed. There were no stairs, no hand- or footholds, nothing vertical that afforded a means of horizontal ascension. But he found himself higher, and that is how they found him, higher yet, as if he were directing the city toward some vast plan. He did not wish to die. He may have wished to jump, but he had no wish to die.

• • •

He holds the notion of his childhood dear. It is stultifying. He is afraid to go home, afraid to look at his mother. "She will ask me why my hair is burning. I will have no answer. I will be terrified." He loves going home. He hates it when he gets there. He has something to say. His mother interrupts him. It was very important, what he had to say. He forgot what it was. He remembered again that when he had something important to say, truly important, he always forgot it. Always. "What is important does not like me to say it."

The priest came to visit him at school. He was shorter than the boy had remembered, and fat. He carried his history with him; inside his fat face the boy could see a thin face emerging, the cheeks and jowls not able to cover the sharp nose, now blurred reddish purple with veins that skated off in many directions like tracks on a frozen pond, and eyes that crinkled and drooped, pulled down by guilt. His gray hair, neatly combed, looked as if it had been tattooed on his skull. He still had a good smile. That, the boy thought, he will never lose.

"I understand you've been through a hard time."

The boy looked angrily at him.

"I mean it's not easy."

"It's OK."

"I guess your mother is taking it pretty hard."

"She's OK."

"That's good to hear."

The boy said nothing. He didn't know how to talk to the priest. It had been years since he had seen him. Many years. The last time had been after Nann's funeral.

"They say you get dreamy, go vacant."

The boy said nothing. He reached into his pocket and took a key off his key ring and tried to bend it.

"I know your father, your grandmother, your grandfather, all your family."

Suddenly the boy knew how the priest spent his Sunday afternoons. He masturbated into a freshly starched handkerchief and then washed it out in a small sink in his room. Then he threw up. He did it every Sunday. He dreaded Sundays.

"I know you think I'm butting in," the priest said, "but I can't stand by while this is happening."

"Nothing is happening."

"Maybe that's the trouble."

"There is no trouble."

"You shouldn't be angry at your father."

"I'm not."

"He can't help himself."

"I know."

"Lord knows he can't."

It was good to have someone talk about his father. It made him seem real, turned him into an object he could touch. Whatever his father did was less important than his physical presence. Flesh, blood, bone, confirmed him in a way that no miscreant act could ever deny. He could commit any atrocity as long as he remained real, as long as he sweated, could bleed, would cough and rage and throw something through the window. Let me smell you, the boy thought. Let me just touch your skin. I'd be satisfied with that. I don't need anything more.

The priest took out a handkerchief and wiped his forehead. It was a cold day, but the effort of his speaking seemed to generate a heat from within.

"I have a question," the boy said.

"Yes?" said the priest, leaning forward on his chair. The boy noticed how worn and greasy the inside of his hat was. He suddenly felt sorry for him. The priest had retired. He didn't have much money. He didn't have to be here.

"Whatever happened to the stones?"

"What stones?" the priest asked.

"Those stones you tried to get me to kiss."

He paused. Something had been wiped clean from the priest's face.

"When I was little."

"I don't know what you're talking about."

"I wish I had kissed those stones," he said.

GONE

NITNY WANTED TO SEE A DEAD PERSON. SO HE NAILED HIMSELF to the fence. The only dead person he could find was himself. But he couldn't see himself dead, he could only see himself dying, so he never got to see a dead person Christmas Day. Nitny vanished. He evaporated. The more I ask about him, the more his whole existence is called into question. His parents are not even sure there was a Nitny. Everyone seems to have forgotten him. But I will remember. I now make it my duty to remember things that others forget. I also make it my duty to unexplain things. Too many things are explained these days.

Faustio and I were talking about him. We were in the alley, behind the garage of the man who wore braces to sit up straight. Faustio called him a jerk.

"Don't call him that," I said.

"I call him that. That's what he was."

We both know what is coming.

"He wasn't a jerk. Just funny."

"Funny like my ass is funny."

"He wasn't mean enough to be a jerk. He never tried. You have to try to be a jerk. It takes effort."

"Hole, as in ass. And he was dumb."

"Dumb he wasn't."

"Beyond dumb. Stupid, very stupid."

It is early afternoon. There is something about Faustio that I do not like. Perhaps it is his name, or the thick black leather shoes he wears. The shoes look too serious, they look like something you can buy at Sears. I want to tell him that you should not buy your shoes at Sears, but I doubt he will understand.

"He was an asshole. Anybody who does that is an asshole."

"Fuck you."

We were on the ground. We had hit each other, but the hitting didn't seem to do much good, so we looked for a part of the body to break, bend, something that would extract pain. Both of us were great believers in pain. Lying on the ground alongside Faustio, each of us locked in the other's embrace, I feel a great sense of anger and eroticism. He has my head cradled in the crook of his arm and rubs something into my face. I try to put my knee in the small of his back. Faustio wants to talk while we fight, but I don't. Talking would spoil the thing we have in fighting.

He has my head in the gutter and rubs my hair in engine oil. I separate the little finger from his hand and bend it back. There is something delicious about the pain this causes him, and I can see him trying to hide the distress on his face, as if pain were shameful, torture not a pleasure to inflict. We move into a new position. Now we are face to face, trying to squeeze the air out of each other's lungs. I would like to crack a few ribs, and try, searching for an unlucky floating rib that I can fracture; he would like to collapse one lung, two if time permits. I would like to do serious, costly damage. We keep shifting arms, trying to get a better position. Now I realize what I dislike about him. His breath smells like cat shit.

I think the reason I am so violent is that basically I am a peaceful person. There is a connection between the two, and I can explain it, though it goes against my principles. Punching someone in the face is an intensely satisfying experience, very calming, a fact I recognized when I was punching Faustio. The truly violent never punch, never push, never bend flesh. That is left to pacifists like myself, for whom a quick shove, a nasty jab, a twisted limb (bent under pressure), leaves one feeling clean inside, very satisfied, hugely competent.

Holding me with one hand, Faustio punches me in the face. It doesn't take much for my nose to bleed. I worry about what my nose will look like after having been smeared across part of my face. I pull his hair back and choke him. I feel he is breathing too much, using too much of my air. Before he loses his breath he punches me in the stomach.

My balls feel like they dropped off, or else were jerked up on a string, where my stomach used to be. I want to tell him that he shouldn't have done that, but the pain is too exquisite, too beautiful. I can chew it. I try to eat the pain, try to swallow it. How can I eat my stomach, eat the pain? There is a snake of noise trying to escape from the back of my throat. Listen, I want to say. Listen here. But that is as far as I get. The only sound my body will hear is the sound my stomach makes.

I once heard a story about a man who was robbed and tortured. To those who were aware of the incident, knew in fact who did it, the robbery was incidental. Some things always have to be apologized for.

A sort of vision comes back to my stomach. Then he has me in a headlock.

Squeezing blood and air, he has my neck within his arms; the muscles in my back go soft, hurt. We have both struggled to our feet. He stands with my head at his chest. I am at his hip, bent over, my arms searching for something to pull, to twist. Tiny pinpricks of light dance in my eyes. He holds my neck hostage, furious at the connection it makes with my head. He keeps punching me in the face. I get angry, indignant over this attitude. Rage swells my arms, and I pick him up, cradling him like a baby, and throw him down. He still holds my neck, and I follow him down on the cement. There is a double whack; first his head, then mine, hit the alley. We are bloodied, unrepentant. He sticks his fist in my face. I kick him. It is only in the leg, but it presses the meat of the leg into the bone. I feel something go soft in his leg. I want to follow this up with a punch, where cartilage joins bone.

Fighting never frightens me, but the moments before a fight do. There is something very calming about the anger in a fight. I can feel the winds of rage rush through my body in a clear *whoosh*. I hear the noise of that wind in my ear, a blue howling.

When I bend Faustio's arm behind his back, when I twist his wrist, when I see the look of pain on his face, I feel exalted, lucky, full of gratitude. Then, twisting out of my grip, he hits me in the chest, kicks me in the ribs. He means to punish me, and is intent on doing this. Sitting on my stomach, he bounces my head off the cement. It is beyond hurt. I do not know how much longer I can keep him in view. Blood is coming from my nose and the back of my head. There is a draft at the top of my head. I feel air coming in. Garages, the alley, begin to rise.

He seems to enjoy this. I would like to kill him quickly, but not too quickly.

My legs rise. I hook my ankle around his neck and flip him over. The blood rushes to my eyes. I wrap my legs around his stomach and squeeze. He punches, kicks my legs. I keep squeezing, seeing less as the blood fills my eyes. The anger rushes into my legs, a huge wind, and squeezes the air out of him. I can feel him deflating. His face is obscured. Evening has come too soon, though it is only early afternoon. I do not know where I will be hours from now. As the air continues to rush out of him, I feel that I am teaching him something, but I do not know what that is.

TESTS

2 3

THE BOY WAS EXPECTED TO PASS A LOYALTY OATH. AS DEVISED by the boy's father, it was a rather simple test. The boy was expected to be home, in his apartment ready to receive him, when the father arrived. The father never told the boy he was coming. That was the test. The boy was just supposed to know. So when the boy's father was fired once again from one of his many jobs (Illinois, Texas, West Virginia), having a little time on his hands, and usually some severance pay, he decided that his son should just know he was coming. The father always knew where the boy lived, though the boy rarely knew where his father lived.

Where the boy lived was a six-flight walk-up, on linoleum steps that slanted away from the wall, with a banister that shook the steps if you used it for support. Climbing the six flights, his new leather shoes clicking on the metal strip nailed to the edge of each stair to prolong its shaky life, the father knocked on the door to the boy's apartment. There was no answer. He would have left a note, but he had no paper, no pen. He had a pencil, but the majesty of his being there demanded a pen. He walked down the stairs to find a store that sold paper and pens, but he found a tavern first and went in and had a bourbon to fortify himself for the trip to the store, then had a shot of rye to fortify himself for buying the right pen and paper, then another bourbon to fortify the previous rye and bourbon, and then went out and bought some embossed stationery and an expensive fountain pen with liquid ink capsules and took the paper and the pen back to the bar so he would have something steady to write his note on. In the cool night of the tavern, the father decided he would write a novel to his son on the embossed stationery. It would be a novel about the journey he was taking, an odyssey of his struggles against the medical establishment, the perfidy of real estate dealers, the shams that used-car salesmen perpetrate, the insularity of the scientific community, the seductivity of women, and the pitfalls of practicing medicine. He would talk about the time he and three friends had a contest at an AMA convention to see who could ski the farthest on a table greased with caviar, or the time a bear wandered on the golf course at another convention, in Banff, Canada, and they persuaded the bear to drive a golf cart into the hotel lobby. The damp air-conditioning in the bar, the stale smell of beer froth, the cold, dim light, spurred his imagination, as if the darkness between the places of light were areas waiting to be filled in by his pen. He asked for a bowl of soup. Soup always went well with writing novels. "We have no soup," the bartender told him. The father looked up, querulous, frowning. "You should, you know," he said. "It's as important as . . . as anything in the world, as important as fish or meat." "We don't have those, either," the bartender said. He would write the novel without soup. It would be short, concise, brilliant to the point of terror, filled with horror. No, he would write notes toward a novel, sketch a plan, an outline.

It would serve as a warning to his son. Beware of this book. It devours. He had another bourbon and rye, wrote three notes, none of which he liked, went to the toilet to throw up, came back, wrote another note, had a rye, then crumpled the note and wrote another, then asked the bartender if he could leave the note and the paper there because he had to go out and buy some Scotch tape, to stick the note to his son's door. Finally, with Scotch tape, note, paper, fountain pen, and ink capsules, he climbed the six flights of stairs and quietly taped the note to the door. He did not knock. He had already knocked, and no one had been there. One knock was enough. He had already put in his time knocking. This was the time for note writing, for sticking the note to the door, and he did it as quietly, as silently as he could. Indeed he did it so quietly that the boy, who was inside the apartment by this time, did not hear him. That was another test. It was the same sort of test that required that the boy be there when he arrived. It was a test that required of the boy that he hear his father quietly taping the note to the door, come to the door, open it, and welcome him. The boy also failed this test. This second test the boy's father had made up on the spot, but the first test was a long-standing test, if not known to others at least known to the boy's father.

Quietly descending the stairs, the boy's father hoped that the note would make the boy feel guilty, or if not guilty, at least like kicking himself for his poor timing, for choosing just that moment, when his father showed up, to be away from his apartment. The boy's father was actually glad that he was not there, because he would have had to explain why he got fired from another job, a tedious explanation at best. He had actually thought about asking the boy if he could stay at his apartment for a few weeks, since he had no place to live at the moment, and now he was glad that he had been relieved of this task. He did not like to ask his son for anything. He was afraid to be turned down. The thought of his son turning him down seemed especially heinous, a sort of primitive patricide. On the cab ride out to the airport to catch a flight to a southern city where he no longer had an apartment (the apartment went with the job), the father recognized his unreasonableness in all this, and gloated over it. He enjoyed setting unreasonable demands, such as asking that his son keep up the payments on a Cadillac he himself had wrecked. It was a way he had of breaking out of his mind, a way around the issue of free will. No, that was a lie. He had done it out of spite, out of perversity. He'd had a few drinks on the plane coming in and had wanted to devise some sort of test for his son. He had realized, almost with a shock, that he had never really tested his son. So he had not done it out of perversity or spite after all. It was very reasonable. In reality, it answered to a deeper logic. He had proven many things to his son. His son had not asked him to do this; he had simply done it by virtue of his being a father, a duty inherent in the role. Now his son would have to prove something to him. He could not tell his son, the boy, what this was, because the telling of it would invalidate it. Part of the test was figuring out that it was a test. Passing something you didn't know was a test could hardly be thought of as a test. The father wondered where he would sleep that night, and for many nights to come. He knew he was no longer welcome in the town he was flying to. That, he thought, was *his* test. He drank a finger-size bottle of Jack Daniel's and watched the slippery colors of the New York sky recede over the silt and sludge of Jamaica Bay, and he thought about the millions of unseen hands that turned on the pinpricks of light in Queens.

The following morning the son came out and saw the note. "I was here. Dad." He called his mother and she gave him his father's phone number in Texas, but they had no idea where he was. The boy guessed, correctly, without them actually telling him, that his father had been fired. His mother was unaware of this. She had long ago given up following him, or trying to follow him. It was like trying to follow a comet. She had gone from Canada to Chicago to Michigan to Illinois to West Virginia and then stayed there when he went to Texas, feeling a great fatigue settle upon her. The energy of his moving was more than she was able to bear; he generated a special heat that burned those close to him. The boy would not call his mother and tell her about Texas. His father would write, as he always did, from another state, another clinic, building up the new job, tearing down the old. He is leaving behind a sea of complications, a history that he drags with him, a net stuffed full of unpalatable fish: sea robins, puffed creatures, bottom crawlers. The boy could follow the trail, from Kalamazoo to Mattoon to Elkins to Dallas, by the angry, vituperative letters that came from each city, some from his father, others from furious doctors, eager lawyers breathless to sue, outraged husbands, angry state medical examiners, bitter hotel owners and bank managers, fuming used-car salesmen, sputtering real-estate brokers. Wherever his father roamed, wherever he landed, he liked to spend, to buy. Never rent when you can buy, he said. A doctor's credit is always good, he said. He bought cars, homes, plots of land, women, and defaulted on them all. He left them behind without leaving himself behind, knowing that it was a temporary misfortune. He beguiled, he charmed, he soothed; he was not to be trusted.

The boy felt a sense of liberation on failing the first test, a sense of freedom that went with not living up to what someone expected of you so that they never again would have to expect anything of you, which would allow you the freedom to live up to what they no longer expected of you.

But there were other parts to the test. He only had the opportunity to fail the first part; the rest of the test beckoned him, Circe to his Odysseus. He would have to find out where his father had gone, and then react properly to finding him. Furthermore, he would never know the results of this test. They could be published in a letter to his mother or brother, conceivably to some television personality or to a United States senator.

The boy had given some thought to failure, and had decided that failures were more interesting than success. Winners were plodders, who when confronted with their victories seemed to have something sucked out of them, as if they were dazed, as if something in them had been glazed over, as if it were necessary to deny life in order to win. But failures, interesting failures, big failures, those who fought for big stakes and lost gloriously, were of much more interesting cloth. (Better to sink with the palace intact than survive with a hot-dog stand.) They were huge samples of humanity. They were larger than any victory, larger than any life had a right to contain. Exploring the wreckage of their lives was more interesting than sifting through the neat order of winners made shallow with victory.

But it seemed as if his father would not let him fail, that he would deny him the victory of his failure. He had called a halt to the test by phoning the boy two months later to announce that he had a new job, as a pathologist at a clinic in Bethesda, Maryland, and sent the boy a round-trip airline ticket. He met the boy at the airport in a pink Cadillac convertible.

"I hate the color," his father said, "but it has features I couldn't resist. If you piss on the back seat, the top goes up. But I don't know if it works by pissing on the front seat."

They passed through countryside that confirmed an image of Maryland: gently rolling hills covered with lush grass and bounded by overly elaborate white wooden fences, herds of fast, fragile horses, sleek beyond imagination, too beautiful to run with humans on their backs, graceful brick mansions with white porticoes and Greek columns in front, dangling at the end of long, carefully guarded gravel driveways.

"Jesus, how they guard these places. You can't shit in the meadow without them knowing about it."

His father drove slowly, almost awkwardly.

"It's got cruise control in case you get a thrombosis in your leg. Put your high beams on and they automatically dip when another car's headlights hit you, in case you have primary nerve degeneration in your hand or foot. The seats go up, down, back, forth, and also tilt, at the press of a button. It also has air-conditioning. The stupidity of air-conditioning in a convertible impressed me. It was that and the pissing in the back seats that made me buy the car."

"On time?"

"Of course."

"Until you accumulate enough capital?"

"In spite of accumulating enough capital. In several months I'll have enough to develop a mile of Chesapeake Bay property. I'm going to be rich. We're going to be rich."

"Me?"

"Of course not. My partner and I. I don't think you'll ever be rich. You don't want to be, do you?"

"I haven't given it much thought."

"I have. I've decided I like money. I've decided I don't have enough of it. Banks have it all. I want some of it. I'd like to buy more Cadillacs, but different colors."

"What are you doing?" the boy asked. "Just what are you doing?"

His father looked at him in amazement.

"I'll show you the property."

In fifteen minutes they were at the bay, driving along the water.

"I'm going to own all that, and then I'm going to develop the hell out of it. You wouldn't be able to recognize it a year from now."

"Why are you doing this?"

"Why not? What's wrong with money?"

"But you're a doctor."

"A pathologist now."

"But why all this?"

"Doctors and money," he explained slowly and patiently, "are a perfect fit."

His father deposited him at a motel.

"The painters and carpenters are still at my place. You'll love it when it's finished: five bedrooms, two Jacuzzis, a tennis court. I'll take you there when it's finished. I'll pick you up tomorrow. I'm on call tonight. Put the motel on my tab."

The motel was garish enough to be soothing. Every possible horizontal surface, and many vertical surfaces, were carpeted. It was impossible to make noise when you walked. The boy felt very relaxed. He was glad to be away from his father for a while. He had a meal in the motel restaurant that tasted like baked butterflies. He slept well, though he dreamt about large, naked black women who chased him with frying pans. The next day his father did not come. He had a meal of sea worms, and slept a sound, dreamless sleep. The next day his father came in the pink Cadillac, a scrape running the length of the right fender and the left headlight and chrome trim smashed.

"You can't trust workmen anymore," his father said. "They put a douche in the bathroom. I don't want any goddamn douche! I told them that. They listened."

They drove silently along a main thoroughfare. The boy read all the local advertisements, feeling that he was swallowing the city through its billboards, that these, more than anything else, told him what the city was like. He saw one sign that said THE LAST BIRD. Where had he seen that before? And where was this creature, this unique, soon-to-be-extirpated organism, gasping its feeble last in some gallery of dodoes?

"Let's drive along the water," his father said. "I want to see if my property is still there."

It started to rain, and the convertible top slowly came up.

"See," his father said, "and I'm not even pissing on it."

The top continued to rise, but at some point the passing air equaled the force of the motors pushing the top up, and it remained in the air, like a black, upraised hand, a sort of signal to the unwary that his father was driving.

"They haven't perfected this damn thing yet."

"I think you're supposed to stop and let the top come up."

"Stop? Why should I stop?"

"It's too much work for the electric motors."

"Of course it is. I know physics."

He continued driving, and then pulled over next to a carpet outlet. The top, poised for an instant in its absolute verticalness, slowly fell over the windshield. They buckled the clasps, securing the top. Rain drummed just inches over their heads. The rolls of carpet left outside seemed to swell, grow, become more than they were. Desolate salesmen watched their waterlogged product from inside the showroom. A drain in front of the showroom clogged, and a pool began to form.

"I think we're going to float away," the boy said.

His father looked at him. "This is a water state," he said. "Never look down on water."

He started the Cadillac, and drove slowly through the quickly forming lake. The boy could feel the power of the water and watched the waves the car made, two sets of waves, that surged over the water. Water was seeping in through the door. They left the lake and bumped onto the street.

"Property disappears," his father said. "You think it's above water, and zip, it's under. It's the old shyster game, the old con, selling underwater property. They're famous for that down here."

They continued driving, out of the city now and into the dead zone between the city and the country, a mélange of junkyards, elaborate restaurants with stone fronts, outlets for pool manufacturers, toy stores that featured plastic tricycles, stores that sold pornographic magazines, liturgical supplies, more ice cream than one should eat, and finally stores that sold absolutely nothing at all, yawning stores, gasping for products to sell, moaning for goods—holes, abscesses in the commercial strip. Sheets of water fled from roofs, bullet-quick rivers shot through the gutters. They continued driving until they reached the waterfront, a gray porridge, the water hard and yet frothy, as if worked over with a bellows, hit on a slant by pellets of rain that raised quickly disappearing dimples.

"My land is still there." His father sighed, satisfied and yet vaguely disappointed at not having been cheated.

"It's a magnificent view," the boy said.

"Just wait till the people from Manhattan come."

"Manhattan?"

"They're the ones with the money. Forget the other boroughs."

"Why Manhattan?"

"It's sinking. Too many people on it. All the big moneymen know that. The people have to go somewhere else."

The boy's father gazed dreamily at the waterfront.

"Maybe I'll only sell to doctors. They won't screw things up, like lawyers."

They drove back to the city, the rain beating at the car as if it were trying to drive it from the road.

"Let me show you my house," the boy's father said.

He continued driving, stopping before a small hill. He pointed to the top of the hill.

"Up there. You can't get up the road in the rain."

The boy could see nothing.

"It's there; believe me it's there. It's just what I've always wanted. I'll send for your mother. She doesn't need any goddamn douche."

He drove him back to the motel and let him off.

"Don't worry," the boy's father shouted at him through the rain. "It's on my tab. You don't have to worry about a thing."

His father kept the window rolled down, looking at him through the rain as if he expected the boy to toss him something, some toy the father had given him when he was much younger.

"I'll call you tomorrow. This has been great. Getting together with you like this."

His face seemed to slip when he said this, his eyes lowered, and the boy felt he was in the sudden presence of truth. He didn't want his father to go, and his father, sensing this, became uncomfortable and rolled the window up. The boy watched him drive off. It seemed to him that the car was a huge trunk on wheels.

Inside, the motel air was oppressive, air-conditioned and yet muggy, a cold dampness. The desk clerk called him over.

"You'll be settling up shortly, sir?"

"Isn't this on my father's tab?" he asked.

The clerk twisted a smile on his face, and said with a hint of menace, "We don't do tabs here. It's not that kind of a place."

That evening he dined on something green and slimy served in garlic butter, something that the waiter said was found only on the walls of stone farmhouses in Normandy. The salad had Thousand Island dressing. He found a small corner of tinfoil in it. He had coffee and too much ice cream. Back in his room, he deposited most of the meal, through proper channels, of course, in the toilet. It was a relief, but he was hungry again. He called to ask about room service, and was informed that in order to provide their guests with better service, there was no room service. He hung up the phone and burped.

The bed was greatly comfortable, and after the meal, put him at ease. He slept well, dreaming in color that he was strapped to the back of an elephant that could, in a single leap, jump over acres of lush green lawn. The next day his father did not call. Nor did he call the following day. The third day he called.

"This is your father," his father said.

"OK," the boy said.

"Guess where I am."

"I don't know."

"Neither do I."

He could hear crying on the other end of the phone before the line went dead.

DEAD UNCLES

ALL MY MICHIGAN UNCLES ARE DEAD. NONE OF THEM DIED
by gun. None of them were stabbed, or bled to death, or were pushed off buildings or shoved in front of railroad engines. None of them were beaten senseless with baseball bats. Their throats were not garroted with piano wire, nor were ice picks jabbed into their brains. None of them drowned. None of them were ground to bonemeal in automobile accidents or had bombs thrown in their faces. They all died peacefully.

"Which is not to say we had peaceful deaths," my hardware uncle said.

They are summer uncles, vacation uncles.

They sit on the porch in summer, smoking, and it is always summer.

Michigan hums, like some horned insect frantic on its back, moaning to be turned over.

All of them are sixty. They are different ages, but they are all sixty. They keep their shoes shined and wear thin soles and thinner socks, through which the hairs on their legs peek out. On my hardware uncle, the fat of his leg dribbles over the elastic band of the sock, but on my eyeshade uncle, the varicose veins peek out of the sock. My cheese uncle wears socks with no elastic bands, and his socks fall in a heap around his ankles. My elf uncle's socks may not even exist; I think he paints his legs.

It is summer and they are waiting for me. They sit on the porch, smoking and talking. Their wives, my aunts, are inside making tomato aspic. They will die after their husbands. They will all be embalmed in a tuna casserole.

"Come here," they say. "We want to talk to you."

They had never *wanted* to talk to me. They had always just talked to me. When someone wants to talk to you they want to tell you how to behave or act or to leave you with a little moral (good for life), but when someone talks to you, that's all they do and you can damn well behave any way you please. My uncles never wanted to do anything. They just did it.

"Look in the window," my eyeshade uncle said.

I did.

"See your aunt working?"

I did.

"What does it mean?" he asked.

"She likes to bake?"

That was my way of saying I didn't know.

"No, it doesn't mean that."

"I don't know."

He lit his cigar.

"It doesn't mean anything," he said.

"It's not much of a lesson."

"It's the only one there is."

"It doesn't seem like such a big deal to me."

"It isn't."

"You came all the way back here just to tell me that?"

"We never left."

"Do you need a good used car?" my elf uncle asked.

My aunt came outside and asked me if I wanted any tomato aspic.

"Sure," I said.

"Who are you talking to?" she asked, looking around the porch.

"No one."

"Come inside; it's getting cold."

"Could I eat it out here?"

"The porch light doesn't work."

"I don't have to see what I'm eating."

She answered me by walking inside, letting the screen door bounce against the doorframe, and closing the glass door, which seemed to suck all the air off the porch. I followed her in.

The carpets in the living room sighed, and the drapes, heavy folds of velvet that propped up the walls, shuddered. There were varnished tables with tiny fences that ran around the edges to keep things from sliding off. There were huge ceramic lamps with washable lampshades that never needed to be washed because they were encased in elaborate folds of plastic. There were underneath rugs and scatter rugs and throw rugs and rugs to be stepped on and rugs to be watched over, there were rugs for the stairways and rugs for the upstairs rooms, these last being very thin. I never saw the wooden floor in the living room, though I once dug down through five layers of carpets trying to find it. In the bedroom, however, the wood floor lay yawning with wide planks that seemed to smile at the ceiling. The bathtub stood straight up on tall horned legs that rested on huge glass balls. It was long and narrow, with high sides for wide skinny people who liked to bathe sideways. The sink had separate spigots for hot and cold. The water was never the right temperature because the rubber stopper leaked. There was a mirror in the bathroom. It was an enormous room. All the fixtures were in the middle. The walls were painted yellow and seemed to be falling away when you took a bath. The entire house reminded me of my uncle's sweater. Years later, when another family owned the house, I got in by a ruse and while the family was in the living room went upstairs and took a bath.

My aunt's face was like fresh pie. The corners of her mouth and eyes were pleasantly browned and wrinkled, and her skin felt like the underside of old, soft fabric left to age in attic trunks and brought out once a year to be dusted. Where my uncle's smile was mischievous, hers was without guile, like scallops cut in an apple turnover. Her hair was neatly pulled back from her forehead. It had absolutely no color. Her print dresses were loose around the chest, and I never knew if she had breasts. None of my aunts had breasts, but they all had busts. I had a small aunt who had a large bust, and several large aunts whose busts were camouflaged as stomachs, but this aunt—her bust was a mystery.

She set some food in front of me and a glass of milk. I had not asked for milk but knew I had to drink it. My aunt looked sad. I remembered a picture of my hardware uncle several years before he died. His entire body seemed to settle into an area just below his belt. He had a round ball there, as if he were pregnant. He kept his face down, looking at that ball, wondering if it would jump loose from his body and fly off.

My aunt made lace cookies. Several years after my uncle died she moved to Florida, bought a condominium, and waited.

"Someday," she said to me, "there's a story I want to tell you."

She sucked her thumb.

"Baking soda," she said.

"What's that?" I asked.

"Your uncle found twenty cases of baking soda in the basement of the store he bought. Five-pound tins. Do you know how big five pounds of baking soda is?"

I said no.

"Neither do I. He never showed me the baking soda, just told me about it. He had big plans for baking soda, but he never told me about his plans. He never told me about any of his plans."

My eyeshade uncle was ninety years old. He thought it was a big joke that he had reached the age of ninety. Why would anyone want to reach the age of ninety? His relatives threw a party for him to celebrate this unlikely event. He howled. One ton of German potato salad was trucked in from upper Michigan, along with five hundred hot dogs and seven barrels of pickles. My uncle smiled at everyone. His white hair stood straight up, like a shoe brush. He could only turn his head by turning his whole body. He shook hands with several thousand people and told them all about his boyhood in upper Michigan. He lived on a farm near Lake Huron. That was all he could remember.

"What did they do . . . that day?"

"Don't you remember?"

One of the uncles started to dance. He was holding an eel sandwich in one hand and a piece of cake in the other. He sang a song:

> *When I'm alone and gray*
> *into your tent I'll creep,*
> *and if that's very far*
> *I'll have to come by jeep.*

Another uncle joined in. He held his clasped hands over his head and danced. There was a quart of motor oil in his jacket pocket.

The bay bubbled with colors as the light receded from the sky. A bonfire was lit, packages of marshmallows were opened, beer was uncapped, hot dogs were stuck on long willow stems, and more potato salad was scooped on plates. All the uncles were up, except my ninety-year-old uncle, dancing in a line. They jiggled and jounced and kicked the sand. Whatever they were doing it was difficult to call dancing. It looked like an erratic display of twitching.

The old man looked up at them. I had always thought of him as an uncle, and therefore invulnerable, but I now saw him as an old man. He had a small white mustache, which he kept ruler straight. His eyes rang with light; I could almost hear the sound of blue coming from them. He had on a white shirt and a bow tie, which was loose at the neck and hanging to one side. I noticed that the top button of his shirt hadn't been buttoned but the area around the button was heavily creased and finger smudged. I suddenly realized he hadn't been able to button it. I desperately wanted to button it for him.

He stood up, a tall figure, amazingly straight.

The other uncles stopped dancing. He walked to the center of the line and they opened to receive him. He put his hands on the shoulders on both sides of him, and, slowly, the other uncles did likewise. Then he began a slow, simple step. The others followed. I had never seen the step before, and never expect to again. I have no idea where it came from. It was simple and easy to follow, and he moved through the sand with slow grace, his long legs stepping and bending as if underwater. The other uncles looked to his legs for guidance, and slowly the line moved back and forth, right and left, in amazing unison.

The bay darkened, the wind came up, more sticks were added to the fire. The uncles danced. The light from the fire flickered against their aging legs. I expected them to smile. They didn't. They watched the old man with calm eyes. He was leading them somewhere. They didn't know where. They followed. I had the feeling they could have danced for hours. I had the feeling they could have flown.

"What was he doing?" I asked my aunt.

"You were there."

"But I didn't understand."

"Oh, yes you did."

I asked my dead uncles what it meant.

"We used to know," my elf uncle said, "but now that we're

dead, we don't. Dead takes something out of you. The part you thought you knew, that's the part that dead takes."

"Wait a second," I said, "there's got to be more than that."

"Oh there is," my cheese uncle said, "but that's the part you won't understand."

MORE STONES

3 $^3/_4$

8 $^1/_2$

1 2 $^1/_2$

2 2

IT WAS THE THIRD THING HE COULD REMEMBER. HE WAS STAND-
ing on a wooden pier with a golden-
brown dog that was as old as he, three,
maybe four. The dog wanted to chew
on something, or chase something. He
didn't know that then, but he knew it
now looking back on then. The dog
kept jumping around on the dock,
straight up, then sideways, as if the dock
were too hot to stand on. He couldn't
remember the sky, but he could remember the water. Pale green, gray, a
flat color; it looked like something solid,

slick, thick, something he could walk
on. The dog kept jumping; it wanted
him to do something. He turned around,
and his father walked onto the dock.

As soon as the dog heard his father
step on the dock he became more agitated. He not only jumped up and down

and sideways, but when he landed on the pier he kept turning his head back and forth, quickly, his tongue hanging out, foam flecking his teeth.

"Let me show you how dumb that dog is," his father said.

He always talked to him like that. He talked to him as if he was eighteen, nineteen, not three or four. He didn't always understand his father. *Let me show you* he knew. *Dog* he knew. *Dumb* he didn't.

"Watch this," his father said.

He took a stone out of his pocket and threw it against the sky. The boy didn't remember the sky, but he did remember the stone. It was white, with something red and powdery in the center. As soon as he reached into his pocket the dog stopped jumping, looked at his father, at his hand, and shutting his mouth withdrew his tongue and followed the pattern of the stone against the sky with his head. Before it fell he started to run.

"Most expensive damn dog they could find, and the stupid dog chases stones."

He was halfway down the pier after the stone, which bounced two, three times on the pier and then plopped in the water before the dog could get it. The dog followed it into the gray water.

"Now watch this," his father said. *Watch* and *this* he knew, *now* he wasn't sure about. His father liked to say *now*. *Now* went with *then*. The dog surfaced, spilling water on water, his mouth full of sand and wood and gravel. He spit it out, coughed, sneezed, went back in the water. The boy watched the bubbles come up. The dog surfaced with more sand and gravel. Panting, coughing, the dog made his way to the beach and ran out on the dock toward the boy and his father. In front of his father he shook himself off. His father tried to step back and avoid the water but wasn't quick enough. His father shouted at the dog, kicked him. The dog was upset, barking. The boy could see that the dog wanted to jump up and down again, go sideways, but didn't because he was expecting something from his father.

"A monumentally dumb dog." *Monumentally.*

The dog started to whine and gave the sort of whimpering bark that precedes a full bark. He expected the dog to give a full bark, throaty and loud, but the dog kept up with his half barks, sounds that seemed to make him more jumpy.

"He never gets it," his father said. "I throw it in the water, he goes after it, but he never gets it."

He took another stone out of his pocket and threw it up in the air. The dog watched, strangely calm. When it started to fall the dog went after it. This one would not hit the dock. The dog jumped off the dock, the stone falling in the water, the dog missing the stone, swimming with chunky, bobbing strokes, looking for the splash of the stone, which he had missed when he was in the air.

"He never learns," his father said. "I did the same thing last year, and he never learned then, either."

The dog looked around in the water, confused, and then put his head underwater. The boy waited for more bubbles, and the dog came up with something green in his mouth. He made his way more slowly to the beach and then trotted instead of running out to his father on the pier.

"He's got a fishhook in his mouth."

His father opened the dog's mouth and with a fishing pliers clipped the eyelet off the fishhook. The dog growled, whimpered, and bled. He pulled the rest of the hook through, holding the dog's face and jaws between his knees, behind the dog's neck. The dog growled again, tried to pull free, and his father jerked the fishhook through his jowls. The dog bled and barked, growling at his father. With his tongue he licked the blood that ran over the gummy part of his mouth.

"Never learn," his father said. "Watch this."

He took another stone out and held it down for the dog. The creature came forward to get the stone and his father jerked his hand away. He threw it the length of the pier. The dog ran after it, but it fell between the boards of the pier. Over the side again, the dog thrashed around under the pier. He came up with a bottle, dropped it, then got caught in some crossbracing under the pier. The dog barked and howled trying to pull himself free but wedging himself tighter.

"He's too stupid to be saved."

His father smelled, lilacs or honey, a wet sweetness like sugar. He wore a white handkerchief around his neck. His skin was pink, there were little blisters on his neck. The boy smelled the sweetness again. Someone shouted at his father from the beach. He walked toward the shore. The boy watched the dog trying to pull his paw from the V of the wood.

"Stop throwing stones to the dog," he heard someone say to his father, pointing to where his father was standing. The wind rippled the thin water into tiny waves, which flicked against the dock. The dog whimpered. A fat man came running, puffing, out on the dock, yelling at them.

The boy kept pace with the dog, saved by the fat man.

Years later, boy and dog eight, almost nine, the dock swept away in a winter storm, he stood on the beach with his father. The sand was as white as paint, and so smooth it hurt his feet. The dog showed some white in his muzzle. He lay twenty feet from where they stood.

"Watch this," his father said. He called the dog over. "Look at his teeth."

His father opened the dog's mouth. Several teeth were missing, several others were cracked. He didn't seem to mind having his mouth opened.

"He chews on them. He breaks his teeth but he still chews on them."

Summer. The trees dripped caterpillars—short, gooey, eraser-shaped slugs the same color as the bay. The bay had pushed up against the beach, flattening it, strewing broken, bleached objects on the sand that were dulled and blunted. His father wore a cream-colored straw hat with a shiny smooth weave and shoes with the same kind of weave but darker in color and not as smooth. He wore a suit on the beach—the only man on the beach who wore a suit, and a tie, knotted to the top button. His father's face was red and parts of it were puffy; tiny purple and red veins were scattered on the bottom of his nose and inside his ears.

He reached into his pocket and took out a stone. The dog got up quickly, looked at him, and started wagging his tail.

"The fat man won't be yelling. He had a coronary occlusion."

He threw the stone high, though not as high as he had once thrown it. This time the boy lost the stone in the sky but remembered the color, a dirty gray, and the smell, something that had aged slightly beyond its time, that blew in from the bay. The dog seemed confused. He no longer jumped up and down, but he was interested in the stone, and as soon as it hit the sand he ran after it and grabbed it in his jowly mouth. Then he dropped it.

"Infected gum. The fishhook. Never healed properly."

The boy noticed that his father was having trouble with his consonants; the boy didn't call them consonants, but he knew they were the part of speaking where you used your lips or tongue and teeth.

The dog picked up the stone again and started chewing on it.

"He won't even bring it back. He's supposed to be a retriever, but he won't retrieve a goddamn thing."

The dog lay in the sand, chewing on the stone. The boy could hear the sounds, like small explosions, as the dog's teeth tried to clamp down on the rounded stone.

"I come out every morning and throw him a stone. He expects it. We both do. It's the only thing I do around here; that, and wait for meals. Did you have lunch?"

A woman in the house next to his uncle's looked at them through a picture window. She held a cigarette in one hand and a dirty doll in the other. She spoke through the glass, words with no sound, her mouth working frantically.

"I could have married her. She's a lush. But I married your mother."

The boy heard something crack. The dog stopped chewing. The stone and a piece of tooth rolled out of his mouth, followed by a string of spittle, onto the sand. The dog looked at it. The boy thought the dog had the most profound look he had ever seen.

"He deserves another treat."

His father took another stone out of his pocket and skipped it over the surface of the water. The dog raced out into the waves, the water smashing his face and chest, the waves carrying him back several times before he swam out to where the stone-skipped part of the water was. Then he couldn't find the stone, and started to swim around in circles. At first he seemed confused, and shrugged off his confusion by swimming in circles, and then, as the idea of swimming in circles seemed to appeal to him, as much as anything can appeal to an animal, he seemed to substitute swimming in circles for finding the stone.

"He'll do that all day until someone calls him in."

The woman in the picture window came to the door and called the dog, but he refused to come. She pushed open an aluminum screen door and stood on a cement landing that led down to the beach and called again, but the dog heard nothing except the sound of his own circles. She walked down to the shore and pushed a battered aluminum boat into the water. They watched her wait until the boat floated, and then step in, her weight tipping it, the waves battering it, so that by the time she started to row, the boat had its nose pushed into the shore. She had to pole out, through the waves, before she could row to the dog. When she reached him, the crazed circle-swimmer would not climb into the boat. She clubbed him with the oar and tried to drag the growling, choking dog over the side of the boat. She was still smoking the cigarette when a wave hit the high side and flipped her into the water, and when she stood up in the water, holding the dog by the wet fur on the back of his neck, she still had the cigarette, damp, unlit, in her mouth. She pulled dog and boat to shore.

"I talk more now," his father said, "now that I'm older."

He was twelve, going on thirteen. He had no idea how old his father was and, afraid to ask, remained ignorant.

"All sorts of things come into my mind. You can't imagine the kinds of things."

He said this almost wistfully, as if he had preferred a strict curtailment to his imagination. They had driven up the night before in the new Studebaker. The old Ford with the pitted grille and the cloth upholstery splattered with liquor and sputum was resting, rusting in a junkyard in South Chicago. The night drive up to Michigan in the Studebaker had been breathless, fast, somehow immune from death.

A new pier had been put in: cement and steel. More homes popped up on the shore, smaller homes, crouched on narrower land, shorter homes, with lower roofs and no fireplaces. His uncle's cottage, a huge, rambling three-story house with a peaked mansard roof and shingled turrets, had been built too close to the water, and the bay had wreaked its revenge, requiring a fat cement-and-stone storm wall to be built that took up most of the beach and a good part of the front lawn.

"The air is very bracing here. Nothing like the tonic of industrial stink." Several tomato factories had just opened up.

His father no longer wore a suit on the beach but tan pants, a blue knit shirt, and shoes. His face looked the same, almost.

"I still keep them."

He reached into his pocket. The woman next door was lying in a hammock. Her husband, confined to a wheelchair, had been rolled onto the new porch that had just been built. The dog, its muzzle, neck, and chest flecked with white hairs, lay under the woman.

His father threw the first stone along the pebble-strewn shore. His arm seemed to have deteriorated more than his face, though both had taken a beating.

The dog had started to get up when he saw the man's hand reach into his pocket, but by the time he had extracted the stone from his pocket and thrown it, the dog was still trying to get up, a process that involved elevating his hind end, and then trying to raise the front, finally doing so, unsteadily. When the dog steadied itself, he walked, hobbled, down to where the stone had been thrown, and then, looking for the stone among all the other stones, was, once more, confused.

"I picked a bunch of them from the beach this morning. They're all alike. He thinks he can find them, but he can't. He'll never learn."

His father seemed to shudder as he spoke.

"You know dogs age seven yea—"

"I know," the boy said.

"Jeez. I almost married her."

The dog sniffed among the stones. The woman called to the dog, which would not come.

"Dog must be deaf now. No longer housebroken; they probably keep it outside."

He threw another stone. The dog looked up, the man in the wheelchair tried to shout, and the woman in the hammock merely sighed. She called the dog again. The dog looked around, expecting more stones to drop out of the air or pop up out of the ground. Then the dog lay down, snoring, dreaming of stones. The woman shouted at the dog, opaque words, as if she had been speaking through glass.

His father threw another stone, and the dog woke up, and then, with great agony and trepidation, began the rise to its feet, a process it accomplished by elevating sections, unsteadily, of its body. It slowly walked over to where they were standing.

"Look at this."

The woman, sitting up in the hammock, shouted at the dog.

When the dog reached them, his father opened its mouth.

"Try to find his teeth."

The boy saw only two; one above, the other almost but not quite directly below.

"He cracked all the others on stones. He still chases them. Watch."

He threw the stone toward the road at the back of the house. It had recently been repaved to serve the new houses on the bay. A speed limit was posted, which had the effect of speeding up traffic.

Large cars with trunks big enough to hold several bicycles flew down the road, which now sported not just new blacktop but a double yellow line down the middle. The dog hobbled toward the road. The woman, getting up from the hammock, shouted after the dog, who now was intent on the stone that lay on the edge of the road. The woman started to walk after the dog and then, seeing that the dog, despite its hobble, would beat her, tried to speed up, walking faster, not yet running. But the dog, hobble and all, was going to reach the road before she did. She swept past them, her face energetically haggard, a cigarette in the corner of her mouth that was damp to the lit end.

"God damn you!" she said.

His father watched her go by.

"Now there's a real lush, a classic lush."

The boy noticed the new dental work in his father's mouth when he spoke. He could smell the same cloying sweetness on his father's breath, but this time from candy, not from alcohol. His nose had gotten bigger, and a whole delta of tiny purple veins had appeared on his cheek.

"Did I tell you I have a new job? A clinic. Internal medicine. I was always partial to the digestive tract."

His uncle died the following year. A stroke. He felt nothing. He keeled over. He had been talking about cheese. The house on the bay was sold.

The boy was twenty-one, twenty-two. He hadn't seen his father for several years. Now he was walking on the beach with him, no longer Michigan but the South Side of Chicago. His father's hair had turned white. His face was full of folds. He seemed to have trouble finding his way. The boy—he still thought of himself as a boy—suddenly realized that every time he was with his father he was between ages, never settled comfortably in any one age. His mother and father had been separated for several years. His father seemed happier with the arrangement, but also more confused, apathetic. His mouth contained the same number of teeth as the dog's, or would have, if the dog were still alive.

THINGS THAT EVAPORATE

IN THE AIR, I

ARISTOTLE BELIEVED THAT THE ARTERIES WERE CONDUITS FOR air. The Buddhists believe that winds sweep through our bodies. My father believed that people were machines that run on air. It is a system of checks and balances, he once told me, and various forms of air live in the body, disease being stagnant air where fresh should be.

He was the first to diagnose leprosy in Michigan. There has never been a case of leprosy in Michigan. He wrote to the state medical journal and called several of his friends, who examined the patient. It wasn't leprosy. He had botched the diagnosis. It was a simple skin rash.

"Anyone can make a diagnosis," he said. "It's what you do with it afterward that counts."

He was fifty-five at the time, five years after he had interned for the second time, in the same Michigan town where he had been thrown into the asylum and walked out as a termite inspector, then bought a green house and settled down to a life of examining patients and testing the air in their bodies. He had a machine in his office that generated electricity in glass tubes.

(My father discovered rashes no one else could: Yellow Mountain spotted fever, Tragnon's syndrome. They all threw him into ecstasy. I was enrolled in a boy scout troop for the simple reason that the scoutmaster had St. Vitus' dance and my father wished to observe it closely over a period of months. The scoutmaster looked like an old root hacked out of a tree, but what amazed me most about him was the way he lit his pipe. He could hold it firmly between his teeth, but the arc his arm described as it aimed for the bowl of the pipe was another matter. The arm looked like a tree buffeted by the wind. He had little control of it below the elbow. I used to watch him trying to light his pipe, failing utterly. He never took the inability of his hand to reach the bowl of the pipe personally, but simply tried again. When it landed near the pipe, he steadied it with his other hand, preferably doing it on a table or next to a column so he could secure his arms. My father told me that the disease was progressive, and that people who had it endured it as best they could until the day came when they simply shook themselves apart.)

And then it was fifteen years of towns like Elkins, West Virginia, and De Kalb, Illinois, Dallas and Charleston, and the jobs seemed to choke him, and he flew, drove, rode away into new enthusiasms and new towns, until something caught up with him and he had no idea what it was but it seemed to be something he had to carry around with him, a physical weight, on his back, or his head, heavy air, that made things go more slowly for him, and him go more slowly for things.

He wrote letters.

"I can't shake it off. I don't know what it is."

Another one.

"Listen, do you know anything about it? Have you heard anything?"

I got a card from somewhere in Florida, deeply stained.

"I've discovered a new formula for soybean absorption."

Mexico.

"They believe me down here."

Arizona.

"What is it? Can you tell me what it is?"

Washington.

"Can you tell me where the center is?"

Then he got a job with a clinic that was desperate for doctors. That was in Chicago. He lived with his sister in the old house, the house of his parents, the house of the burning. He was on the verge of something, waiting patiently for the weight to be removed from his head and back. I asked him what he was doing.

"I'm practicing nigger medicine," he said.

It was a black clinic on the South Side of Chicago that needed another doctor. My father was the only one available. They knew about him, but their need was great. He worked five days a week, five hours a day.

He dispensed aspirin and swabbed throats and gave shots (horrifying to think of his unsteady hand plunging a needle into someone's arm). His colleagues were black, and while he didn't care for blacks, he did like the black doctors he worked for. They were different. They'd had to put up with so much to get through medical school he admired them at the same time he despised their patients.

"Your aunt's afraid of getting raped by a nigger," he said.

He was sitting close to the television. He watched a lot of television, and because of his eyes had to sit close. He talked to me but kept on watching the television set.

"That's all she thinks about," he said.

Johnny Carson was on.

"Can't take her mind off it," he said. "I think it would do her good to get raped; then she could forget about it and think about something else."

Chicago had changed. The neighborhood had changed. Which is another way of saying it was now all black. My aunt and he were surrounded by blacks. All the Irish were gone. My aunt walked the streets as if there were prearranged steps for her to place her feet in, invisibly painted on the sidewalk.

"You get the Jews coming in and they're going to sell to niggers. They make a lot of money selling to niggers. Then they move."

"The neighborhood was all Irish."

"Irish Jews."

Johnny Carson was wearing a wig and a huge hat. He was talking to a lady who had a big snake wrapped around her head and shoulders. My father never talked about what he was seeing on TV.

"What's that you got on your face?"

"A beard," I said.

"I don't think I like that."

The snake had shit on TV. I'd never seen that happen before. Strange, what snake shit looks like.

"I'll die of a heart attack or cancer," he said.

"How are the cataracts in your eyes?"

"Classmate of mine, Jack Something-or-other, is going to remove them."

His glasses were like the bottoms of Coke bottles. He looked like an old Harry Truman, a man he hated.

"What are you doing?" he asked.

"Advertising."

"Lying."

I said nothing.

"Jews and niggers are taking over the country."

"That's not true."

"What do you know?"

He turned away from the TV to look at me. "What did you ever know?"

"How's your book coming?" I asked. "The one about jazz in Chicago during the twenties."

"It's upstairs. It's in a drawer."

"Is it finished?"

"I knew Bix. I knew Bunny Berrigan. I played for Paul Whiteman."

"Is it finished?"

"That was a real bastard, that Paul Whiteman."

He fell silent, eyes glued to the TV.

"What are you doing now?" he asked.

"Advertising."

"Oh."

He was playing with the remote-control buttons.

"I go to work tomorrow," he said. "You might think I can't make it."

"Watch much TV?"

"Quite a lot. Hard to read. Cataracts."

"When is the operation?"

"Next month. Classmate of mine . . ."

"Jack . . ."

"How'd you know?"

"You told me."

He stiffened, resenting what I said.

The conversation was over. He put on a pair of tiny earplugs and the sound disappeared from the set.

I don't know how he got to work.

Then my aunt told me.

I walked around the neighborhood. The houses, all black owned, seemed to be in as good shape as when I was a child. Except they were smaller, much smaller.

"There's something good on TV tonight," he said, thumbing through a *TV Guide* he couldn't read. "Raymond Burr as Perry Mason."

We watched Perry Mason and then a rerun of *My Little Margie* and then a rerun of *Our Miss Brooks* (Eve Arden, Gale Gordon).

We had seen these shows twenty years before, when we first bought a set. Stromberg-Carlson. They're out of business now.

"I like the Channel Five news," my father said. "We watch it always."

My aunt was sitting in the next room. She watched the news, nothing else. She knitted, did puzzles, bought all the papers, made potato dumplings. She was retired, taking care of my father, waiting.

"After the news comes a movie," my father said. "I can't read what it is. Can you tell me?"

I flipped the listings.

"*Pillow Talk*, Rock Hudson, Doris Day, somewhat amusing comedy with trivial plot. Best scene, Rock in drag."

"Like him, hate her."

I went upstairs to sleep in the linen closet. It was just big enough to contain a foldaway bed. I could touch the four walls from the center of the room. Shelves full of sheets and blankets and plastic mattress covers filled one wall. A single window looked over the porch roof and out onto the street. Across the street was a school with steel window grates up to the third floor. The linen closet was next to my father's bedroom. The toilet was across the hall. The staircase, spiral, ended at the entrance to all three rooms.

I heard the buzz of the set downstairs. My father wouldn't come to bed until two or three, and then he would pace around his room or the rest of the house until five or six. He would sleep until late afternoon, having been fired from the clinic (my aunt said the clinic only put up with him for two weeks), missing breakfast and lunch, eating just a light dinner. I could hear him downstairs, shuffling papers, scuffing over the carpet in his slippers. Sometimes he was up all night.

I would wait to hear him fall, expecting a soft series of thuds on the carpet as he slipped to the floor. He bumped into bookcases, disturbed plants, jarred tables; the whole house trembled before him. As I waited for the sound of his falling, my stomach flew to the ceiling and then out the window in a sudden rush as I heard him bump into something. I pictured him doing a cartwheel down the spiral staircase, limbs entangled in the spokes of the railing, snapping off, leaving the rest of his torso to tumble down the stairs. I would rush to the head of the stairs, be afraid to go to him, pretending that I didn't hear, rationalize it as something else, while he lay at the bottom of the stairs twisting and moaning, refusing to cry for help but desperately needing it. I knew I would not be there when he needed me. I would jump out the window and run along the porch roof. My aunt would call to me. Go see to your father, I think he fell. But I would be somewhere along the street, running in my pajamas.

I listen to him coming up the stairs.

They creak under an incredible weight. If you hold on to the staircase railing, there is not enough stair near the center to step on, but if you step farther out, toward the perimeter, where the stair widens, you can't reach the railing. I plot in my mind which way I want him to come. He fights the stairs, teetering. I can't see him teeter, but I can imagine it, which is worse, and I can hear the argument the stairs will have with him, he will have with the stairs. If he falls, I wonder how soon I should rush to him. Or should I go and tell my aunt first? No. I should go directly to him. But if anything is broken it would be a mistake to move him, especially if his spine is injured, so what good would it do to rush to him? Rather than bend his spine, or irreparably twist a broken limb, it would be better if I called an ambulance. They know how to handle these things.

I resent his making me lose so much sleep. He always does it. I think it is his way of getting even. Maybe it is Nann getting even. She could be standing at the top of the stairs, waiting to push him down. I can't figure out how to get her out of the house. I am afraid of Nann. She might be in bed with me. Watching. Sitting on my brain. Seeing what I think. He is halfway up the stairs. From now on, if he tumbles down, the danger starts.

THINGS THAT EVAPORATE

IN THE AIR, II

3 7

HE WOKE UP WITH A START. HE WAS DREAMING HIS FATHER was shouting, and then his father was shouting. There was no word he could attach to the shout. It was a yell, a scream, a sound he had never heard his father make. He fell out of bed, not used to the closeness of the walls and the shelves jammed with linen and blankets and sheets. He pulled them down and then the folding cot doubled up on his leg, his calf caught in the steel scissors of the folding legs.

He thought his father had fallen down the stairs, and he rushed out of the room, almost tumbling down the spiral stairs himself. He ran down but saw no one lying at the foot of the stairs. He heard the shout again. He ran up the stairs and looked in the bathroom. The light was on. It was the whitest room he had ever seen. The light beat against his eyes, batted by white tile and whiter porcelain.

This time a scream that would wake his aunt, sleeping next to the glow-in-the-dark disaster phone with all the emergency numbers (Catholic churches, Catholic funeral homes, Catholic relief agencies) and the calendar with the markings of the saints' days, the feasts, the retreats, the times of penance, the times of holy obligation, and the votary.

There were no more screams, but he knew where they had come from.

His father was sitting on the edge of the bed, feet over the side. His eyes were pulled farther apart than he had ever seen them. The room seemed to be shorn of something, as if someone had just been in the room and yanked pictures off the walls, chairs from the floor.

"Look," his father said. "Look!"

He looked at his father, and then didn't know what else to look at. His father said nothing, demanding him to look at what it was he wanted him to look at. He looked around the room and had the strange feeling the walls were in danger of falling. A cigarette was burning in an ashtray. A dead cup of coffee was on the desk. In the cup, floating, was the corpse of a cigarette.

"Look at this," his father said, grabbing his own arm.

He looked at the arm, and saw nothing.

"Don't you see? Can't you tell?"

He forced a smile on his face, thinking that his father would be pleased.

"It's going—can't you tell? It's going!"

"What?"

"This."

His father grabbed his hand and placed it on his own arm.

"Can't you tell?"

"Tell what, for God sakes?"

"Look."

He suddenly realized how old his father was. Why had he forgotten about it for all these years?

"Open your fucking eyes," his father said.

It was the first time he had heard his father use that word.

"Dad, look, sit down, relax."

He had said it automatically, not realizing he was already sitting.

"Don't you see what's happening? Tonight? Right now?"

"No. No, I don't."

His father sighed and seemed to settle further into the bed, slumping over. He kept sighing and getting smaller and smaller. Then he straightened up.

"I'm evaporating. Can't you see that? I can't stop."

THE LIFE OF HIS DEATH

HE SET HIMSELF ON FIRE. He was sitting at his desk with a cigarette in his mouth when his mind drifted. He opened his mouth and the cigarette fell. On his lap, or the cardboard blotter on the desk.

When I ran upstairs the fire danced and sang on his face and feasted on his skin, and to me it looked as if he were wearing a brilliant new dressing gown with a glowing feathered hat (a balaclava of flame), as if the sun had burst into the room and spilled on his face.

My aunt was downstairs. She smelled the smoke and came running up. My father's pajamas were burning and his hair and eyebrows were on fire. She called the fire department. He stood in the middle of the floor, mumbling, trying to shake the flames from his head, but failing to do that, he looked almost amused, and worried. He seemed to be in a trance, believing that he was not where he was but in some other region of his mind. The flames looked solid, hard, and then quickly melted. He stood in the middle of the room, burning. He was too surprised to be shocked, too amazed to be upset. I had never seen anyone on fire before, certainly not my father, and the sight of a man in pajamas burning, as if he were a magician reciting a secret phrase, startled me.

I pushed him through the window and rolled him in the snow. Charred bits of skin and hair formed peppers of black against the white of the ice and snow. Shards of glass stuck in his body, and tiny veins of blood, shattered screens of red, sprouted. I helped him pick the glass out of his skin. It was pleasant work, almost relaxing, and I kept thinking of fire and snow, first one and then the other, as if they were both part of the same thing.

The room was a ghost gray, painted in some undefined color or amalgam of colors, and the wallpaper and woodwork seemed to bubble up, threatening to burst into the room. He had lived here for the last ten years, compressing all his belongings into this one room. Each time he had threatened to outgrow the room by getting a job, something happened: his past, the ravaged trail he had left, was uncovered, and once more he was forced to shrink back into his room. It was relief, and agony. His whole life had been built on hope (rather than in hope), and now he realized that he had been sitting on air. There was nothing to support him.

Except for the room.

He was fond of the room.

He liked to buy things for the desk: blotters, staplers, pens, inkwell, letter openers, filing drawers, anything that assigned something to its place. He liked gadgets and he liked machines. He wished he were a machine. He felt that having the tools one needed to do the job was more important than doing the job. It showed a sense of readiness, of willingness. He preferred becoming to being. Completing something was anticlimactic.

My aunt came into the room again and screamed, sounding as if she had forgotten to scream when she had been in the room the first time. She refused to stop screaming, just stood there, a siren of aunt fat turning red and then blue, her lungs reaching for air all the way down to her knees. We looked at her. I noticed how funny my father's face looked, red and full of blisters, the forehead pushed back and the nose and lips puffy and the eyes looking as if they had Ping-Pong balls under them; and I saw golf-ball blisters on his chest and arms.

She finished screaming and went downstairs and called the police and the fire department once more. "There is no fire," I told her. In any event, I didn't think the fire department was very skilled in putting out fires on people. She went back downstairs, this time to call a doctor, forgot the number, came back up, took up where she had left off screaming, then remembered when she went down again that there was also a phone on the second floor, right beside her bed, with a lighted dial and a glow-in-the-dark Lord's Prayer. "Goddamn fool," I thought I heard my father say.

I pulled the glass out of his skin with a tweezers. It was like pulling glass out of rubber, or getting the sand out of spinach. You could never get it all out. When he walked, little bits of crystal would grind in his skin. If I put my head close enough I could hear the grinding and ringing of the glass as it bumped its way back and forth inside his body.

"Goddamn," he said.

He spoke as if he had a mouthful of marbles, his lips peeling and puffy, his nose the light bulb in a darkroom. I could hardly see his eyes. They were hidden under ridges of swelling tissue. I had never seen the shape of his head so clearly. It looked like a pumpkin. His long hair was gone, replaced with curled stubble.

He tried to say something else and couldn't, the words caught in some swelling in his throat.

A doctor came up the stairs, breathing heavily, yet still managing to look as if he had pranced into the room.

"We won't even try to take his pajamas off," the doctor said, and I wondered whom he meant by "we."

I was glad he would be in bed for a while. He wouldn't be able to see and couldn't talk. I could stand and look at him; he wouldn't know if I was standing there, if anyone was standing there.

There was a noise that seemed to keep coming out of him, some nascent eruption, like singing to a hidden ear, or a high-pitched note that only dogs and a certain part of one's body could hear. Why was I able to hear it? My ears weren't involved. Another part of my body, perhaps my fingers when I placed them on his hands (and shuddered), heard the sound. It was a bone sound. His bones were singing. And the notes traveled from his bones to mine, up to the cranial nerve, through the auditory channels, into the brain. He wanted to embrace me. I would collapse if he did. I wanted to run away. He wanted to follow me. Why are you afraid of me? he sings. I don't know, I sing back. Please don't ask. There is a word you don't want to hear, he sings. Please, I say, this time not even trying to sing. Please.

I kept thinking how the room hadn't been touched by the fire, how the fire had wrapped itself around his nose and eyelashes and devoured his hair, flew in and out of his pajamas, licked at the buttons, leapt into the air at the sight of his glasses. It was the air that had kept the fire off the room, kept the fire on his body. It was brown air, body air, air waiting for flesh to burn.

I watched his face change colors in the hospital. It went from a beautiful red, a flaming sunset red, to a sort of urine yellow, and then to an old laundry white, and then almost, but not quite, to green, lime green, no lighter than that. I wanted to tell him about all the colors his face was going through, wanted to tell him about the rainbow that was happening on his face, but didn't, not knowing how he would take it, or if he would, could, hear. I had expected that his face would be swaddled in bandages or coated with something yellow and greasy, but it wasn't. It just changed colors.

My aunt came and made cream cheese and jelly sandwiches,

which no one ate. She left these on the radiator and the janitor took them and fed them to a cat he kept in the boiler room, which had had a leg removed by some medical students.

He looked like a vegetable garden. One day he was a beet and the next day a turnip, then a squash, a tomato, and finally a leek. When he got to be a leek I thought he must be getting better. There was no reason to believe that leeks were healthier than any other vegetable, but there was something about a leek that seemed to suit him, perhaps the color of the skin or the shape, or maybe just the sound of the word: it sounded of drippings, something that would twist and strike back at you when you weren't looking. There was something sinister about it, and also something healthy about it, a sort of straightforward deviousness.

There was no place to put his body. It was becoming a thing of the air.

I keep looking for the dying tube on his bed. It makes no sense, but I cannot help thinking that there is such a tube, a long tube with a large end that sticks up at the foot of the bed and when someone dies or is dying they turn on the dying tube and the dead person or soon-to-be-dead person is sucked into the tube and down into the dead room. I can't find the tube. Maybe the nurses have hidden it.

There is a red nurse and a green nurse and a blue nurse on this ward. He had the blue nurse. She had huge breasts that looked like sand castles, and her hair was a coil of snakes. Every day she took his temperature and reached under the sheets and did something else to him and when she was done she rolled him over and stuck a needle in his ass. She pulled the needle out and looked at it, hoping to discover some secret. If she didn't like what she saw in the needle she would take another needle out of her pocket and screw that one on her syringe and stick him in the ass again. But there was increasingly less ass to stick something in.

Burning, he had nothing left to hold him in. Burning, there was no way I could hold his hand, no way I could touch him. Burning thin, he sang, now that his skin was gone, and left between us a wall. A machine managed his breath. Quite well, I thought. And in place of skin he left a certain wariness, a displaced membrane, stripped, shrunken, burned clean. Go away, go away, he said. I am not half the man you knew. I do not have a hand to hold you.

He made lots of money and drank it up. He had no will. He had planned to leave me some socks and shirts and pajamas that smelled of bleach and several manuscripts that smelled of something else, a pair of rabbit-lined gloves, a doctor's bag with out-of-date medicine, a suitcase, twenty or thirty outdated medical texts, a book on pornography and a book on Darwin, some pencils, a stethoscope, an otoscope, many wooden tongue depressors, about thirty or forty uppers and downers, a seven-year-old air-conditioned Cadillac in Texas that was sold for storage charges, and twenty-three hundred dollars in social security checks, which went to pay for the funeral.

I keep thinking about fire. The other night there was an electrical storm and I thought a bolt might hit me and I might sizzle, become air, just as he did.

I kept waiting for something. For years I waited, and then I realized there wasn't anything to wait for. The funny thing of it is, I didn't know what I was waiting for.

I pushed him as I pushed the others. It is time to go, I told him. I wanted him so I pushed him and he fought back and I pushed him. It is beyond crying now. I kill what I love. It is hateful. I kill what I love so I can love it more. I pushed him and he pushed back. I knew he would. I can't cry anymore. I pushed him. When will you die so I can truly love you? So I can see my love for you? I pushed him he pushed back or else he didn't. God how I love that man oh God it's unholy. You have to go so I can say I love you.

He is gone.

I never saw him go.

He's gone.

He's in the air. And that's it. He is a pronoun. He is dead in the air.

He can't tell you anything now.

A NOTE ON THE TYPE

The text of this book was set in Garamond No. 3, a modern rendering of the type first cut by Claude Garamond (c. 1480–1561). Garamond was a pupil of Geoffroy Tory and is believed to have based his letters on the Venetian models, although he introduced a number of important differences, and it is to him that we owe the letter we know as "old style." He gave to his letters a certain elegance and a feeling of movement that won for their creator an immediate reputation and the patronage of Francis I of France.

The display type in this book consists of Alternate Gothic No. 51 and Airport Tourist No. 602 (designers unknown), photographed and then photocopied eighteen times from a Baltotype brochure issued on July 1st, 1939, and purchased at a flea market in State College, Pennsylvania, during July 1987.

Composed by Crane Typesetting Service, Inc.
Barnstable, Massachusetts
Printed and bound by Fairfield Graphics,
Fairfield, Pennsylvania
Book design by Chip Kidd